Bell

Book and Claw

V.C. Sanford

341 Enterprise

USA

Bell Book and Claw

Published in the United States of America
By 341 Enterprise
Rossville, Georgia 30741 USA
www.bellbookandclaw.com
Copyright 2019 by
ISBN: 978-0-578-62340-5

This is a work of fiction. Except for historical and famous characters, all characters, names, places, and events appearing in this work are a product of the author's imagination or used fictitiously. Any resemblance to real persons, living or dead, is entirely coincidental.

DEDICATED TO ALL THE SURVIVORS OF STROKES
AND THE ONES WE LOVE WHO DIDN'T.

THE ONE WHO WRITES THE STORIES,
RULES THE WORLD

One

Dust fell from the ceiling, coating everyone seated at the table with a thin white powder. Serving dishes vibrated and crystal wine glasses tipped over, sending tendrils of burgundy flowing down the hairline cracks in the old wood. Overhead the ornate iron chandelier began to sway back and forth, the sibilant squeak adding a discordant counterpoint to the already irritating booming sounds. Almost as soon as the peculiar noise faded, the sound came again, a loud banging that reverberated throughout the dining hall, followed by a faint vibration and a shifting of the floor that caused everything on the table to slide from its current position.

Asmaris Shalestone, elected head of faculty at the exclusive Rosemount School of Elemental Magic, reacted without thought, stretching his arm across his table-mates plate in a desperate attempt to save his goblet of Alaric's Gold as it worked its way toward the edge of the ornate mahogany table. Sipping the delicate apple-pear concoction once more, he set the fragile crystal carefully back in the center of the table, then leaned back in his chair before addressing his companions.

"Master Stolinn, what exactly did you cover with the first-year students today?"

"We discussed gravity and its effects, as well as going over the basics of levitation and feather fall spells. You don't think--- Mekiva? Drasst it! Not again!"

Master Shalestone didn't have to finish his sentence. Despite one hundred twenty-six years of experience teaching at the academy, Stolinn could not recall another student that could raise his blood pressure half as fast as Mekiva Bell. He truly prayed the school could survive her. He prayed he'd survive her. It wasn't enough that she disrupted every class. Mekiva had developed an annoying habit of interrupting his dinner at least three times a week.

"Perhaps you might consider…"

"I would get disbarred for everything I have considered. Mekiva has the potential to wield powerful magic. As a natural sorcerer, she has an innate ability to command and manipulate the elements. She could become an extremely powerful Elementalist-- if we can figure out why her spells exhibit such erratic outbursts of power. I am not going to turn my back on her, you'll just have to suffer through the next few years." Rising from his chair with a resigned nod to his fellow diners, then moved his fingers in an intricate pattern that left a trail of glittery motes of light upon the air. Abruptly he stopped. "I hate cold fish", he said. Stepping back to the table, he snatched one last bite of the pecan encrusted trout, wiped his mouth with a slightly dusty cotton napkin, muttered two final words and vanished.

Almost instantaneously he reappeared just inside the doorway of a small dorm-room directly above the dining hall. His eyes widened slightly at the chaotic scene before him. Sure enough, standing on top of her bureau, clutching desperately at a small tattered book that strained to escape her fingers, was Mekiva Bell.

"What in Ligazra's Nine Realms are you doing now?" he thundered.

"It was supposed to simply float up a few inches."

She paled as her fingers slipped and once again, the book slammed into the ceiling.

Stolinn managed to control his anger long enough to snap a few quick words, followed by a tight flick of his hand, quickly dismissing her spell. Face frozen, he bent over to pick up the now tattered leather book. Silence filled the room, broken only by the soft pattering sounds of plaster and dust drifting slowly to the ground. Even Twizzle, her ever-present Dra-cat, made it a point to be conspicuously absent, probably cowering in the bottom of the overturned wardrobe.

"Next time, you might consider the use of an alternative to your spellbook when you experiment. Something in lead perhaps? It would be exceedingly difficult to recreate all your hard work. And could you perhaps practice outdoors, I truthfully don't know if the building can handle it." His face twisted wryly as he struggled to keep a stern expression on his face. Realizing he wasn't going to be able to keep the smile from his face for long, he nodded abruptly to his favorite student, turned and left the room, slamming the door to the room against the wall as he exited. Immediately the room started to fill as everyone ran to see what 'Mekiva Bell had done now'.

Thankfully, the dust from the ceiling covered her face so no one could see the crimson flush of her cheeks. Mumbling a few words about getting a broom and bucket, she used the cover of the other students' laughter to escape the crowded room. Ducking into the first supply closet she came to, she shut the door behind her, turned a bucket over and plopped down with her hands covering her face. Once again, she'd managed to humiliate herself and her instructor. Despite her best efforts, she was still a misfit… unable to complete the simplest incantation without everything getting completely out of hand. She sighed, leaning forward and listening at the door.

No, they were still out there, waiting, like vhulls circling a dead rabbit. I hate when they stare. They could be so hateful. The idea of disappointing Master Stolinn once again brought her to tears. Despite extensive study and her every precaution, she couldn't recall the last time she'd completed an assignment without mishap. Notwithstanding it all, Master Stolinn never seemed to grow jaded, despite continuous derision from his fellow instructors. Ever pessimistic, they failed to understand why he was wasting his time on a student with so little control. Instead, he confessed to her that it didn't matter what others thought, it was what she thought of herself that mattered.

She wiped the last stray tear from her face with the sleeve of her robe, then grabbed the handle of the bucket she'd been using as a chair and a well-worn straw broom. Head high and eyes shining from unspent tears, she returned to the scene of her latest misadventure.

Two exhausting hours later the room was once again spotless. Damage was minimal, apart from the large section of exposed ceiling lathes left bare after the remaining plaster fell. Mekiva made one last quick check around the area and then gathered up her cleaning supplies to return them to the supply closet.

Twizzle, now fully recovered from his frightening ordeal, flitted past in an intricate aerial ballet as he chased a moth that had been unfortunate enough to fly in through her open window. Mekiva knew the pursuit would only keep him busy for a few moments, hopefully, long enough for her to snatch a brief moment of relaxation before the rambunctious kit demanded her attention after another of his never-ending exploits. Closing the door behind her she raced down the hall, stopping briefly at the storage cupboard to put away the broom and bucket. Twizzle would grow tired of his game and find her soon enough. Now to enjoy my time off, --- but first a quick dinner and a hot bath.

The institution's enormous kitchen was a madhouse. Everyone was racing back and forth trying to finish up their chores in time for the evening's festivities. Cook, a middle-aged woman almost as big around as she was tall, was standing in the middle of the room on a large meat cutting block that she often used to observe her small kingdom. From her designated perch the portly chef would merrily wave a rolling pin, pointing here and there as she urged the potboys to hurry up and finish putting things away. Ensconced in an alcove near the rear door, two young housemaids sat shelling peas, enjoying the antics as their young beaus scampered around the room like chickens with a fox chasing them.

Mekiva smiled as she entered the crowded room, it was always so entertaining in the kitchen. Most any time of day you could find bakers singing over their rising dough or butcher boys pulling feathers from hens while racing each other to see who finished first. And the smell was wonderful, so different from the pungent odors that surrounded her all day in the labs. It always reminded her of growing up on the farm.

"An what mite I be a-gettin' for ya, Miss Kee`vahh," Cook drawled, hopping down from her perch on the butcher block. "Dinna is long ov'ah an mos everthin is put to for da evenin'." She looked over Mekiva's shoulder anxiously, certain that a diminutive winged bandit was hiding somewhere nearby, ready to pounce upon her wildly curling grey locks at any moment. It was bad enough some twisted sorcerer had bred a housecat with a lizard, but then to give it wings… it was sick, that's what it was. Sick.

Mekiva resigned herself to another night without a hot dinner. Lately, it had developed into something of a habit--- an unwanted habit at that. Hesitantly she responded, "Twizzles stalking a moth, so we have a few minutes of peace before he shows up. I know it's late, but I wonder if there is anything I might use to make a picnic? I could take a basket and a blanket with me and eat while I watch the festivities."

This would be an ideal solution, as well as giving Gwendolyn an opportunity to escape her mother's store. The two teenage girls often spent their free time watching people passing by, making up little stories about how they imagined their lives to be. Considering how poor the town was, the stories were invariably more interesting than the actual lives of the average passerby.

Cook cracked a big smile, Mekiva was so different from the usual gaggle of arrogant brats that demanded, instead of asking, treating her as though she was a common bondservant. Twizzle, though a pest at times, had definitely cut down on the vermin infesting the grain bins. "I got jus de thing, you wait." She trotted into the storage pantry humming merrily under her breath.

"Please tell Cook I'll be right back, I'm going to take a quick bath and change my clothes."

Without waiting for an answer from the overworked pot-boy, Mekiva raced down the long hallway toward the students' bathhouse, barely avoiding two-floor maids and a startled house cat as she swept past. Upon entering the steamy room, she was pleased to find it totally empty. Today she was lucky, no waiting in line and getting stuck with a quick tepid dunk and scrub bath. Hastily she stripped off her dirty clothes, bundling them up and tossing them into a basket of similar items waiting to be washed. Luxuriating in her choice of tubs, she sank to her chin, soaking in the warmth for a few moments. It would be so easy to slowly drift off to sleep...

Startled awake by the water closing over her head, for a moment Mekiva had no idea where she was. It seemed only seconds had passed since she'd stepped into the tub, but the water was tepid, almost cold. Gwendolyn would be furious but she hated a cold bath. She quickly jumped out of the tub, dipped in a finger and whispered a warming cantrip, grinning when the bath temperature increased about twenty degrees. Sighing happily, she slipped back into the steaming water. She'd made the mistake of staying in the tub once. It was weeks before she'd shed all the burnt skin.

Dunking under the water to wet her hair, she used the hard lye soap to cut the dust and dirt that had changed her usually bright chestnut hair to a dull copper brown. Two buckets of cold water to rinse later and she felt ready to face the world again.

Slipping the ugly standard grey robe over her head, she turned and studied herself in the long full-length mirror on the wall, for once truly satisfied by what she saw. The slender body in the mirror was due to her lanky father. Her mother had gifted her with thick, dark chestnut hair that reached the small of her back and freckles that spattered across her small pert nose.

Well, I'll never be a beauty but all in all, not bad. My eyes are my best feature-- green like the foam of the sea and flaked with gold. I could be a little taller but at least I'm not tiny like Gwendolyn. No poets will ever pen epic poems about my beauty, but I usually manage to find plenty of partners at the local dances. Drasst, I'd better hurry or Gwen might think I'm not coming at all.

The kitchen was empty except for Twizzle, who was hastily finishing the last few bites of some unknown tidbit. He sat licking the last bit of grease from his paws as Mekiva examined the covered basket Cook had provided. Inside were the picked-over remnants of a cold roasted chicken, several half-eaten chunks of cheese and two soft loaves of brown bread. A ceramic container of three-band golden bees honey was tucked in beside it. Even better, wrapped inside a scrap of red cloth and somehow undisturbed by the inquisitive carnivore, was a raisin cake with buttercream icing.

"Pig!" she squealed as the Dra-cat fluttered overhead, eyes on the last bit of cold chicken remaining in the basket. "I guess I should be happy you left me any at all."

The voracious Draccat had not left enough to feed a real cat much less a half-starved human girl and her best friend. Once again, she'd have to improvise. Luckily, the money in her pocket made her feel comfortable, if not exactly flush with wealth. Gwendolyn would not have to foot the bill again. Time for fun!!

Two

It's said that time heals every wound, but no matter how much time passes, the scar will always remain. Yeah… be great if all I had to deal with was a stupid scar.

Balanced defiantly against the ship's figurehead as the Sirens Breath rose and fell with the outgoing swell, Vondal Botherton stared out across the inlet, enjoying his first view of Cabrell, the city of his birth. Cool bursts of early winter's breezes rising off the seawall whipped his shoulder-length hair around his face. Unaware of his childhood habit, he ran the tip of his tongue over his cracked lips, licking the crusty salt that had formed from the water in the air.

Dawn… at last. It'd been a long night. Crimson fingers of bright light breaking over the northern horizon signaled the imminent arrival of the first of Omission's twin suns. The early morning heat enticed the mists on the ocean waters into a naiad's dance, beckoning the heavily laden ship into the sea. Distant spires cast faint grey shadows across the vivid green and cool blues of the water, broken only by the hazy form of a gray shirk as it swam a lazy crisscross pattern around the ship while scouting for his breakfast. In the distance, a single bell rang hauntingly, announcing to all concerned that the Sirens Breath had finally arrived in port.

"Something's bothering you?"

Startled, Vondal lost his balance, grabbing hastily onto the breast of the bow's scantily clad figurehead in a desperate effort to keep from falling into the brackish water below. For a moment, he flinched, embarrassed as his hand slid along the breast before his fingers wrapped tightly around the upright nipple. Caught deep within the tangled nets of his ill-timed daydream, he'd failed to notice his silent friend standing nearby

"Nothing gets past you, does it?" He kicked out at his friend's head, not really trying to hit him, but clearly not caring if he did land a lucky blow.

"Hey, I'm not the one feeling sorry for myself. You've been moping around like a condemned man heading for his own funeral." Untouched by Vondal's display of self-pity, Jaxx made a halfhearted gesture with his three middle fingers before turning back to his bucket. He dunked the unwieldy mop he was carrying into the pail of soapy water and then slapped it down onto the worn wooden deck, sweeping it back and forth across the salt-stained planks a few times, before ducking it into the pail again.

Vondal swung his leg over the battered copper stanchion, wavered once or twice before catching his balance and then dropped gracefully down onto the deck, landing just to the right of his friend.

"I keep second-guessing myself. I should've killed that son of a mangy Wyvern while I had the chance. Every time I close my I eyes, I'm inundated by visions of my mother's battered body, there's blood everywhere. I still wake up screaming. Now I'm going back? Am I crazy?" Kneeling slightly outside the sodden mops arch, he reached down and picked up the end of a rope from a tangled pile and began winding it up, looping it over his shoulder and around his arm until it was too short to continue.

Jaxx struggled with an answer. Vondal hated his memories of Cabrell, it was a sore spot in every conversation. But Cabrell was situated on the main trade route between the Dyrropian Sea and Alliance. There was money to be made transporting food and supplies through the mountains to the mines nearby. Establishing a trade route between Cabrell and Alliance was their best chance for a successful business. He'd debated it with Jaxxx for five years. Once they'd even come to blows over it. Now was the time to either start their business or forget it completely.

He gave himself a mental shrug. It wasn't fear that held him back. There were very few things he was afraid of... nothing came to mind except the idea of facing his father again.

Jaxx fought back a smirk. The young entrepreneur rarely left himself this wide open to one of his ripostes. This could be a great opportunity to score a few points while recouping some payback from Vondal's earlier pranks. He debated, enjoying several possible retribution scenarios for a few seconds before deciding against it. Vondal had been right to tear into him after he got wasted in that dive in Altair last week. It was only by Tyche's grace that he'd escaped with only a scar on his wrist to remind him of his lack of judgment. One day his temper was going to get him in serious trouble.

Shrugging, he shoved the oversized horsehair mop across the deck a few more times and then dropped it into the bucket of grimy water. Vondal drove him crazy at times. He was always overanalyzing everything. He'd given up arguing with him long ago but that doesn't mean he had to let him off easy. But how...

"Stop complaining, you sound like a crabby old woman. Poor little Vondal...always whining about what might happen. Let's finish up what we started and lay low until we reach port." Jaxx's pales green eyes narrowed. "I never want to lay eyes on a mop again. Why the captain insists we scrub this old scow from bow to stern escapes me. It'll just get filthy during the offloading. Drasst!" He jumped back, cursing loudly as another watery white offering was deposited on the section of the deck he'd recently cleaned. "Stupid flying rats don't make it any easier." He swung the mops handle in a futile attempt to annihilate a pair of seagulls who fought over the remains of last night's dinner that had been recently dumped overboard by the ships cook. He felt better, but he would still need to re-clean it. Disgusted, he wrung the dirty water from his mop, then swiped at the bird droppings.

Vondal grinned, allowing a slight chuckle to escape at his friends' crude outburst before bending to pick up the end of another length of twisted hemp. Jaxx made life aboard the ship easier. The work was hard, everyone was expected to pull their own weight, but anything was better than his previous life. That part had sucked. He'd spent the better part of the last five years trying to forget. Now, he was going back, to Cabrell and to what was left of his family. Yes, of course, he had doubts. The idea of facing his father had him feeling like a ten-year-old again. Not that his father would have missed him, he doubted the sadistic drunkard had even noticed he was gone. He only sobered up when he ran out of money. It was his mother who'd made life bearable. Unconsciously Vondal wiped away a lone tear that fell from his bad eye. He'd never cried, not once, since he'd found her that night, her lifeless body lying at his fathers' feet, with him passed out drunk at the table.

That was the moment everything changed. Nightmares brought back bits and pieces, but he was never sure how much of it was true and how much was just wishful thinking. All he remembered was swinging, blow after blow until his father stopped moving. Then he ran until he was too tired to run anymore. He was still covered in blood when the ship's cook found him, asleep inside an empty water barrel. Unconsciously, his finger traced the jagged scar that marred his handsome features, a constant reminder of how fickle fate could be, fate and a cold-hearted woman.

"So, we go?" Jaxx asked. "This is it, your last chance to change your mind. Leaving the ship is a big step. If you can't hack it, now would be a good time to speak up."

"You can't do it alone," Vondal replied. "And it was my idea." Yeah, Jaxx's is always willing to try my ideas----especially when a profit was to be made." His mouth twisted slightly as he struggled to keep a grin off his face, so many of the memories dancing through his mind were of good times.

"Glad to see you're through doubting yourself. It was starting to get on my nerves. Yes, it'll be hard, anything worth having is. My mamma always told me: 'You gain strength and confidence when you look fear in the face'. Not sure where she heard it, but it makes sense."

Jaxx paused, remembering how she'd died. After all this time it still tore at his heart. He allowed his gaze to shift once more toward the small town growing closer as each minute passed. No, it wasn't going to be easy. Being the half-blood son of a Duaar chieftain had taught him that many years ago.

Stone-faced, he wrung the dirty water from his mop and then began talking again as he swiped at the salty buildup.

"We've been on this ship nigh on five years---five very

long years. We've torn up and been thrown out 'a more places than I'd care to admit to around the rim of the Star-Mist Sea. Some we survived, a few survived us. Together we can face anything, including your family."

"I know---I know, and I'll do what I need to do when the time comes." Vondal studied the piles of cargo waiting to be offloaded once the ship docked. "Right now, I only want to do two things, get this drassted ship unloaded and then get good and drunk." He glanced up at a group of coin girls walking by, hips swaying in time to the soft jingle of the bells around their ankles, and grinned. "Let's make it three things."

Jaxx quickly agreed.

The two young men spent the morning lounging alongside the ship's rail while the Sirens Breath awaited the Harbor Master's signal to unload. One ship, moored beside the Wyvern, was just finishing up. Stirred by the sight of a slaver's coffle of nubile flesh destined for the evening sale, the Sirens Breaths' crew let out a series of whistles, catcalls and cheers, followed by a loud united guffaw as one overly enthusiastic sailor leaned too far forward and lost his hold, dropping into the icy saltwater. The elderly bosom, torn between laughter and duty, finally tossed the half-drowned youth a line before his fingers grew too cold to hold the line. The excited crew waited, fidgeting impatiently as the ship edged ever closer to the wharf and their long-awaited furloughs.

As soon as the harbormaster gave the signal, Vondal grabbed up a nearby box and slung it onto his shoulder. Not to be outdone, Jaxx grabbed two equally large bags and carried them both toward the wagon waiting at the end of the loading ramp.

"I shoulda know'd it, las three years I practically 'ad

to beat ya to get much of anythin' done." Captain Myles Brannigan leaned forward to get a better view of the two young men at work. "Now, yer ready to unload the whole ship by ye'selves, just so ye can be off." He watched the two young men as they worked, knowing that it was going to be the last time he saw them again. It was going to be difficult to replace them. Vondal was a born leader, he often managed to keep the peace aboard the ship during the long stretches away from shore when tempers ran short and hot. Other than one incident that earned him the scar that parted his eyebrow, he couldn't remember a time when the boy had ever stepped out of bounds.

As for Jaxx, he was fair-haired, with startling blue eyes that appeared to bore into your soul and an angelic face that could charm the sourest maiden into a smile. Just average in height, but that was all that was average about the young Duaar. He was one of the strongest men the captain had ever chanced upon, and fast too. Many a fool had mistakenly wagered on a much bigger man, only to lose his hard-earned pay to the wiry muscles hidden beneath the well-worn clothes. He'd have to hire two men in hopes of getting the same amount of work done. He grinned. "Should I call a few of the cooks up here to help you boys out?"

Vondal raised an eyebrow, offering the captain a rakish grin as he deposited another heavy box on top of several others that had already been brought ashore. Captain Brannigan was like that, always complaining aloud, but never meaning anything he said. Both men had long ago learned that his bark was much worse than his bite. Jaxx was already halfway back up to the deck. If he didn't hurry his brother might get snappish, and unlike the captain, Jaxx's bite hurt.

Not much later Vondal dropped the last bolt of cotton on the dock and signaled the harbormaster that the job was complete. Captain Brannigan nodded his approval before shaking both boys' hands one last time.

"Sure'n ye boys twon't be for changen ye minds?"

Neither hesitated.

"No way, Captain!" they shouted as one.

The Captain shrugged and turned away. There'd soon be two more just like them ready to see the world from the deck of a ship. The sea was a harsh mistress, but her arms were always open to those who heard her siren call. In fact, I see a promising candidate already waiting at the end of the gangway. A big boy, too. A sad smile creased his features for roughly a second, then he motioned for the first mate to bring the lad aboard. Too bad he wasn't Duaar…

Jaxx raced Vondal to the gangway, reaching the deck before the mate caught up with the potential cabin boy. "First thing, we need a place to eat and sleep, and then we need to find a way to earn some money. Let's get going." He gathered up his seabag, shifted his ax so that it didn't flop around while he walked and headed towards shore. Jaxx winked at the gangly youngster waiting to board as he passed. Vondal shifted own bag, took a deep breath and followed him away from the busy docks.

Three

"You're kidding, right? When you said this place was a bit of a dump you were being generous."

Jaxx swallowed, retching from the stink of the rancid sewage flowing down the street nearby. He found himself silently praying that Vondal was teasing him and had no intention of dragging him into the ratty looking wharf dive. The cool breeze off the sea was as familiar as a woman's touch, and as welcome, as it brought with it a welcome relief for his overworked nostrils. The reek of rotting garbage piled near the entrance of the public house had announced the location of the tavern long before the two friends were close enough to make out the faded sign that hung by one rusty nail above the door. Someone had made a halfhearted attempt at painting what could be loosely interpreted as a woman's leg wearing a ladies dancing shoe. Only the faded lettering "Silver Slipper Tavern" saved it from being an abject failure. He doubted a slipper had ever graced the inside of the bar. Most of the women in this part of town went barefoot except for the coldest days, and heavy leather boots cost much less than thin silk.

He reached for the door, then jumped back as a plump rat slunk around the edge and trotted casually down the sidewalk. Stretched out on top of a nearby rain barrel enjoying the afternoon sun, a local cat greeted them with a yawn, then calmly turned over and went back to sleep, ignoring the nonchalant rodent.

"What was wrong with the other four dumps we passed? This one serves a better quality of swill?" He kept his eyes open for another rat, but none were in sight.

"Yep. My father's second home. He's usually here until he passes out. Sometimes the city watch will bring him home and dump him before our door. Cheaper than taking him to jail I guess."

Old Maggie had named the place 'The Silver Slipper Tavern' in a deliberate attempt to fool unfamiliar travelers into believing that the flophouse was a respectable tavern. Instead, it became the dark heart of Downside, a section of Cabrell usually skirted at all costs by any sensible person. This included the vast majority of Cabrell's City Watch, a police force made up of the lesser sons of local businessmen with enough money to buy them a commission.

The two friends stood for a moment listening to the sound of a badly played piano floating on the night air.

Old Mort's still banging away at the only three songs he knows. Nothing changes. Once his good eye had adjusted to the dim lighting in the doorway, Vondal pushed open the swinging doors and entered the smoky room. Looking around, he was astonished to find out that something had changed! His father wasn't inside.

"Well… are we going to stand here until we grow roots or are we going to get that drink?" Jaxx pushed past Vondal, passing through the swinging doors of the room. Despite the dim lighting provided by the three smoking oil lamps, he had no problem seeing, one of the traits he'd received from his Duaar father. He stepped to the right to circumvent a couple of men who lounged against the wall in whispered conversation, then made his way to a vacant bench along a wall near the Bar. Content, he dropped all the packs he carried into a pile and sank down on the hard planks beside them. Then he laid his head back against the wall, closed his eyes and did his best to go to sleep.

Vondal ignored his lack of demeanor. Jaxx could be such a boor at times. It was better to accept his quirks then make any attempt to explain his bad behavior and tactless comments. He'd often contemplated what drunken debacle had induced the lust of the demon that spawned his recalcitrant brother. He might have the face of an angel, but he had the personality of a denizen born of a distinctly different locale. It was the only explanation that made sense. Since Jaxx never talked about his parents it left a lot of room for his imagination.

Vondal let his eyes roam around the room, re-familiarizing himself with the furnishing and decorations he'd not seen in over five years. His expression softened as he studied the single oil painting that hung behind the polished mahogany bar: a portrait of a titian-haired, sloe-eyed beauty with a come-hither smile and a body that would turn a strong man into a blithering idiot. Especially the eyes; there the artist had captured a glimpse of the devilish personality that had made Maggie such a sensation amongst the youth of Cabrell. But that had been a long time ago and he'd seen the real-life version of the painting too many times to fantasize.

The rest of the room seemed the same, a scattering of mismatched chairs and tables filled the middle of the room. Along the entire perimeter of the wall ran a narrow board bench, offering seating but little else. There was a curtained door to the rear, leading to a staircase used to access the rooms upstairs. The dirty unkempt condition of the tavern worried him. Something had changed dramatically in the years he'd been gone. Maggie might run a dive, but it had always been a clean dive. Even the dance halls already disreputable clientele had devolved, if that was possible, into an even smarmier group of characters. His eyes narrowed as a smallish, rat-faced man, who had been lounging back in his chair as he studied his cards, nearly fell in his haste to scramble to his feet. He managed to grab the rickety table and steady himself, losing his hat in the process and disrupting the game in progress. Despite the man's attempt to nonchalant while looking his way, he kept glancing in their direction, a sure sign that he was watching them. Vondal was about to turn away when a subtle hand gesture from a second man reclining on the bench nearby made him look more closely.

Drasst! Watch yourself Vondal! Don't jump to conclusions. There's doubtless a simple answer for their behavior, probably too much of Maggie's Best. He observed the rat-faced man wander around the room for a few moments, stopping here and there for a brief conversation, before he made his way out of the swinging doors and disappeared.

Vondal scanned the room once more before making his way over to a weathered wooden bar made from cast-off planks from salvaged ships, where a haggard-looking barmaid stood wiping at a spill. Silently she poured two shots of rotgut without waiting for his order, the bar minimum.

"Is Maggie around darling?" Vondal leaned down and placed his hands against the bar, so he could look the scrawny, once pretty, young woman, directly in her eyes.

She stopped her half-hearted attempt to clean the dirty countertop, a scarlet flush slowly creeping across her cheeks as she shifted her threadbare bodice to better show her meager assets. It worked. Her body, though on the smallish side, was well rounded, after three months at sea, she easily caught his attention.

"Wait and I'll get her." She winked, offering him a wicked smile that hinted of interesting possibilities, before walking over to a swinging door that divided the main room from the kitchen beyond. "Maggie!" She called, "Someone here askin' for ya!"

There was a lull in the rattle and bang of the kitchen pots, then a familiar voice answered from behind the stringy curtained door.

"Who is it?"

"Don't know, never laid eyes on him before." *Not that he's bad on the eyes at all. That scar adds just a hint of a bad boy, doesn't hurt his looks at all…* The barmaid picked up another glass and half-heartedly wiped it clean, but continued to keep her eyes on the handsome young man before her.

Seconds later a skinny old woman came through the half door behind the bar, drying her hands on an equally old and well-used apron. At one time she must have been a beauty, but years of hard work and harder living had taken their toll on Maggie's appearance, leaving her haggard and tired looking. Her hair, once an eye-catching titian halo, was now a dull and lusterless mop of rusty copper threaded with salt and pepper grey. She moved closer, peering through squinted eyes at Vondal, and then gasped aloud, a wide smile erasing the years from her face.

"Lands sakes nephew! Never thought I'd see your handsome mug around these parts again. What brings you back to this hell hole?" She waved the bemused barmaid away, directing her to take care of another customer.

Vondal winced as she spoke. The last time he'd visited, she had been leading the crowd in a boisterous roundelay.

She wouldn't be singing any time soon, her voice, once soft and seductive, was now frail and wispy, as if she was having trouble catching her breath.

"Good to see you too Maggie, we came here straight from the ship."

He moved forward drawing the old woman into a warm embrace. Drasst! What in the hells had happened to his beautiful aunt? Times may be hard, but.... he'd seen bodies laid out for burial that looked livelier than the wizened old woman standing before him.

"Almost didn't recognize you with that long hair. That scar over your eye, it's new, too. Came in on the Sirens Breath, did you?" The old woman pointed her withered arm in the direction of the bay. "Best be leaving the same way. Better still if you had never returned."

"I'm looking for my father Maggie."

"He with you?" she asked, looking across the room at Jaxx, who was now stretched out on the bench, his head resting on his ship's bag.

Vondal nodded.

"Then get your friend."

Vondal could tell from her expression it wasn't going to be good news, but any information would help. A lot had changed in Cabrell, most apparent, the absence of street vendors and beggars around the city that had once been the main supply lines for gossip and information. He'd passed several watch stations, manned by hawkish men in blue uniforms on the way to the bar and figured that might have something to do with the lack of indigents.

He whistled once sharply to get Jaxx's attention. Jaxx sat up abruptly, his hand moving toward a well-used ax lying nearby. Once he realized Vondal was not in trouble, he calmed, got slowly to his feet and made his way through the tangle of tables to join his friend at the bar. Green eyes narrowed slightly as Maggie reached up to a shelf overhead, but he relaxed as she grabbed two clay mugs, filled them with a foamy amber mix, and then sat them on the bar in front of them, removing the rotgut and dumping it back into a keg standing nearby.

"Better ta drink up boys, ya ain't gonna like hear'n this." She waited until both had swallowed a few mouthfuls, then poured their mugs full again. "Your father's dead now--- gone three years. The watch found him in his bed--- or at least what was left of him---the house picked clean by thieves. Ain't seen a sign of your brothers since right after you took off. No use in going back home, what was left of the house caught fire and burned soon after he died. Nothing left but a small pile of burnt timber. Even the rocks got totted off."

Vondal swept Jaxx's face seeking advice, but his friend merely shook his head, not willing to offer an opinion without knowing more about the situation. Unsure what this news would mean to his plans, Vondal took a long sip from the brimming mug and gathered his thoughts. Another woman might be taken aback by his lack of immediate response, however, his aunt had years of practice in dealing with drunken alcoholics. His little delay in answering would not raise an eyebrow.

"You know who did it?" he asked after pondering a moment.

Maggie's face furrowed as if she'd eaten something sour. "Rumor has it he crossed Samsara. I know Castillo was looking for him at that time. But I don't buy it. Samsara's too flamboyant. He likes to make a public spectacle out of anyone ignorant enough to cross him. Says it keeps order. Simply killing your father and burning the house doesn't fit his protocol. No ceremony, no lesson."

She cracked a wizened grin. "Truth be told, most people around here don't want to know what happened to your father---or who did it. The least known, the safer they feel. Things ain't like they used to be. Samsara's got big dreams, once he got control of the Bottoms, he expanded his interests from petty thievery to politics. Don't know how he did it, maybe extortion or bribery. Either way, he now runs the city. Not that his lordship the mayor and his cronies don't do everything they can to line their own pockets Between the two of them, most of the smaller businesses are just skimping by, praying we make enough to stay in business.

Maggie looked around the room and noticed that a few of her regulars were missing. "Gossip says your uncle was asking after you about that time. He's Lord Botherton now--made it big in the shipping business and bought the title of Mayor. Your uncles offered a big reward for information leading to your whereabouts. Strange…he didn't mention your brothers. Bet there's two or three of my regular customers knocking on the back door of his mansion as we speak."

She sighed. "Gonna be big trouble for me once Samsara hears tell I helped you, instead of sending word to Castillo. But you're my nephew and blood is blood."

"So there is no one in town that I can get information from?"

She paused for a moment to gather her thoughts and then nodded sympathetically. "You might try old Mathias. He knows a lot of things about a lot of people… she cracked a toothless grin and continued, …if you can get him sober enough to talk."

"What's wrong with you?" Jaxx asked forthrightly.

Maggie didn't try to pretend she'd no idea what he was

asking. She smiled, briefly allowing him a glimpse of the broken remains of her once pearly white teeth and when she answered, her accent was back. "Taint nothing ya kin catch, so don't be worryin'. Old age and wild living 'ave caught up with me. The healers say ain't no cure, not that I can afford ta pay one anyways."

" Shi'i?" Vondal asked.

"Boy, the Shi'i-Lakka care for the rich and entitled. Not the likes o' me." Her eyes were constantly moving, scanning the bar as she talked. Momentarily they darkened, then the sparkle was back. She didn't look happy.

Vondal followed her gaze across the crowded room, finding only dark glares and silence. A few of the sharper clientele were quickly clearing up their business and making an obvious move to leave the premises.

"Like rats from a sinking ship," he thought, as two brightly painted coin girls gathered their things and left through the door without customers. This alone would have been enough warning to signal something bad was coming…soon.

Though nothing usually upset her, Maggie was alarmed at the rapid desertion of her regular patrons. Her eyes darted to the door.

"Troubles coming, time for you boys to go." She spoke slowly, her voice little more than a whisper. She opened a latched gate at the end of the bar that acted as a barricade against drunken customers before addressing the barmaid who hovered nearby. "Bev, take over here and make sure nothing wanders off."

Maggie turned back to the boys, "Don't let that goofy grin fool you, nothing gets by Bev. Took her a while to get the insipid look right, but now she's got most of the watch completely fooled. If anyone comes by looking for you, she'll stall 'em as long as she can. You boys get your things and come into the kitchen with me. Best I slip you out the back way. If you go down the alley to the market, with luck, you might lose them in the crowds."

Shouldering their packs, they followed Maggie through the swinging doorway into a surprisingly clean and well-stocked kitchen. Vondal couldn't help watching over his shoulder as Maggie unbarred the back door and motioned them outside. Jaxx let his eyes drift to a tray of hot buttered scones he noted on a warming stand near the hearth, his growling stomach reminding him it was long past dinner. Maggie failed to offer the tempting repast and they didn't have time to debate the issue, so he kept his mouth shut and suffered in silence.

Behind the building was a small grassy courtyard surrounded by a high wooden fence. Slipping quietly through the dark to the fence, Vondal put his hands on the top of the slats and felt no broken glass or nails. It was safe to go over.

"Feels clear, you go first," he whispered.

"Give me a bootup," Jaxx grunted to his slightly slimmer companion. He was already regretting his missed dinner and the haunting odor of freshly baked bread wafting through the open door only made it worse. Using Vondal's crossed hands as a step he managed to raise his stocky frame up and over the top.

Vondal kissed his aunt lightly on her cheek, and then quickly clambered over the fence, dropping down to the ground beside his friend, only to have his feet slip in the muck. His arms wind-milled wildly as he unsuccessfully fought for balance, before landing on his backside. His antics startled some feral neighborhood cats that were searching the rubbish piled outside. Screeching loudly, they defended their territory with claws and teeth before disappearing into the nearby shadows.

"Stop playing with the drassted cats. I don't know why I bothered whispering when you make enough noise to wake the dead," Jaxx jibed, pleased with the opportunity to deliver the one-liner. Cackling like a hen, he pulled Vondal back to his feet.

"Stop giggling like a moron, it wasn't that funny. Shut up and let's get going."

Gwendolyn is going to be furious. The crowds around the market are ridiculous today. Mekiva cautiously wove her way through revelers intent on enjoying the harvest festival. Catching a glimpse of movement from the corner of her eye, she hastily stepped backward managing to sidestep around two heavyset women coming out of a clothing shop, their arms piled high with packages. A more pragmatic person would have kept walking without consideration. It was as much her right to be on the street as it was theirs, and Gwendolyn was waiting. But the way her luck was running the two women would be married to highly placed school officials, maybe even one of her own instructors.

"Best to be safe than sorry… Hope Gwendolyn feels the same." She paused to consider her options for a moment. Her basket held the basics but there was nothing in it that would soothe her best friends' wounded feelings, especially since Twizzle's teeth marks eliminated any chance the meticulous Shi'i-Lakka maiden would partake of the cheese or chicken. The frosted cake was untouched, and the bread and honey, but there wasn't enough food remaining for one, much less two hungry girls. "I'll stop in the market and pick up a few special things. It's not really out of my way and I'm already late."

Brightly decorated food stalls and booths lined both sides of the busy market street in celebration of the on-going Harvest Festival. Mekiva was drawn in several directions---the enticing smells of freshly baked bread, hot roast mutton dripping over coals, hot meat pies and sweet fruit pastry all making her mouth water. She chose a stall she often frequented, ordering one of Gwendolyn's favorite dishes ---sliced mutton in a spicy sauce cooked with chopped nuts and mushrooms. A sweet vendor nearby provided a sack of sugared figs and dates for dessert. Twizzle must have tired of shopping. He vanished on one of his jaunts, probably looking for an open window facing someone's kitchen or larder. Mekiva grimaced, remembering the last time the unruly Mir cub had gone scavenging, helping himself to a link of blood-sausages hanging in butchers' window. That little escapade had cost her several days of hard labor as well as an entire week's stipend. He'd show up tired and famished and then finish off anything leftover in the basket.

Spying a busy bake shop, she hesitated for a moment. Gwendolyn loved the sweet sticky buns with white icing, so she dashed in to buy a few. After paying out the last few of her coins, she was finally satisfied with her small repast. She placed her purchases into her basket along with the food she'd brought from the school. Now, it would be enough for both Gwendolyn and for her to enjoy. And maybe Gwendolyn won't be quite so annoyed…

Four

Vondal fell heavily against the wall of a sadly neglected wooden building, taking advantage of the cover provided by a half-collapsed awning to catch his breath. Despite the uproar from the crowds gathered in the market nearby, he was certain each raspy inhalation was loud enough to draw the searchers' attention directly to their current position.

Jaxx's breathing was worse. The two friends had been running nonstop since leaving Maggie's Tavern, down back alleys and dark streets, using buildings, trees, and other objects to hide them in hopes of evading capture by the men following close behind. He listened, studying the people nearby. If anyone was interested, they were good enough to hide it. For the moment they were safe.

Vondal was worried about Jaxx. The Duaar was great in a fight being strong and well-coordinated. But running… After ten years aboard a ship even walking on a flat surface was difficult for him. He needed a place to rest.

"How'd we manage to get the city watch on our trail?"

"I guess all ---the noise you made--- playing with the drassted cat." Jaxx struggled to get the words out.

"Haw. Haw! So now it's against the law to play?"

"Who knows--- maybe thieves--- have been working-- the area. The watch -----might think—we're working --- with them. Not--- that there's ---anything worth--- stealing back there."

"Musta heard you were looking for a date and wanted to protect their daughters," Vondal fired back. Tired or not, he hated to waste any opportunity to get one over on the arrogant ex-marine.

"Ain't it nice--- to be popular?" Jaxx offered with a wry grin, refusing to take the bait.

"Just shut up and run," Vondal called back over his shoulder.

Jaxx didn't bother to reply.

"Yaaga blast you all to the Nine Realms! If they escape, it won't be your jobs you'll be losing." He pointed to two of his men. "You men cover that side, the rest take this one. They're heading for the market. Cut them off before they reach the festival crowds." After affirming that for once his orders were being followed, Prefect Aku-Ballar paused to wipe his forehead and take a sip of water. Over an hour had been wasted chasing the young men and he still had no idea who they were or why they were wanted. Standing orders were to bring in the tall man with the scar and his Duaar friend, or else.

It was the "or else" that worried him, as he'd received his own stripes after his last commander had failed to act in accordance with a similarly worded request. Resigned to a few more hours of pointless searching, he sighed deeply and resumed the chase.

He was getting too old for this kind of thing. He should retire. Unfortunately, the desk jobs offered to the officers of the city watch were expensive to obtain, ... much too expensive for a middle-aged letch with both a wife and five children; and a young and quite expensive mistress. Only last night he'd noticed her eyes traveling to a younger, handsome, cadet. He knew once his gold was gone, she too would become a pleasant memory.

After following the distant sounds of drums and flutes, Jaxx and Vondal turned the corner that brought them into sight of the shopping bazaar. Colorful banners hung from poles, dancing in the flickering light of the torches that burned at almost every stall. Revelers of all races could be seen in the crowded lanes. Despite the danger, both boys paused to watch three scantily clad maidens with bells on their ankles swaying provocatively before a colorfully dressed Ransooni. His fingers danced along the strings of a musical instrument neither boy recognized, the melody both haunting and provocative. Nearby, a stoic dusky-skinned mercenary stood silent vigil over a jeweler's stall, his eyes constantly moving as he attempted to keep watch on the milling crowds while guarding his employers stock against opportunistic thieves. He gave the two boys a once over before dismissing them as a prospective threat.

The crowds were thickest around the food stalls. Jaxx motioned for Vondal to work his way toward the busiest section of the bazaar hoping the spectators would hide them from view. At least for the moment, the desperate escape plan appeared to be working. The two groups chasing them kept getting in each other's way, allowing the two boys some small glimmer of hope that they might get away among the milling populace.

Realizing that a chase was on---and who it was that was doing the chasing--- many of the shoppers, as well as quite a few merchants, turned their attention from haggling over gaudy merchandise to the entertainment in the street. Eagar to get some small amount of payback, many of the poorer citizens of Cabrell utilized any obstacle available to interfere with the pursuit. One or two of the smaller children began pelting the pursuers with discarded fruit and vegetables from the garbage piled nearby.

A scattered cheer rose up from the nearby market stalls as the harried teenagers barreled through a basket weaver's booth, jumping from table to table to escape the pursuers. The unfortunate proprietor's merchandise rolled out into the street, further hampering the chase as the men in pursuit dodged awkwardly around the bulky baskets.

Hoping to cash in on the unique opportunity, a gaudily dressed Bezonite started taking bets, offering odds on the outcome of the hunt. There was intense speculation over which team would catch the erstwhile young men. Depending on the bets the odds changed constantly. This added to the confusion as some of the gamblers took the opportunity to hedge their bets by delaying the opposing team of pursuers as often as possible. Many others sought to slow the chase by misdirecting the pursuit, calling out false directions to the group they had bet against.

Utilizing the height of a nearby wagon, Prefect Aku-Ballar managed to detect Vondal just as he made his desperate dash through the basket shop. He immediately began screaming out orders, using his sword to point out directions to his men. With faces down to protect them from the rotten produce, the soldiers made a halfhearted attempt to push their way through the throngs of shoppers.

Their commanders bellowing only provoked the milling crowds into further turmoil, many ignoring the shouted orders to move out of their way. Only after the two escapees were once more out of sight did the jubilant gamblers move slowly to the sides of the street to allow the guards a clear path.

Less than a block separated Vondal and Jaxx from the pursuit when the two men finally dropped to the ground, exhausted, behind a vegetable vendor's cart to once again gulp mouthfuls of air.

"Jaxx, ---this isn't ---working." Now Vondal was also straining to catch his breath, his chest burning from the run, "let's separate--- and try--- to lose them--- in the crowd."

"We've--- got to try---something," Jaxx agreed between each ragged breath. "I can't handle---this pace. We need--- to try separating." He hated running, his well-muscled body was built for short bursts of speed, not stamina. His heart was pounding, his lungs ached, and the slight twinge in his side had developed into a series of sharp muscle spasms.

Vondal realized he needed to buy some time for his exhausted friend. He studied the surrounding area, then a sly grin came across his face. "Jaxx, I'm going to lead them away. Find someplace to lie low."

"You know ---you can't ---do anything ---without me."

Vondal glared and reluctantly he nodded agreement. He puckered up his lips and blew a kiss at his friend, overly exaggerating his action between gasps of air.

Despite his exhaustion, Vondal laughed aloud at his friends' antics before clutching his aching side. "Jaxx, just go--- I can't handle---any more pain." He took off again, looking for something to cause an uproar. Spotting an unguarded vendors cart filled with cabbages parked nearby, he gave it a push, trusting that the natural slope of the street would keep it moving. The unwieldy conveyance rolled true, bowling over several browsers gathered before a jewelry display before finally coming to a stop. It was now wedged between a fountain and the outside wall of a stone building, effectively blocking the passageway --- and access to most of the city guard. A group of tradesmen intent on being among the first to inspect the newest offerings freshly offloaded from the Sirens Breath found their passage blocked. Immediately they started pushing and shoving one another, blaming each other for the delay.

Vaulting upon the cart blocking the aisle, Vondal began hurling heads of cabbage, striking one pursuer in the side and another upon the head. Once he was satisfied he had their full attention he drew his sword, yelling aloud and waving it over his head to draw the notice of the remainder. His objective met, Vondal ran, taunting the crowd and swinging his sword around his head wildly.

To give Jaxx as much time as possible he began tossing anything within reach, overturning stalls, large baskets of fruit and vegetables, and cages of live fowl behind him, furious vendors joined the mob further slowing down the chase.

Glancing at a nearby storefront, Vondal caught a brief impression of an unkempt body reflected in the glass, just before someone clamped a hand onto his shoulder. Caught completely off guard, he panicked. Twisting left, he kicked out with his foot, catching the unknown man directly above his knee. His assailant crumpled, allowing Vondal to break free. Fear overwhelmed sense, sending him into a panic-stricken run that took him up and down alleys, through buildings, over fences and random stairways, and occasionally back toward the festival until he could no longer see anyone on his tail.

Gradually he slowed his pace to a walk. Now he needed to rest and get his wind back. But where? Spotting the crowded shop of a meat vendor Vondal took a chance and slipped inside. Instantly, he realized his mistake. Dropping flat to the ground, he somehow managed to duck below the heavy metal meat cleaver as it passed over his head. Chips of lumber flew through the air as the blade bit deeply into the shop's wooden framework. The angry proprietor strained to dislodge the cleaver, eager to remove his uninvited guest before the ongoing pursuit arrived to wreak further havoc on his business.

Vondal scrambled for an opening, hoping to escape with his head intact, slipping under the low wooden counter at the rear of the butchers' stall and out into the crowded lane. Somehow he avoided a collision with two desert clad revelers who were passing by.

Faced with a choice between the two unknown nomads (and possibly two experienced swordsmen) and the hotheaded butcher and his cleaver, he panicked and froze. Which way? To the left was a busy market lane, to the right a narrow alley that opened into another crowded market district.

Right. His decision made, Vondal lunged, only to be tripped up as the corpulent butcher tackled him from behind. Pain shot down his left side as his shoulder slammed into the rough stone corner of the building facing the alley. The jarring pain brought tears to his eyes and caused him to drop his pack. The meat cutter used his weight to his advantage, rolling on top to pin his face down. Vondal reacted without thought, snapping his head back into the face of his assailant. Blood erupted from the man's shattered nose. The butcher sat backward, his hands clutched to his bleeding face, swaying slightly from the pain.

Finding his arms miraculously free, Vondal heaved his body upwards, throwing the dazed man off balance. Squirming free, he snatched up his pack, grinned at the two amused desert men and sprinted away.

Jaxx studied the crowd from his hiding spot beneath the brightly colored tarp surrounding a closed pottery stand. No one seemed to be paying any attention to him, everyone was watching Vondal's antics with the sword. Now was his chance. He crawled toward a nearby weaver's booth. Once inside, he wove his way through the stacked bolts of cloth to the rear of the booth and out the back of the canvas. The crowd gathered near a hand pie vendors cart looked large enough to block him from view, he took a chance and joined a group of women heading in that direction. The food vendor's cart was backed up to an old stone building, and better yet, next to it was a dimly lit alley. Offering a silent plea to whichever God might be listening, he made a break for the narrow opening.

Ten feet into the passage he hesitated, overcome by the horrific odor. The nearby businesses must have been using the alley to dispose of their urine and other waste matter, the smell was appalling. Circumstances being what they were, Jaxx decided he could stand the stench a lot easier than he could handle jail...or worse. That decided, he continued onward. Twenty feet farther the alley widened, offering him a slight breeze and more room to maneuver. Better yet, the foul odor was less noticeable.

He shivered, as his sweat cooled in the breeze. It was growing noticeably colder, and it looked like it might start snowing soon. He could handle the cold for a while, but snow bothered him. They needed to find a place to stay soon.

A hearty appetite also came along with the Duaar bloodline, and his empty stomach reminded him once more that it had been hours since he'd last eaten. Now his nose joined in. The heady scents of yeast and baking bread seeped through several cracks in an older chimney that had lost its chink. A bakery and it was still open for business from the sounds coming through the wall.

There were three possible entrances to the bakery from the alley, however, all three were securely locked. One rusty lock looked promising. A nearby trash file provided a bent piece of wire. He easily picked the rudimentary lock and entered the small room. It was not the bakery, but at least it was warmer than the streets. Pressed up against the side of the warm chimney he slumped to the dirt floor, asleep almost before his eyes closed.

Lost them, I knew I could. Vondal slowed, walking slowly and blending into the milling crowd as he moved in the direction of the harbor. Jaxx was always lecturing him, warning him to be careful, so he paused occasionally and listened for the sounds of footsteps following. Nothing… he was safe for now.

Despite his sketchy memories of Cabrell, Vondal was certain that if he crossed the street at the corner, it would enable him to take a shortcut down a nearby alley. That would allow him to cut out about three blocks of travel while placing him near the infamous cabbage cart. Jaxx would be nearby, safe in a bolt-hole out of the weather. He was certain he could find him. Whistling a familiar sea ditty, he began jogging down the alley, not slowing down as he reached the end and turned the corner onto the busy bazaar street.

He managed about five steps before crashing into a young woman coming out of a bakery. Startled, the young woman grabbed onto his arm to try to slow her fall, dropping her basket at his feet. Somehow, she managed to look graceful throughout it all.

"Don't you ever look where you are going?" Her green eyes flashed angrily. Cursing under her breath she dropped to her knees, scurrying to pick up the scattered contents of her basket from the crowded street before someone stepped on them. She brushed off each item, checking it for damage, and then placed it back into the basket.

Vondal cringed. Raised with three sisters he was familiar with angry women, and this one was really mad. Muttering an apology, he attempted to help her to her feet.

"Put me down, you Orrog's whelp. Haven't you done enough damage?"

How could such a tiny body produce such deafening noise? Vondal pondered, awestruck by the diminutive redhead before him.

She dusted off the front of her gown, continuing her angry tirade. "If you used your head for something besides a hat rack, you might have noticed me exiting the bakery."

Vondal pushed his long dark hair away from his face and smiled down at the auburn-haired beauty scolding him in the middle of the crowded market. Noticed her? Hells! How could anyone miss her, she's lovely. Or she would be if she wasn't frowning. Her eyes are gorgeous, green like Jaxx's, but darker now. I wonder what color they are when she wasn't angry. Sea mist maybe?

He'd heard the expression "looks could kill" before

but until today he'd never experienced it. Vondal found himself thanking the Gods she didn't have a knife handy. Not that he blamed her, it was his fault he'd run into her. He'd been so busy watching behind him, he was blind to anyone coming from the front.

"My apologies mistress." For some reason, he was finding it hard to force the words out of his mouth. "No harm meant. I often do the first thing that pops into my head, and then realize afterward I'd made a mistake." He flushed, realizing it wasn't helping the situation.

"Well, that's no reason for your behavior, merely a flimsy excuse." She continued to glare at him, heedless of the people beginning to gather around them.

Vondal couldn't take his eyes off her. She was tall for a woman, but the top of her head barely reached his chin. A little thunderstorm, loud and blustery but not dangerous, in fact,---

"I know you!" he blurted out. He blushed a bright scarlet as he realized he'd uttered the words out loud. "I mean, we used to play games. Ummm, …when we were children,… in the hayloft…on the farm." He was steadily digging a deeper hole.

Embarrassed and once again at a loss for words, he hastened to think of something to say, anything, that would make him seem less a fool. There was plenty to use for inspiration. Hair the color of a ripe chestnut and a cute button nose, with barely a sprinkle of freckles. And a body that made you … Drasst, he was doing it again. Get your mind back on the matter at hand. He was considering just how he was going to slip away without cringing in shame when Jaxx's cynical voice broke into the silence.

"Not wanting to intrude on this magical moment, but I think you might be interested in knowing that we have company coming."

Vondal tore his gaze from Mekiva's face, staring up the street in the direction Jaxx was pointing. Sure enough, he detected the plumed tops of two watch helmets above the crowd, and they were heading their way. If the watch had found them, Castillo's men were nearby. He was certain that watching him being jailed would ruin any chance he had of reuniting with the mysterious young woman. Then someone in the crowd yelled a warning that a couple of thugs were in a nearby bar, asking questions. Vondal decided he'd have to leave the conversation for another time.

"Sorry about your basket. I'll make it up to you somehow. But now I've to go. Come on Jaxx, now might be a good time to get a room." The two young men trotted off in the direction of the harbor. After a few steps, Vondal suddenly stopped and looked back to see if the girl was still standing there. She was.

"Don't forget me," he yelled. Mekiva watched him until he was no longer in sight, then she hurried off to meet Gwendolyn.

"Sorry, I'm late…but Gwendolyn, you won't believe what happened." Mekiva launched into a description of her day, starting with the misfired spell, the chase in the market and ending with the astonishing young man she'd literally run into in the lane outside the bakery.

"I don't why…", she gave a brief shudder, "…but he made me feel like I was on display. It was like he was judging me." Those eyes…

"Probably making sure you hadn't picked his pockets."

"Honestly Gwendolyn! It wasn't like that. I felt like he

was appraising me, deciding if I was worth his time." What if I wasn't? What if he thought I was an ugly shrew?

"Makes me glad I'm Shi'i-Lakka," Gwendolyn remarked wryly. "No man will ever affect me that way." She tied a small knot in her sewing, cut the excess thread and placed it into a basket to be ironed. "Toss me that blue tunic."

She giggled as Mekiva stuck out her tongue, before wadding the freshly laundered shirt into a ball and throwing it at her head. Now she'd have to iron it again.

"It's strange, he seemed so familiar," Mekiva continued. "But I've no idea where I could have met him. I've never been anywhere… except for my family's farm and the school. I'm positive he's not a student at the school. Goddess knows I've been laughed at by every one of them at least once."

"Mind your stitches! You girls and your fantasies, a handsome face is all you care about. But if you must dream, then dream big… make him a wealthy Bezonite merchant? Or maybe he's a dusky-skinned Zarrni sheik, in town to purchase a new concubine. Perhaps he'll ride up on a white stallion and carry you off to his hareem across the sands." Brianna, Gwendolyn's' foster mother, enjoyed teasing Mekiva. The girl was like a daughter and with Gwendolyn soon taking the Shi'i-Lakka oath, Mekiva was as close as she'd get to a possibility of a grandchild.

She sighed as she snapped off the last few threads. "Your stories make me happy I'm long since married. It's been many years since a man affected me that way. And well that is," she continued with a sigh. "Between my everyday chores and the store, Gwendolyn's father leaves me little time to spare for nonsense. Better forget him, girl, and concentrate on learning enough magic to keep old Stolinn happy."

But Mekiva could not get the strangers' eyes out of her mind. Why did she feel like she already knew him?

Five

"Smells clean," Jaxx stated as he pushed open the heavy wooden door of the Blue Moon Inn and Tavern. "It'll do. You get us a room, okay?" He didn't wait to hear Vondal's response, six strides took him across the common room floor. He un-slung his heavy pack with a heartfelt sigh, then he plopped himself down in one of the well-used chairs sitting directly across from the stone fireplace, stretching his legs out before him. Paradise!

Shaking his head at the brusque Duaar's rude behavior, Vondal picked up the battered brass bell prominently displayed atop a leather ledger. Before he could ring it, a petite white-haired woman of about sixty years swept into the room, wiping her hands on her apron as she approached. She tucked an unruly lock of snow-white hair behind one ear, then flipped it back impatiently when it refused to stay in place.

"Can I help you?" she inquired, casting a wary look at him and a sharper one at Jaxx, who'd removed his boots and was holding his rain dampened stocking feet closer to the fire to dry them. Her eyes narrowed for a moment, and then she shrugged, allowing a tender smile to cross her features. Vondal noticed that her eyes sparkled with suppressed mirth as she struggled to keep a businesslike demeanor.

"A room with two beds." He could tell by the way her eyes darkened that he wouldn't like her answer.

"We've no rooms available." She glanced again at Jaxx, who was starting to doze in front of the fire. "Have you boys come far?"

"Aye mistress, we came in on the Sirens Breath, but we finished our pledged time of service and hope to find work here in Cabrell."

"Jobs are scarce, what with everyone looking to hire out for the festival. I could use a cooks' girl, but even my tired old eyes can tell you two don't fit that description."

Vondal sighed, not looking forward to a long and futile search for an empty room in the snow. He reached into his pocket and unconsciously counted the coins there. It was easily enough for a room and food for the pair, but only if they were frugal. Their plans had been simple, sleep in a real bed for a day or two and fill up on good home-cooked food. The main portion of their savings was safely secreted in special belts the two had purchased in Hyperion last winter. Nothing about the pair would attract the attention of thieves. If they kept the money out of sight no one would ever suspect them of being anything more than two down and out sailors looking for a cheap place to lay their heads.

"Maybe you'd allow us space on the floor near the fireplace? The weather's getting worse and we really need a place to stay, even if it's only one night." Vondal smiled warmly, a look that had often melted lonely female hearts in the past. The old woman's eyes twinkled as she recognized his good-natured ploy.

"Wait here, I need to talk to someone." She winked, before disappearing through a set of swinging doors. Vondal could make out the murmur of voices and the sounds of things being moved about, then the innkeeper returned, followed by a portly, dark-skinned woman, with dark curly hair. Vondal caught his breath. A Zarr! He found himself wondering how a member of that secretive desert tribe had come to live so far away from her native land.

The Zarrtina chef was covered in flour and carrying a pewter pitcher and a tray with four ceramic mugs on it. She stopped and looked him up and down, open suspicion evident in her expression. Vondal squared his shoulders and looked her straight in the eyes. Despite his consternation, he kept his composure as her ebony eyes bored into him, seemingly straight into his heart. He shifted uncomfortably, and her eyebrows rose, then she turned away with a chuckle. The two women exchanged a brief conversation in a language he didn't recognize, and then the Zarrtina gestured toward the door to the Inn.

Vondal groaned inwardly. Snow had begun falling as they approached the inn, by now it would be building up along the pathway, making it difficult to navigate. His shoulders slumped, and he closed his eyes, whispering a brief prayer to whatever god might be willing to listen.

"When you are through talking to yourself, you might want to join us for a mug? I don't know about you, but I've been on my feet all day. I could use a rest."

Vondal's eyes widened. Had he heard correctly? Were they not being asked to leave? He was certain that he'd made a mistake. The older woman was placing the night bar across the entrance. She smiled broadly at the astonished boy, dimmed the lantern hanging just inside the entrance, and followed the dusky woman to a great trestle table. Settling down in one of the overstuffed chairs, she motioned for Vondal to join them, indicating with a wave that he should wake Jaxx and bring him too.

"I could really use a break," she said, filling two of the mugs and passing them to Jaxx and Vondal, then pouring one for the Zarr woman before pouring one for herself. She took a long swallow, taking time to savor the pungent flavor before placing the mug on the table again. Content, she sat back in the chair. Removing a small leather bag of smoke-weed from a pocket, she offered it to the others before filling her own pipe.

Vondal was never one to miss any chance to enjoy a smoke. Happily, he filled his pipe, having been out of smoke-weed for some time and no opportunity to restock.

"I have a proposal. It's a busy time for us right now, and we're short-handed." The Innkeeper took another pull on her pipe, cast a weary look towards her friend, and then spoke again.

"We could use your help for the next few days, just till the festival is over and things get back to normal. It's a bit too much for the two of us to handle." Her eyes turned soft and misty and for a moment a touch of fear appeared on her wizened features. She paused to take a drag, then exhaled and continued. "No pay, just room, and meals. But it'll give you a place out of the weather until you can make other arrangements. Mind you, the rooms not much to look at, it's tiny. Truth is, it's more like a big closet. The cooks' helper slept there till she ran off with some boy from Alliance three weeks ago." She sighed, remembering her own days of young love, and then took another sip from her mug before continuing. "If you boys could help with the heavy lifting, maybe feed the animals and such, it'd be a great help to us."

Jaxx sniffed and yawned sleepily, grateful to be sitting in a warm room. All he cared about was filling his stomach and getting some rest. A few chores in exchange for a place to sleep sounded great to him. He rested head on the table, leaving the decision up to Vondal.

"Jaxx, mind your manners," Vondal chided, then blushed as both women chuckled again. He knew it was futile to expect his partners' behavior to miraculously improve. "I'm Vondal Botherton, Vondal to my friends, that's Amberjaxx Stoneshield. He doesn't make many friends. Those few he has, call him Jaxx. We'd appreciate the opportunity to trade."

"Then wake your sleepy friend and follow me," the landlady said warmly, gathering up the now empty mugs and passing the tray to the cook, who had sat throughout the entire conversation without saying a word.

"You can call me Addie, cooks name is Tula. She can't speak but a few words of our language, so unless you speak Zarrni, don't expect her to answer if you call out to her." She led them up a dimly lit flight of stairs, then down a carpeted hall past several doors, to the backside of the Inn. There she opened another door, entering a dimly lit hallway leading to a second and much narrower set of stairs. Beckoning them to follow she started up, climbing briskly, as nimble as a much younger woman. Turning left at the landing, she opened the third door, gesturing for the boys to enter before her.

The garret space room was little more than a tall man's height in length and width, with sloping ceilings and exposed rafters. Vondal tried not to scowl when he saw the battered old bedstead. Along the wall sat a small wooden chest and a chair that had seen its better days about the time Vondal was born. On the other side of the room was a small cedar bureau. One drawer was broken but the other was still serviceable. Sitting on top was a white china bowl for washing along with a chipped ewer of water. The chest also provided a battered copper lamp with a cracked glass dome, which would give them some light after dark.

Addie crossed over to the small garret window and opened it wide, allowing a slight breeze into the musty room. "I know it's not much but times being what they are, it's better than the streets. At least it's warm, being right above the kitchen, with the chimney and all. You boys come down for supper in about an hour, we'll talk more then." She set the lamp on the chest, then turned and went back downstairs.

Vondal continued smiling until the door closed behind her, then the smile was replaced by an expression caught somewhere between disappointment and abject disgust. He closed his eyes tightly for a moment, mumbling a half-hearted prayer to any God willing to listen. Then he opened his eyes. It didn't help. It was still a dump. Clean … but still a dump.

The rickety bedstead was topped with a thinly stuffed mattress of straw. Over the mattress were threadbare linen sheets covered by a tattered blanket that looked as if someone had pieced it together from scraps of worn-out clothing. There was a pillow so thin it might as well not be there at all. However, the room was warm, the heat radiating off the exposed bricks of the chimney flue making it seem almost comfortable. Overall it was a sad but secure place to sleep. Still, it was better to be safe than sorry, so Vondal checked underneath the bed, finding only a chipped and well-used chamber pot hiding amongst the dust and cobwebs.

"Move out of my way before I drop this." Vondal moved aside to allow Jaxx a chance to deposit his heavy load on the ancient bed. The life had gone of Jaxx's face when he realized there was only one. They'd have to share or take turns, the other sleeping on the floor.

"You take it tonight, I'll take tomorrow." Vondal stepped over to the small window and looked out at the city, thinking about all that had happened in such a short time. But mostly he was thinking about her, glowing auburn locks that hung down to her waist, a face that was speckled with freckles and eyes, unlike any color he'd ever seen, green like the foam of the sea and flaked with gold. Almost unconsciously, he shut and locked the window to keep out the chill.

Jaxx watched his friend through slitted eyes. After the Alliance incident, Vondal had settled into a long stretch of one-night stands. Jaxx had sworn he'd not harp on it, at least until the memories faded, or his tall friend decided he was over it. But today, he'd recognized the dazed expression on his face. Vondal was infatuated, and that always meant trouble. At least it was trouble he could deal with it another day.

Jaxx poured some water into the chipped basin, washing his face and arms before changing into fresh clothes. He gave his filthy trousers, shirt, and still damp socks a quick hand laundering, and then hung them over the back of the old chair to dry. Only then did he sink down on the bed, pushing himself up toward the head and stretching his aching back in the process.

"You think I'm crazy, spending all my time thinking about a girl I just met?" Vondal asked as he rolled out his bedroll on the floor beside the chimney.

"Can't put anything past you, can I. You realize that you'll never see her again. That girl probably forgot you by the time you turned the corner. Forget her and be happy you did. Are you really ready for another relationship after what happened?"

Vondal hesitated. He'd been a jerk since Kira's untimely death. It still hurt, but that pain hadn't dimmed his lust for the next beautiful face---as long as they left his bed the next morning. But something about this girl was different. "You're right. You know me, I have a one-track mind. And right now, my mind is set on getting to know her as soon as possible."

"And what makes you think she might be interested in you? You don't even know her name. Did you even notice she was wearing grey robes? She's young, so she's probably a student at Rosemont. Beautifully gifted mages, even student mages, are not interested in bedding unemployed sailors turned adventurers---he laughed soundly---or in this case, cook's helpers and stable hands."

"But do you think I have a chance?" Vondal's voice held a hint of hope.

"You have a chance all right, a chance on getting us thrown in the town lockup. They are already after us, and we don't have a clue as to why. We need to lay low for a while, give everyone a chance to forget what we look like. That girl is only going to bring more trouble."

"Probably, they all do." He laughed. "I don't think the watch even noticed her. I'm sure I know her. Its Mekiva, I know it."

"Well, she didn't recognize you. You haven't changed that much. It's probably just a coincidence."

"Yeah, you're right. It's been five years since I last saw her. Her family would have married her off long ago. I bet she's fat as a sow from birthing two or three scrawny brats. Probably lost half her teeth, and that red hair has gone dull with stringy gray streaks." But even as he spoke the words his mind refused to let it go, all he could see were those eyes, …and those lips, …and those breasts, … and…

"Are you ready? That roast certainly smells good." Jaxx decided to change the subject.

"Yeah." He closed the window and let the curtain drop. The pristine snow was deceptive, like the city he'd returned to, it was easy to look at the surface and forget what hid beneath the beauty.

His attention was drawn to a trio of men talking among themselves just outside the inn's courtyard. The two men were speaking rapidly, but they were too far away for Vondal to make out what they were saying. He could tell from the agitated gestures one man was making, that their discussion was important. It was a shame he couldn't get close enough to eavesdrop on their conversation. He'd an awful premonition it somehow concerned them.

"You're sure it's the man I seek? Make no mistake, it won't go well for you if I find you've wasted my time." Lord Torrin Botherton adjusted his cravat, admiring his reflection in the ornate mirror that decorated the wall directly behind his desk, before turning his attention once more to the trembling man before him. His cruel stare reflected his quickly diminishing patience, a not so subtle warning that the man would deeply regret every word if the information failed to pan out.

"Aye, it's him all right! That scar on his face, that's new. It's downright ugly it is… cuts his temple, down through his eyebrow. Hood made it hard to see his eyes. But everything else was spot on. Just over six feet, heavily muscled but slim, aye and some might say handsome, like yer self. That long black hair pulled back in a horse's tail, it's new, like the golden ring decorating his left ear. Your lordship, this boy's a man now, nothing like the young pup I kicked around." Tibby shifted his weight, uncomfortable standing on the fine silk oriental rugs. He self-consciously attempted to scrape the mud from the bottom of his boots then stopped abruptly when the majordomo grunted a warning.

"No one is to know what you've told me." He tossed the grateful miscreant a small leather bag of coins. "Take this for your trouble. Any further information about this man and his actions will earn more of the same."

He motioned for a page to come forward. "Take this man to the kitchen and see that he's well-fed, and then have a cart return him to his home."

Bowing respectfully, the young page ushered the groveling man out of the study and toward the back of the house, happy for any excuse to escape the room and his tempestuous lord's attention. He was still sporting a blackened eye, courtesy of the last unpleasant message he'd delivered.

Lord Botherton remained sitting behind his desk, sipping a glass of brandy as the servant hurried to do his bidding. Once the door closed, his eyes flashed triumphantly. Casually he licked his lips, reviewing the information he'd newly received. The fact that his nephew was back in town interested him greatly. His late brother was worthless, his only marketable quality had been the families' debonair good looks, which they'd both utilized to enhance their personal fortunes. Uncharacteristically, the fool had fallen in love. She was a beauty, an entitled woman of good bloodlines and an even better face and figure, but no dowry. As her beauty faded, so did his brother's devotion. He'd returned to his earlier love…Duaar ale. Her death had been unexpected, however, it had provided his brother with an unforeseen treasure… or at least the rumor of one.

Lord Botherton frowned, remembering the months of manipulations, searching out and feeding his brothers perverse and often sadistic addictions, and then---when he'd finally convinced the drunken sot to trust him with the location of the map---the pathetic fool revealed his late wife had never disclosed the secret to him, deciding instead to entrust her youngest son Vondal with the information.

Vondal… that whelp had disappeared soon after her death. He set my hunt back months…if not years. I'd given up all hope of ever finding the crux. Now, he shows up, acting as if he'd never been away.

Fate was finally smiling his way. A few days with his nephew and he was certain the boy would tell him every-thing he needed to know. And then maybe, just maybe, Iza-bal would give him some peace about that damned book she wanted. He glared at the gilt frame mirror that covered most of the wall, trying not to show his interest. Izabal had eyes everywhere. He was certain that the witch had spies within his own household. There was no loyalty among the servants, a handful of silver Qip's would buy details of every surreptitious meeting that took place within his halls, possibly some he wasn't even aware of.

He forced himself to look away from the ornate look-ing glass, staring instead out the window at the snow drift-ing down. He'd do well to remember that a mirror could be used to observe as well as reflect. Best that he does not show his hand so early. He turned away from the window, pacing up and down the room, going over his options in his head. The boy's the answer. But convincing Vondal to tell me where the medallion is hidden won't be as simple as it once was. My nephew's older, and not as naïve. Young or not, he and his companion managed to evade both the watch and Castillo's goons, an impressive feat considering how much gold I've offered. For now, I'll wait and watch, give young Vondal a chance to relax his guard. But the Duaar … he reminds me of another man, one I'd like to forget. A very dangerous man… No, the resemblance must be chance. It's possible he could be one of Raskur's by-blows, but why would he show up hundreds of leagues away from his hold. Best that the Duaar he took out of the equation before he turned into a problem. Time to call in a favor.

Returning to his chair, he opened his desk drawer, removing several sheets of parchment and his pen and inkwell. His hands shaking and tremulous, he slowly inscribed a short missive, lightly dusting it with sand to set the ink, then signed it by dripping hot wax and using his ring as a seal. He needed to be careful, any word of what he was requesting could create repercussions large enough to affect his status in the community. Luckily, there were many who owed him favors who didn't owe their living---or their allegiance--- to Samsara's Dark Society. It could be arranged without implicating him in any manner. He rang the bell on his desk. Almost immediately a second prepubescent page appeared in the doorway.

"Take this immediately to the Sirens Breath's purser. Place it directly in his hands. It's important that it reaches only his eyes. Trust it to no other."

Lord Botherton motioned for the trembling boy to come closer, so the boy couldn't fail to hear his parting words. "Insist if you have to---there must be no mistake. Wait until the purser has read it, and then return with both the original and his answer."

He stared straight into the eyes of the now terrified youngster. "Don't make me regret that I entrusted you with this. Now go!"

He siipped his wine as the boy ran from the roon, and smiled. It would soon be his.

Then he began a second missive.

Six

Two days after her run-in with the handsome rogue outside the bakery, Mekiva was still thinking about him. Despite Gwendolyn's arguments, she was convinced it was her destiny to see him once again.

"You've got to consider the risks from all sides. I agreed to help you find this mystery man... and I did. But now I'm asking you again. Please forget him." Gwendolyn was not going to give up her opinion.

Mekiva sighed, she couldn't tell if her friends' shadowed eyes were hiding amusement... or concern. No matter how much she argued, Gwendolyn was certain she was walking straight into more trouble than she could handle. According to Gwen, the young man could be everything from a sadistic pervert bent on destroying her innocence, a murderer intent on strangulation, or a destitute mercenary intent on selling her into a life of slavery. She had problems imagining herself as a coin girl, obviously, Gwendolyn didn't.

"Mekiva, be reasonable. You can't just cast a spell and follow it to whatever Inn he's staying at. What are you planning to do then? Walk in and ask for him? Use some common sense for once. You don't know anything about him. He might be a thief---or worse." Gwendolyn has stated the obvious for so long her already quiet voice was now barely a whisper. "I agreed to help you find this mystery man... but now I'm asking you again. Please forget him."

"Why should I?" she snapped before turning and stomping back across the room. "Women go into Inn's every day. It's perfectly normal."

"Yes, women with no morals. The ones who make their living by selling their bodies. Coin girls in chains, not young girls barely sixteen who are still in school. Mage school at that! What if it is Vondal? What makes you think he'd remember you? You were eight the last time you saw him."

"He told me not to forget him. He must want me to find him." Not that they needed to go into the Inn once they find him. They could send a messenger with a note arranging a meeting in a public setting. That would be the proper way to do it.

Mekiva grinned. No one had ever accused her of being proper.

Exasperated, Gwendolyn threw up her hands, admitting defeat. "Give me a minute to get my things. If you're going to make a fool of yourself, I might as well be there to watch." She hastened into the house behind the small sewing shop then reappeared in moments carrying a leather bag. "I'm ready, let's go".

Mekiva nodded.

Once they reached the bakery Mekiva cast the seeker spell. The bright blue hesitated for a few seconds as if it was catching a scent, and then it began moving along the street in the directions the boys had been traveling. They hurried to follow.

Jaxx allowed a soft, self-satisfied grunt to escape as he tossed the last bale of hay into Vondal's waiting arms.

The hours had crawled by, but the tedious day was finally nearing its end. He was tired of horses and the overwhelming smell of urine-soaked horse droppings. He considered then decided against hiding the rake and shovel that he'd dropped after his earlier efforts at manure removal. She'd never believe they were stolen.

Vondal broke the hay into sections, stuffing them into the wooden slatted managers above each horse's stall. "Let's get out of here before Addie thinks of something else that "just has to be done." He checked one last time to make sure the barn was sealed against inclement weather and slid the heavy barn door closed.

The weather had been unpredictable, and today's sky was filled with the signs of probable snow… again. He peered upwards, eyeing a vee of low flying geese rushing southward. Their scattered cries echoed against the mountains surrounding the sleepy town as they struggled to out-fly the rapidly approaching storm.

"Stop dawdling, let's get inside. It's going to start snowing again. It'll probably freeze over tonight." Jaxx trudged toward the door of the thatch-roofed inn, confident that his equally worn-out friend would follow.

"Right behind you," Vondal called. He stopped to check the latch on the barn door. The way his luck had been running the wind would blow the door open, probably about the time he got comfortable for the night. Worse yet, he'd be right in the middle of a great dream, possibly one staring that green-eyed vixen. He satisfied himself that nothing short of a hurricane would affect the latch, then ran across the open courtyard, eager for the warmth that awaited him inside.

Jaxx was already relaxing beside the fire, enjoying a mug of hot mulled ale and Tula's spicy onion potatoes.

The Inn was full, many travelers driven inside to escape the inclement weather. A heady buzz of conversation spoken in several languages made it seem even more festive than normal.

"May Lady Fate's wheel ever lands on your number," Jaxx exclaimed, raising his mug in the traditional toast of adventurers.

"Seems like it already has," Vondal responded, raising his hand in greeting.

Jaxx was surprised to see the young girl from the market coming through the Inns door, accompanied by a second figure draped in desert style clothing. The dark-colored robes completely covered the head and body except for a narrow space for the eyes, offering no hint of sex or appearance. Even the hands were bandaged in heavy strips of some darkly tanned skin. There was something about the way she stood that convinced him it was another girl. A tall, slim girl, but definitely walking in a feminine way.

Before he had a chance to comment on their presence Vondal was already halfway to their side, ushering them across the common room to their table.

Addie was beaming as she swept the dirty plates away from the table, replacing the boy's empty mugs with fresh spiced ale. It surprised her that the two young men had somehow found the time to make friends, especially one of the elusive Shi'i-Lakka since they had only arrived in town two days before. "Would you young ladies like spiced ale or would you prefer a nice cup of hot tea?"

"Tea please, for us both if you don't mind. I'm Mekiva, and this is my friend Gwendolyn I hope you don't mind that we dropped by. It's just---it's just so rare that I meet anyone like you---ummm--two. I mean---," she hesitated, her already pink cheeks somehow flushing an even brighter shade of scarlet, then continued, "---I felt comfortable. Like I've known you for a long time." She stopped talking as Addie returned with the tea.

As Addie poured she talked, curiosity evident on her face. "Na'Keevah is an unusual name, not from around here, are you?" She pronounced it in the old manner, something most people failed to do. Mekiva liked her immediately.

"Actually, Mekiva and I are old friends. I didn't recognize her at first. We literally ran into each other in the market yesterday." Vondal gave Addie a brief description of the story, playing down the chase but including the embarrassing collision in from of the bakery.

Jaxx smothered a laugh at Vondal's choice of words. The girl showing up as they did could be a good sign--- or a hint from Tyche to run for the ship before it sailed. This Mekiva girl seems okay if a little too pushy for my taste. But the other one, something about her makes me uncomfortable. Why the secrecy? What's she hiding under that thing she's wearing? Vondal's way too trusting. Strange. Her choice of clothing doesn't seem to bother Addie at all.

Jaxx determined it was just his overactive imagination, deciding to dismiss his doubts and enjoy the evening. He leaned back in the chair, relaxing and sipping his drink. That's when the door from the kitchen opened, and Tula came in. The strange old woman whispered something to Addie and then handed her a leather-wrapped parcel. She went back into the kitchen without another word.

Addie turned to Vondal, laying the sealed package by his mug. "This just came by messenger to the kitchen door. Tula didn't open it, she gave the boy a tip and hurried him on his way."

The seal on the pouch belonged to Captain Brannigan so Vondal wasted no time in opening it. The pouch contained a wooden message cylinder inscribed with the emblem of the local messenger guild. Inside the cylinder was a note requesting Jaxx's return to the Sirens Breath for a meeting, the time to be two candle marks after dark. It was specified that he come alone.

"Yours." He tossed the note to Jaxx, who quickly scanned its contents.

"I can't imagine what he needs," Jaxx said, after scanning the short note, "but if the old man felt it was important enough to send a bonded messenger out in this weather, then I'd better go." He excused himself and returned to his room for his heavy cloak. He needed to hurry. It would take about a candle mark to walk down to the shore and the storm was getting worse, they were in for a long cold night. There was something about the message that worried him, but he couldn't quite put his finger on what it was. It wasn't the wording, that was simply a request for his presence. Regardless, it had to be serious for the old man to call him out on a night like this.

"It's strange that the captain paid a bonded runner to deliver the message," Vondal informed the girls after Jaxx left the table. "Any member of the crew would've jumped at the excuse to get out for the evening. I'm going to hate myself for doing this---- but I need to go with Jaxx, even if the note says differently. Let me get my sword and cloak from my room, and then I'll walk you home." He decided that even though the letter specified that Jaxx report to the Captain alone, there was no reason for his friend to walk there by himself in the storm. Besides, he was certain the girls both lived in the direction they would be heading---allowing him the opportunity to escort them home. He hoped that might diffuse the disappointment of an early end to their evening.

"Of course, we can get together another time," Mekiva replied. "You should accompany your friend, especially if you feel something isn't right."

"I'll tell him you felt uneasy walking alone in this storm, that you're afraid the drifting snow might cause you to lose your way in the dark." Vondal's face was smiling, but his eyes were shadowed and dim. Both girls could tell he was really concerned about his friend's wellbeing.

One more point in his favor. Mekiva glanced at Gwendolyn. Instead of her usual twinkle, Gwendolyn's stare was dark and cold. Something was bothering her friend. She wondered what it was.

Darkness pressed close about the shadowy figures, extending her protection and welcoming the umbrageous pair into her warm embrace. Both were seasoned killers, but only one was for hire and he waited impatiently for his targets arrival.

"It seems a shame to take money for this." The younger man said. His hand drifted to his waist, finally resting his palm on the pommel of a thin-bladed dirk.

"Your business is murder," cautioned the second. "Why should you feel any different about this man?" He never considered the guilt or possible innocence of the man he'd been hired to kill. Like most men in his profession, he didn't care one way or another. It was a job, one he hoped to complete before the storm hit. He carefully wiped his dagger to remove traces of the snow and ice that swirled around their hands.

"I still got my own code. The Duaar ain't done nuttin'

worth getting 'is neck slashed."

"There's no such thing as an innocent person, even a child knows how to tell a lie. Trust me, this Duaar is far from innocent. Your orders are specific, take him out fast. If his one-eyed friend is with him, you're to leave him alive and unhurt. Don't overthink it." He resumed his efforts to clean his weapons, making sure the grips were dry and protected from the weather by placing them inside pockets in his cloak to keep them ready.

"A lot of money just to take out one man. Why's he worth so many qips?"

"To help you keep your mouth shut. Just get this business over with. I have a much more interesting body waiting in my bed at home."

"---much gold for a ..."

Castillo found himself battling a powerful urge to drive his newly cleaned blade deep into the ignorant henchman's heart. "Then make sure you earn it. Use knives, go quietly, and if you're spotted, lead them off toward the water. You'll have assistance." With that said he turned away, walking back toward the center of town before vanishing into the shadows.

"I can't imagine why the captain needs to see you tonight. The weather is getting worse by the candle mark. The town is going to be frozen by morning."

"It must be important, what with him paying a runner. Cheap as old Longbottom is, I wonder why he didn't send the cabin boy. Or come himself?"

"I expect it's because the boy's new, he may not know his way around Cabrell. Maybe the captain felt guilty about sending him out in the storm. Or he already got tired of the old man's bellowing and jumped ship."

"Captain never felt bad about sending us out, no matter how bad the weather."

"He probably found an old gambling debt that you failed to clear up. Or maybe he needs you to deliver some special freight, something that he doesn't want to trust to a stranger. This could be the start of our new business."

"Then why did he specify that I come alone?"

"Make sure you ask him that when you see him."

Despite the early snowstorm, the streets were crowded with festival-goers and others out enjoying any excuse for a party. Warmly dressed revelers frequented the festivities, confident the city guard would keep the undesirable elements away. Half a mark of walking took them past several saloons, various general businesses, two boarding houses, and one surprisingly busy hotel before reaching a much seedier section of town located just outside the main dock area.

Now both men slowed, aware that the seaside district they were entering attracted a more unsavory crowd than the neighborhood around Addie's quaint hotel. Coin girls, some beautiful and some a man would have to be stone-cold drunk to bed, touted their wares from windows and the front doors of the less respectable bars in a futile attempt to stay out of the cold. Beggars, knowing from experience that the weather would keep any potential marks inside by the fires, picked up their tools of the trade, and headed off to find a warm, dry spot for the night. The occasional drunk unlucky enough to pass out away from the safety of home, awoke naked, stripped of everything of worth--- if he was lucky enough to wake at all. Even Samsara's crew of con artists and snatch and grab cutpurses were conspicuously absent, the streets rapidly emptying as the storm grew stronger. It was too early for a deep freeze, but until the warming sun melted it away, Cabrell was an unwilling victim of nature's fickle whims. Vondal studied a pile of crates and boxes sitting outside the entrance to a narrow alley, deciding they were close enough to the ship to offer a clear view while providing some small degree of protection from the cold wind.

"I'll wait here besides this building out of the wind until you return." He straddled one of the crates and leaned back against the wall watching as Jaxx continued on his way. The building blocked the wind, but he couldn't get comfortable. Something kept nagging at his consciousness about the ship. But what? The Sirens Breath rode deep in the water, her cargo holds full of outgoing freight. The smoky scent of pipe tobacco drifting across the water was a familiar welcome back for the ex-marine. Her gangway was extended, the hazy light on the landing pole a dim beacon shining through the wintery flurry. A lone guard stood post, stamping his feet for warmth and to keep the snow from building up on his boots. It's too quiet. The Sirens Breath's usually swarming with rowdy drunken sailors and cheap whores while in port. A snowstorm wouldn't have stopped the crew's carousing. Liquor doesn't freeze.

He noticed a man in the dark grey uniform of the city-watch making his way down the dockside, stopping at each ship to check the tightness of the ropes tied up to the piers. He paused briefly under a lantern and adjusted his cloak before moving on to the next ship. Something about the way he was behaving drew Vondal's attention. He was too controlled, spending the same amount of time at each landing. Looking closer, Vondal noticed that there was no insignia on his uniform or identification of any kind on the weapons he carried. His path would take him near the dark loading ramp leading up to the deck of the Sirens Breath---at about the same time Jaxx would start his climb.

Thank the Gods Jaxx is already at the ship. I can hear his scathing remarks about my paranoia. Now's not the time for me to start jumping to conclusions. But it might be good to be a bit closer to the ship, just in case. Stepping away from the shelter of the alley, Vondal noticed another vague shape standing deep inside the shadows of a nearby doorway. He paused and waited to see if the indistinct figure would say or do anything. After a few moments, the watcher faded back into the darkness without incident and Vondal relaxed. But he kept an eye on the approaching watchman.

Jaxx's skin prickled as he approached the ship, the same disconcerting itch that had saved his head many a time during the last war. Despite familiar surroundings, he couldn't squelch his sense of impending danger. I served on the Sirens Breath seven years. I know every man in the ships' crew, but I've never seen the guard stationed on the gangway. The first mate would never trust an untried man on watch duty. Besides, we trained our replacements. So who is he?

Habit made him draw his ax. He swung it a couple of times to loosen up, just in case. Vondal was watching, he hoped his friend recognized his silent signal and was ready to help if anything happened. Now fully alert and prepared for trouble, Jaxx walked up to the guard and announced his arrival.

The guard didn't respond to his hail. Expressionless,

he merely removed the chain blocking access to the gang-way, then silently motioned for Jaxx to precede him up to the ship. Jaxx hesitated, glancing back, hoping to spot Vondal moving in his direction. No such luck.

All senses heightened, Jaxx stepped forward, using one hand for balance on the ice-slicked planking while the other hand gripped the hand ax hidden from view under his coat. His heart pounding, all senses alert, he began climbing the gangway to the ship

A flash of torchlight on metal drew Vondal's atten-tion. The unknown guard had moved from his position on the dock and was now moving stealthily up the gangway behind his friend, a wavy dagger in his hand.

"Drasst! Jaxx look out!" Fearing the worst, Vondal rolled out from behind the cover of the crane. Losing his footing, he grabbed a nearby chain to help him balance on the rime coating that covered most of the dock. He was screaming as he fought for balance but Jaxx showed no sign that he'd heard the frantic calls. Vondal could only watch in horror as the blade fell.

Already alert, Jaxx had heard Vondal's warning but continued moving upward as though everything was nor-mal. At the first hint of movement, he stepped to the left, evading the assassins' first strike. Instead of the expected killing blow, the blade caught on Jaxx's heavy sea-coat, carving a long strip in the fabric but failing to strike flesh. Immediately the assailant lunged forward, slicing the heavy blade across his shoulder and down his back. The force of the blow spun the solid Duaar, turning him so that he was now facing his attacker. The bogus guard followed the first dagger strike with an underhanded jab from a second shorter blade, slashing at Jaxx's groin, hoping to sever a vein in the attempt. He missed. Off-balance and sliding on the icy planks, Jaxx launched himself back off the ramp, landing none too gently in a frost-coated pile of sailcloth he'd noticed earlier on the dock.

Intent on his friend's danger, Vondal almost missed the sound of a second assailant closing in behind him, his sword blade moving in an overhead slash meant to remove the teenager's head from his shoulders. The uneven wood of the dock threw Vondal askew, then an icy patch brought him to one knee seconds before the blade of the assailant's sword passed over his head. Hastily, the young man brought his own blade up, barely evading the second stroke. Without pause, the killer swung again, this time Vondal took a solid hit in his ribs. His chest felt like it was on fire. He could feel the warm blood running down his back and side. Confident that the kill was his, the ruffian picked up speed, slashing and parrying Vondal's blows effortlessly.

Now it was all Vondal could do to stay ahead of his strikes, --- and somehow stay alive. He was rapidly losing blood and knew that unless the fight was over soon, it would not matter. His vision blurred, and he was finding it difficult to concentrate. Taking a wild chance, Vondal fell forward onto his stomach, then he grabbed the other mans' legs and twisted as hard as he could. Unable to balance on the rime slick pier, he fell backward, entangling his sword blade in the ropes supporting the gangway. Desperately, Vondal struck out with the hilt of his sword, the heavy metal striking the ridge above the eye before ripping a long gash in the man's face. Before the man could recover from the blow, Vondal kicked him squarely in the groin. The reflexive attack had the desired effect. The injured assassin dropped his sword and rolled up into a ball as waves of intense pain shot through his groin. Blind fury replaced fear in Vondal's mind, he swung the heavy blade once more, a clean blow to his forehead that left his attacker semi-conscious.

Seizing his tunic, Vondal pulled him forward, rolling him off the pier and into the icy water. The panic-stricken man twisted, clutching desperately at an icy rope with his one hand, sliding ever closer to the inky darkness of the boiling water below. Vondal turned away. The man was still alive when he hit the water, but in the dockside swell, he'd be dead within minutes, either from the icy sea, or the sharks and other scavengers that were drawn to the smell of his blood.

Jaxx rose slowly to his feet, his attention riveted by the fight between Vondal and the second assailant. His shoulder was bleeding profusely, sending waves of pain throughout him every time he moved. He could feel the warm blood cool as it trickled down his arm. Despite the small amount of blood coating his coat sleeve and gloves, he knew the injury was probably much worse than it appeared. If Vondal needed his help he would let him know.

It was better to wait and let the approaching watchmen handle it. Cabrell city guardsmen were not known for their tolerance, especially when said criminal offenses required them to undergo a sprint down an ice-covered wharf. What's taking him so long?

Vondal braced himself, expecting to see Jaxx take a

lethal hit. His vision blurred in and out as he feverishly concentrated on the distant fight. One body was slowly crumbling to the ground, but which one? He was almost certain he'd seen Jaxx falling toward the dock. The Watchman didn't seem to be interested in the fight, in fact, he was looking back in the direction from which he'd come as if considering turning back. Suddenly, he jerked upright, grabbing at his neck with both hands. Was his friend okay? He tried to walk that direction, but he could not get his legs to move. Silently, he slid to his knees.

Jaxx watched as the dock watchman fell forward onto the pier, his fingers groping at a knife lodged in his throat. Blood spurted from the wound, the droplets a warm red shower that began freezing almost as soon as they hit the ground. Who'd thrown the knife? He couldn't see anyone. And what happened to the one that attacked him? No matter, he didn't have time to worry about men he did not know, Vondal needed him.

Confused, bleeding from multiple wounds, and faint from loss of blood, Jaxx struggled back to his feet. The cold weather intensified the effects of his blood loss, making it difficult for him to stay upright. Staggering and sliding, he used the freight stacked along the wharf to pull himself along, gradually working his way down the frozen pier.

Vondal's inert body lay face down in a snowdrift stained pink by the blood seeping from his left side. Jaxx dropped beside him, checking for life signs. Finding a slight but irregular pulse helped, but he knew that unless he could get him to help immediately, Vondal would die. But where could he go? Until tonight he'd have trusted his mates aboard the Sirens Breath with his life. Now he wasn't sure he could trust anyone. Some friends, he thought, spend five years with them and they try to kill you. Overwhelmed, he looked back at the ship, calling out for help.

The Sirens Breath was gone, replaced by a weather-beaten scow barely able to stay afloat in the storm. The derelict ship was dark and quiet, there were no signs that anyone was even aboard her. What the hells?

Jaxx forgot all about the mystery as Vondal struggled to take a breath, pink bubbles and a bit of blood dribbled from his mouth. He groaned and tried to raise his body but fell back again as he was racked with pain. The Inn, Addie will know what to do. But it won't matter if I can't slow his bleeding. He searched the area nearby, finally locating a length of rope lying on top of a broken crate, half-buried in a drift. Hands shaking from the cold he cut a strip from his shirt, folding it into a pad to cover the gaping wound in his Vondal's side. He tied the rope tightly, to hold it in place. The makeshift bandage seemed to slow the flow but made it difficult for his friend to breathe. He lingered in and out of consciousness, one moment aware that Jaxx held him in his arms, the next, fighting for his life on the pier.

Jaxx fought to gain his feet. He wavered a bit, shifting Vondal's body over his shoulder and then began trudging through the blinding snow and ice. His slashed back muscles strained to support the extra weight. He could feel the cut on his shoulder bleeding profusely. The storm had intensified. He knew if he stopped, even for a minute, both would die from exposure. Already it was impossible to see more than a few inches in front of his eyes. He lost his footing on a patch of black ice, falling hard against the side of a building and scraping his injured shoulder. Despite the pain, he struggled onward in the blistering cold, breathing in labored gasps through partially frozen lips. The pain in his chest grew. He feared that if he ever stopped moving, his lungs would freeze solid. He no longer felt his injured shoulder, the blood from the knife wound had soaked into his shirt, and then the material froze, slowing the bleeding and helping to preserve his life. He prayed to Bel and Namim but didn't expect either God to listen. Tomorrow I'll come back and track the assassins. Someone will know who they work for, where they hang out. I'll find them and then I'll find the man who sent them. They made a big mistake, allowing me to live. First, I'll help Vondal. Then someone will pay.

Castillo cursed. Three men dead and none of them were the targets. He'd lost a favorite throwing knife when the bounty hunter toppled from the gangway into the water. To make matters worse, Vondal was injured. If the boy died he'd never hear the end of it. Some fool had called the watch, and for once they responded. What else could go wrong?

Seven

Addie opened the hot oven with her empty hand, careful to balance the tray of cookies with the other. "Why is it that regardless of the order that it went in, everything always needs to come out at the same time?" Shifting the pan of hot scones, she placed both trays down onto the flour-dusted kitchen table.

Tula smiled softly but didn't answer. It was a question she'd heard many times over the last ten years. Besides, she was up to her elbows in cornbread stuffing for the bird she'd plucked, ready to place the unlucky hen into the oven as soon as she finished filling up its cavities.

She raised a flour-covered hand and wiped the perspiration from her head with a kerchief kept handy for that reason. It might be cold outside, but the little kitchen was stifling, what with the heat from the oven, and the kettles boiling in the fireplace. Steeling herself for the expected blast of cold, she opened the door to the back courtyard to retrieve a crock of milk set out to cool in the snow. The milk jar hit the floor with a crash, startling Tula, who turned around just in time to step backward, as two bloody forms covered with snow fell through the open door to land at Addie's feet.

The morning sun streaming through the window of the tiny room woke Jaxx from an uneasy sleep. He shut his eyes, wincing against the brightness. He felt weak as a kitten, and his head pounded like he was coming off a three-day binge on cheap sour mash whiskey. He tried to set up but gave up as pain racked his body. He knew he was in the tiny attic room in the inn, but he had no memory of how he got there. In fact, his last memory was of… Vondal!

Steeling himself against the pain, the stalwart duaar forced his aching muscles into reluctant activity. One of his arms was bandaged and his shoulder was tight, feeling as if he hadn't used it in a long time. How long had he been asleep?

By pushing against the footboard and bracing with his left arm, he managed to sit upright, while further entangling his body in the blankets covering him. He was shocked by the effort it took to remove the coverlet with one arm, gasping in agony as red-hot flashes raced across his back and neck. Finally, upright but unsteady, he paused, allowing the trembling to stop and the pain to recede, then he swung his feet off the bed, hesitating at the sight of his bare legs.

Drasst it all, where were his trousers? He spotted his boots sitting beside the chair, his socks drying across the back. His chest was bandaged and was wearing a clean shirt, but his pants were nowhere to be found. Oh well, someone has obviously seen me without them. Bracing himself against the bedpost, he slid his legs out and struggled to his feet, but before he could take the first step, the door to the room opened and Addie entered, followed by of all people, the odd girl that had been with the redhaired girl Vondal was mooning over.

"Stop yelling! Vondal's downstairs sleeping, something you should be doing yourself." She gently helped him lie back against the mattress. "Now calm down or you will reopen your wounds."

"He's all right then, I got him here in time?"

The two women exchanged an apprehensive glance. Addie struggled to form a response that wouldn't further alarm the already distressed young man. Finding nothing she could say that would alleviate his anxiety, she chose instead to calmly ignore his pleas for information, finally adding another pillow before answering.

"He's hurt Jaxx, much worse than you were. I did the best I could--- but I'm not a healer. He's lost a lot of blood. And he's developed a fever in his chest, being out in the cold didn't help. I don't know if he'll make it." She paused, seeming to gather her thoughts, and then continued calmly. "He hasn't regained consciousness. The temple of Nin-isinna is empty, all the priests are on a pilgrimage. I don't think he would survive the trip to Rheaaz's temple in Alliance. The only thing we can do is pray that the Gods find him worth saving."

"Drasst woman, Gods can't be counted on. Get my pants. I'm getting out of this bed one way or another---and I'd prefer to be wearing them when I do." He tossed the tangled blanket aside, then sat up and swung his feet off, using the headboard for support. The bandages pulled on his chest and his cracked rib made it difficult to breathe, but he refused to let that stop him.

Strangely affected by the sight of the half-naked teen, the young Shi'i girl hastily tossed a pair of pants his way.

Red-faced, she averted her eyes, so he could put them on.

Addie chuckled at her rapidly coloring face. She'd overcome her own shyness many years ago. It was apparent Jaxx had too. Evidently, he wasn't going to stay in the bed until he'd assured himself that Vondal was going to be alright. Despite her worry, she couldn't help admiring the young man's valiant struggle to dress with only one arm.

"Here boy, let me help you with that. You're going to tear open your shoulder." Once he was decently attired, she offered her arm for support and then helped him down the narrow stairs to a room that backed unto the Inns fireplace.

Finding Vondal in this room alarmed Jaxx more than her words. The heat from the fire kept the room toasty, making it a favorite among paying guests. The loss of the room rent would be a severe hardship for the kindly innkeeper, especially during the festival when charges increased to almost double the usual rates.

Vondal still shivered, even though he was covered in blankets. Someone had placed a warm brick at his feet. Mekiva sat on a milking stool beside the bed, her hand grasping his tightly. Her usually beautiful face was taut with worry and almost as pale as Vondal's. She realized his chance of awakening was becoming less likely with the passage of time.

"It's in the Lady's hands. If it's her will that he lives, he shall," she whispered "I dreamed last night of blood, and of you and Vondal. We've been here since the snow let up. The sun is shining, and the ice is melting, so why do I feel so cold?"

Addie located another chair and urged Jaxx to use it.

Jaxx smiled gratefully, his legs still too weak to support him for long. He fought to hold back tears, his stoic resolve shaken by the condition of his best friend. Scarcely three days past the two had joked about becoming old men in rockers, surrounded by their grandchildren. His mind refused to accept the idea that Vondal might not pull through. Addie squeezed his shoulder, silently acknowledging his pain, before moving back to give him a bit more room.

"So, we sit here and watch him die?" his face reflected his worry.

Vondal groaned aloud, and the blood drained from Jaxx's face, he suddenly felt as weak as a newborn babe. "Tell me what to do."

Addie swallowed, fighting her own tears. She glanced at the silent figure standing beside the tiny window. Gwendolyn wasn't yet a sister, but she might be able to help. Shi'i couldn't volunteer assistance, only wait until someone willingly offered payment.

"Can anyone pledge the price," Addie asked quietly.

Jaxx turned his head at the question, noticing Gwendolyn standing behind him and wondering what price she meant. She wasn't looking at Addie as she spoke, however, the girl seemed shaken by her words. But before Addie could answer, Mekiva spoke up.

"I willingly offer to accept the onus."

"No, sister of my heart, your offer is refused. The cost is too high and the value you offer too great."

"Gwendolyn, you can't refuse. The payment was offered willingly." Mekiva was crying openly now, clutching onto the tiny shard of hope before her. Gwendolyn wouldn't refuse her, once she understood how much she cared about Vondal.

"I am not yet sworn, my prayers may be ignored."

"You have to try. I have not learned any spells of healing, and know of no mage that sells potions in the area. Please, Gwen, you may be his only hope."

"I do this only because I know the pain you bear would be much worse if I refused. But know this, the gift you offered had best be appreciated… or tenfold I will reclaim." The desert girl crossed over to the bed and knelt by Vondal's side. Slowly she untied the knots holding the thin bandages that covered her hands. Jaxx was surprised to see how small and delicate her hands were once the heavy cotton bindings were removed. He'd assumed the bandages were covering some type of burn or similar damage. Pressing her hands hard against Vondal's chest, she began to pray to Rheaaz, begging her Goddess's help in healing the wounds and driving out the fever that ravaged his body.

For one confusing moment, seeing the Shi'i-Lakka girl's hands pressed against Vondal's chest, Jaxx believed she was trying to finish the assassins' work. The 'accidental' meeting could have been a setup. The girls could be involved. Enough coin could buy anything. No--- he couldn't start thinking that way. Once he realized how silly that thought was, he tried to relax. But his overwrought imagination wouldn't still the silent whispers. They didn't know anything about the girls. They appeared to be concerned but was it only an act? But why? Why would anyone want to kill Vondal?

Deep in prayer, her eyes closed, Gwendolyn knelt beside the bed, as her pulse slowed until it matched the stricken young man. She chanted the same words over, and over, again, petitioning her god's help to heal his wounds. For several minutes nothing happened. Then her hands began to radiate a warm glow that gradually spread across Vondal's body. Many heartbeats passed as Jaxx watched anxiously.

Suddenly Gwendolyn opened her eyes and screamed. Vondal's wounds began closing, the flesh flowing back together seamlessly. Once clear and dainty, her hands now appeared swollen and red. Blood dripped from jagged tears in her flesh. Her chant wavered as she fought to control the healing process throughout the pain she was now enduring. When it seemed like she was about to lose control, the light around them both flared brightly, then the pain hammered Vondal mercifully back into unconsciousness. With a sigh, she slipped to the ground beside him.

"The watch pulled two bodies from the water near the pier this morning. Neither was the target. Nor was it a tall man with a scar across his eyebrow."

"That's unfortunate to hear," the richly robed nobleman replied softly." Perhaps I made a mistake by placing my trust in your hands?" He wasn't particularly worried about being connected to the attack. Bodies turned up daily in the portside neighborhood of Blackbottom, Most simply called it the Bottoms. Besides the wharf and warehouses along the pier, there was a saloon or two, a few rundown stores and the usual fishing shacks built down by the waterline. The local citizens had long since learned it was better to keep their eyes… and their mouths closed. However, it was disappointing to know the duaar was still alive to disrupt his plans.

"My Lord, my only mistake was in allowing your bounty to remain posted. Rogue hunters seeking to collect your offering followed the pair to their assignation on the dock. As instructed, my man stepped in to preserve your nephew's life, he lost his own during the fight. He was unable to fulfill your request to eliminate the other at that time, he felt it was critical that the target was allowed to carry your nephew to a healer." The speaker narrowed his eyes. "Or was I wrong?"

"My nephews' survival is essential. His friend is unimportant. Merely a nuisance I prefer to remove before he becomes a problem. Speaking of problems, will anyone connect his body to you?

"No. The uniform he was wearing had no identifying marks or emblems. Even if someone cared enough to hire a priest to question the body about his death, it would be impossible. His body was burned along with the others. The ashes are scattered. There is nothing left to question."

He paused, giving the nobleman an opportunity to assess his comments before continuing. "I do have some information that might improve my lords' disposition. The shipment you've been expecting has arrived. I arranged delivery to your warehouse."

The news brought Lord Torrin some small amount of pleasure, diminishing his anger over the failure of his original plans. Things had gone damnably wrong in a hurry. It seemed that both his nephew and his obstinate young friend were more competent than he'd previously believed. If he hoped to salvage some type of favorable resolution to the problems that he now faced he'd have to come up with a different plan.

Glancing thoughtfully at the ornately carved mirror that hung behind his desk, he motioned for the City Watch Sergeant to rise.

"Have your men continue to keep an eye on them. If the opportunity arises to quietly remove the target, do so. It's imperative my nephew must not be hurt again. Continue until you receive different orders. If the target continues to be a problem that your men cannot quietly remove, I'll arrange something suitable myself. You'll be compensated as usual for your service. You are excused." He rose from his desk, indicating there would be no further conversation.

The sergeant bowed briefly then withdrew. He'd no idea what distracted the sadistic lord from his original tirade, but it had come at an opportune moment.

As soon as the man exited the room, Lord Botherton moved over to a large ornate mirror on the wall. Instead of the expected reflection, the mirror displayed the visage of a tall, slender woman dressed entirely in sapphire silks. Lord Botherton waited impatiently as the image in the glass began to shimmer, and then fade away. The woman stepped through the shimmer and was now standing, only to reform in front of the ornate looking glass.

"I assume you heard everything?" he inquired, once the woman had fully materialized after passing through the mirror.

"That your hired men had failed? Or that Vondal is back in Cabrell? Both are of interest to me. But neither surprises me in the least."

Lord Botherton waited impatiently as Izabal helped herself to a glass of wine. No other woman could try his patience as this one. She picked up a delicate pastry and took a bite. Now she lounged on a dark leather chaise, the elaborate brocade robe she wore draped loosely around her lithe body revealing more than it concealed.

Torrin had to admit she was a beautiful woman, mahogany waist-length hair piled casually atop her head, perfectly sculptured head thrown back provocatively, the ruby liquid in the crystal goblet a perfect match for her luscious lips. She cocked her head slightly and gave him a wide-eyed stare. He found himself drowning in those beautiful cat-like eyes, eyes that could look right into your soul and tear it apart. His eyes wandered down to her breasts. Lust vied with humiliation as he recalled the last time he'd sought oblivion in those soft curves. Izabal could bring intense pleasure, but that pleasure came with a high price tag, one becoming increasingly difficult for him to pay.

"It seems that the gods must be smiling upon me at last. I gave up my efforts to locate my nephew years ago. Now he walks into my arms as if he had simply been out for an afternoon stroll."

"He might decide to take another long walk. Perhaps you should ensure he doesn't." She didn't appear to be overly concerned.

"I must arrange to talk with him before he vanishes once again. I'm certain his mother entrusted him with the map before she died. She didn't trust my brother and the other boys disappeared long before she fell ill. Your scrying has produced no usable information. This is our last hope, everyone we questioned is dead."

"Yes, that hasn't produced many leads. However, it has been quite enjoyable, has it not?" She smiled, and Torrin was once again reminded of a snake playing with its prey. He often wondered how something so beautiful could be so sadistic. "The watch officer, is he to be trusted? Is the information you received accurate?"

"Who knows," he replied. "The information was provided in exchange for gold by a man with no honor. I maintain the man's cooperation, but only as long as he fears discovery. The story may be a complete fabrication, yet somehow, I doubt he would risk my anger for a handful of Qips."

"Yet you felt it worth your coin?" Her eyes narrowed

momentarily, and a slight frown marred her perfect features.

"Certainly. The coin is easily replaced. It isn't as easy to replace someone in a position of confidence. Of course, Castillo has already verified the events of the night."

"Now that one interests me," she simpered.

"He does not come cheaply, yet I would pay several times the amount for the information he provides. He is highly placed in Samsara's organization and has already proved his ingenuity to me on many occasions. I also admire his manual dexterity. He has a way with knives that would please even someone with your exotic---or shall I say---hedonistic tastes."

"The entire fiasco was a waste of time and money if you ask me," Izabal stated frostily. "My men could have taken care of the problem without the cost."

"The coin is mine to waste," Lord Torrin snapped, he paced across the room, glaring angrily. "It's time to proceed with a new plan."

"And our plan is?" Izabal asked calmly, totally ignoring Lord Botherton's irritation. She made her way over to Lord Botherton's well-stocked bar and refilled her goblet with burgundy, swirling the blood-red liquor around several times before taking a sip. She frowned, and muttered a few cryptic syllables, the waited as frost rimmed the crystal chalice and cooled the liquid within. Satisfied with the temperature, she reclined against the edge of the desk, nibbling on a piece of cheese, and waited for his answer.

"First we need to neutralize the outside influences. Once he's alone we can easily convince Vondal to help. If he doesn't have the map, at least he can tell us where it's hidden."

"How will this affect our other business interests? Do

we continue as planned?"

"I see no reason to stop. It's serving two purposes. One way or another I'll locate the medallion, even if I must kill every relative of my late brothers' wife to find it. That I get to enjoy the process is merely a bonus."

"My interest is limited to my own pleasures as you are aware." She smiled. "But if we're both happy, who am I to complain. That is, as long as we find the location of his crypt."

"Soon. I know it is difficult to remain patient after all this time. I'll talk to my nephew, and then it's only a matter of time before the prize is ours."

Eight

Lost in thought, Vondal stood at the window of his room, staring out at the evening fog that covered most of the city. There was no moon to lighten up the silvery wisps, the only break in the glistening white carpet was from the scattered street lamps that glowed dimly in their attempt to lighten the paths of passersby as they trudged thru the ice and snow. He rested his head briefly against the pane, enjoying the coolness of the glass against his skin. It had been two days since the attack and, thanks to Gwendolyn's attention, and Addie's good food, he was feeling much better. Now, he was bored.

"I could really use a change of scenery. How about a short walk, followed up by a cold mug? I really need to get out of this room. I feel like the walls are moving closer every time I close my eyes."

"I could use a break myself." He put aside the book he'd been thumbing thru, stretched and reached for his boots. "How about that new dance hall…the one just off the square? I hear they serve a killer Briar-berry wine. It'd be a welcome change after all the watered-down ale I've suffered through lately."

"You didn't seem to suffer too much, considering how much of it you drank. I'll tell Addie where we are going in case the girls come by. Meet you downstairs."

Less than a candle-mark later, the two young men walked quickly toward the market district, eager now that they were out of the inn and on the way to new adventures. The first sun had set and the second was sinking toward the horizon, surrounding everything with a rosy twilight glow. There were plenty of everyday inhabitants to gawk at, along with one or two shady characters who were just starting their nightly business. Vondal laughed as a particularly long-legged courtesan was whipped around by a sudden burst of wind, bringing howls of laughter from two coin girls working a corner nearby. She cursed them both soundly, brushed the icy slush off her smock, and moved to a more sheltered alcove. He noted the location, frequenting bars and brothels were an essential part of their lifestyle. A mug of Duaar ale and a three qip coin girl could solve many a problem. No one cared who you were or what you did if your gold held out.

His thoughts trailed off as Jaxx suddenly staggered into a pole, then grabbed it and slid down toward the ground, flailing until he was sitting on the curb of the cobbled street. Startled, Vondal stopped walking and turned back toward his longtime friend, unsure what had caused him to act so oddly. Jaxx looked up and winked before the same silly expression came back to his eyes.

"Starting a little early tonight, huh? Usually, you wait until after a few drinks to fall down." He offered his hand for support. Jaxx wavered as he stood, using the pole for support and pulling Vondal close, weaving and swaying as though he could barely stand.

"I'm not sure, but I think someone's following us," he hissed through clenched teeth. "After what happened down by the dock I'm not taking any chances. If he thinks I'm drunk, it might make him a bit careless. Keep your eyes open to the right and I'll check out the left. That way if it's a trap, we're ready for it."

Jaxx had a sixth sense about things that never failed to surprise him. If he said they were being followed, they were.

Vondal allowed his gaze to travel to the opening of a nearby alley, noting a water barrel and a door propped open for air to enter. The narrow alley continued onward until it ended in a high stone fence with an elaborately carved gate covered by a decorative metal grille. There was no obvious place that anyone could be hiding. He turned abruptly, hoping to spot the man but there was no one in sight. When his eyes returned to the road he discovered Jaxx had wobbled on without him.

The Dancers Veil, though newer, was identical to pubs the teens had frequented in countless seaports during their time of the ship. A recently painted sign hung over swinging doors still glistening with new paint, brightly colored letters spelling out the Taverns name. Overhead was a painting of a striking woman, her torn veil offering a hint of her 'come hither' smile. Stepping aside to allow two working girls and their escorts to leave, Jaxx paused for a moment in the shadows of the doorway and then beckoned to Vondal to enter before him.

"You go on ahead, I want to give our shadow a chance to show again. I promise to behave." He lounged against a hitching post outside the light, the shadows deep enough that he could see the door, but no one could see him. From the corner of his eye, Vondal saw him bend over a nearby sewer grate, followed by a retching hack and a series of coughs. He grinned. Jaxx had plenty of experience to draw from. If he wanted someone to think he was drunk, then that's what everyone would think.

Whistling a soft all clear, Vondal pushed the swinging doors open and entered the noisy bar. Two or three customers glanced his way as he entered but no one seemed to be particularly interested in him. It wasn't anything like the Silver Slipper; there was no sawdust on the floor, nor was the air heavy with the smell of last night's swill. It wasn't exactly the dark wood paneling and crystal chandeliers of the Golden Chalice either. The owners had gone with function over aesthetics when they built the L-shaped bar that ran the length of the main room. The salvaged wood counter already showed pits and burn marks from inebriated customers missing the ash buckets scattered along its length.

Little attempt at decoration had been made; the one exception being the heavy velvet drapery that almost succeeded in drawing your eyes away from the cheap pine tables and chairs. Bought second hand, the well-worn burgundy color hadn't faded enough to disguise the coat of arms of the late Earl of Scallrock woven into the cloth. Several sturdy wooden tables were scattered randomly around the room yet spaced far enough apart for conversations to remain private. The stale air smelled of people who spent their days at work and their nights forgetting their days. The musky scent of the long unwashed mixed with the odor of cheap sour mash, skunky green pipeweed, and overly perfumed courtesans. Not a high-class salon, yet all in all, it was a pleasant surprise.

Pleased with his decision to check out the new bar, Vondal picked a table in a quiet out of the way corner. He received the usual once-over from the staff as he crossed the room but nothing out of the ordinary.

Whenever a stranger entered Maggie's place, one of

the regulars would come over, and secretly size him up with some casual conversation and one or two pointed questions. He couldn't tell if the overt lack of interest displayed by the Dancers Veil's patrons was a good thing or a sign that trouble would be coming sooner than he'd expected.

For a split second, he was certain he was being watched. Cautiously he studied the crowd, finally lingering on a petite auburn-haired wench perched on the knee of one of the more affluent looking customers. She kept glancing his way from time to time, offering a shy smile that hinted at very pleasing possibilities.

His interest piqued, Vondal returned her looks, wishing he had more time to delve into the secrets hidden within her cornflower blue eyes. She managed to keep her expression blank as she ignored the way he was studying her. Then, with a little laugh, her cheeks flushed as she realized he knew exactly what she was doing… and why.

A sassy young waitress with perky breasts and a saucy manner sat down at the table beside him. She propped her head on her crossed hands looking him directly in his eyes. Vondal caught a glimpse of one pink-tinged nipple before she shifted her body out of the candles dim glow. Interesting--- and what he couldn't see was even more intriguing, stealing his interest away from the little redhead completely. He took in her tiny five-foot frame, a fun-sized temptation with golden hair, cornflower blue eyes and lips that were made for kissing. He sighed deeply--- beautiful women were his weakness, one he fully recognized. However, the girls would be joining them shortly and he was certain Mekiva would not appreciate her assets the way he did.

"Two coppers for sour mash, three for ale or spiced wine. I'm Kiska, what can I get you?"

"Filburr's Berry Blend...for two." He smiled as she hurried off to get it. Most females flinched at the first sight of his scar, so he'd enjoy this opportunity to flirt with a pretty girl. From the small leather bag at his waist he pulled out a handful of coins, counting out the six needed plus one extra for the waitress. He thought about teasing the barmaid a bit, making her search for the coins, then sighed and placed them on the tabletop. No use thinking about what wasn't going to happen.

Kiska returned with two clay mugs of the plum red beer somehow managing to place them on the table with one hand as she swept up the coins with the other. She 'accidentally' allowed him a quick peek at the scattered freckles that dusted her outstanding breasts. He decided to keep that in mind for later.

"Is there anything else I can offer you?"

"Not now, ..." he let his answer trail off enough to keep her interested.

He wondered if he should offer assistance to the auburn-haired wench. She struggled to get away from her customer, who appeared to have drunk too much beer in too short a time. Then she laughed and poured a mug of sour mash over the young man's head, after which she kissed him soundly on the lips. From his reaction, it was obvious that this wasn't the first time she'd done this. Relaxing, Vondal sat back more comfortably, and then reached slowly into his vest.

"No weapons allowed without a peace bond," Kiska called out, as she passed the table with a fully laden tray, "only wish I'd a way to enforce it. Of course, I could pat you down." Her eyes traveled slowly down his body.

Vondal played along, enjoying the easy banter. "Only one weapon I'd pull on you. But if you insist on a strip search I won't resist." He opened his hand to display the contents, a hand-carved burl-wood pipe and a leather packet of pipeweed. He reached into his vest a second time and removed a wooden firetwig, casually struck it on his boot, then cupping his pipe with his empty hand, put the flame to his pipeweed and took a long slow draw. Content, he leaned back in his chair, letting it rest against the back wall. Jaxx was missing out on an exceptional brew.

His eyes made a circuit of the room, registering in his mind the location of every occupant. One thing he'd learned early in life was that you could never be too careful. The red-haired wench had changed her target, now she was flirting with an older Bezonite mercenary who seemed more interested in playing cards with two men wearing the uniforms of the city watch, than playing with her. Two tables away was a burly man wearing woodsman leathers, maybe a very tall Caldarean, or a short Misoot. That bluish-black was a distinctive hair coloring. Two young Zarrni warriors, still wearing long white thobes, loose sleeveless striped sidriyeh waistcoats, and distinctive kufiyahs sat near the rear exit. He noticed that though both men were dressed similarly, the agal of the younger one was woven with threads of gold and scarlet. Wonder what brings desert royalty so far from home?

"I like this place. Is it always like this," he asked as Kiska returned with an empty tray."

Kiska wrinkled her nose. "With the festival going on, the town is full of strangers. But today's the last day so it should calm down tomorrow. Those four, she nodded at the card table, play here every night. Or every night Tucker is out ah' jail. Ol' Pin sleeps here more often than he goes home, to hear his wife talk anyway. That bunch---, she waved her hand toward several young men in gray robes flirting with the other barmaid, ---is from the Mage School. The only problem with them is their coins have been known to vanish after they leave for the evening. Caleb keeps an accounting behind the bar and collects from the school the next day. Those two are new--," she added, pointing toward the table where the two desert tribesmen were now talking to another young man, "—'cept I heard one say they were waiting on a cousin."

Vondal tensed as the jingle of a small bell announced Jaxx as he staggered through the doors. He made his way to the bar and ordered rotgut in a loud voice, ignoring Vondal completely. Jaxx hated rotgut. Something wasn't right.

Vondal decided to improvise. He whispered something to Kiska that caused the attractive barmaid to gasp, giggle, and slap him lightly on the cheek. Her action allowed his gaze to move slowly across the shadowed room. At first glance, nothing seemed unusual. Then he noticed that the card game had broken up, everyone was anxiously collecting their winnings and preparing to leave. Even the city watchmen. Drasst, not again.

He tapped his pipe against the rim of his mug, watched the ashes fall into the tepid brew, then put his pipe back into his vest pocket. Swallowing the last of his Berry-blend, he set the now empty mug on the table. Better to leave and meet the girls somewhere else, than risk them being injured.

Then three men entered the bar, their appearance justifying Jaxx's strange behavior.

The first two were hulking brutes wearing mismatched boiled leather armor and carrying knives darkened by soot. They walked side by side as they passed through the swinging doors. Immediately they separated, moving to either side of the entrance before stopping. A third, slender man stopped just inside the doors. Even though his face was hidden by shadows Vondal immediately realized he was the most dangerous of the trio. From the corner of his eye, he spotted two others as they entered from the rear, pushing aside the beaded curtains hiding the doorway. It was clear these men had experience working as a team as they entered back to back, instead of side by side. One was tall and slim, carrying a well-used set of matching Sai. He held the melee weapons in hand, ready for use.

His partner was shorter and heavier with a hangdog face, not even a mother could love. An Orrogg knife fighter, he carried a darkened baselard and wore a bandoleer across his chest designed to hold throwing blades close at hand. Like the first two men, they continued to wait silently.

Vondal concentrated on the first trio after deciding the distance across the crowded room was too far for the men at the back to pose an immediate threat. Cautiously he untied the peace knot wrapped around the pommel of his sword and waited.

The leader ignored the remaining patrons, walking directly to his table. "Are you Vondal Botherton?"

"I am." He braced for any sudden moves but when the response came it wasn't what he'd expected.

"I have a message for you." He handed him the rolled white missive, turned and walked out of the bar without waiting for a response.

Vondal noticed the message was sealed with wax and embossed with the emblem of Hyperion. It seemed innocent enough, except his henchmen had remained in the bar. Their eyes kept straying toward Jaxx, who was now leaning against the bar. He was about to read it when he spotted Mekiva and Gwendolyn passing through the swinging doors.

Time slowed as everyone reacted.

Gwendolyn caught a glimpse of the man to the right of the door as he raised a hand-held crossbow and pointed it at Jaxx.

"Look out Jaxx!" She kicked over a small keg placed beside the door for ashes. The heavy barrel crashed into the archer's knees just as the crossbow bolt was released, causing it to veer off target. The bolt came to rest in the wall about a foot above the heads of the two desert nomads. With nothing else to slow its forward motion, the heavy keg continued across the room until it came to rest against the far wall, leaving a trail of ashes across the floor and making it difficult to walk much less maneuver at any speed.

Rheaaz, forgive me!! Gwendolyn ducked, somehow managing to evade the heavy crossbow swung at her by the irritated bowman. Spotting a nearby table, she overturned it and ducked behind, dragging Mekiva with her. Her entire body shook as adrenaline coursed through her body. This was great! Instinctively she palmed her small throwing knives in case she'd another opportunity to help.

Mekiva took longer to react. She didn't know that many offensive spells, her options were mostly defensive. Calmly she gathered a few spell components from the bag she carried at her waist and then began a series of complex passes while chanting the words of a spell.

Alerted by Gwendolyn's cry, Jaxx turned his head in time to see the Orrogg blades-man running toward him, swinging the razor-sharp baselard dagger as though he were playing with a child's toy.

Instinctively Jaxx dropped to the floor. Even so, the wind from the swing kissed his cheek, and he silently thanked Gwendolyn for the warning. The taller assailant was thrown off balance by the missed strike, allowing Jaxx time to move. He began crawling toward the open floor in front of the now-empty bards stand. Then the air shimmered and Jaxx vanished.

The Orrogg began cussing vehemently at anyone who dared to look his way. Enraged by his quarries escape attempt, he began swinging wildly in hopes of landing a lucky blow. Chips and flakes of wood flew all around as he chopped his way through two chairs and a solid wood table.

Vondal glimpsed the purposeful motion of Mekiva hands as she stared at him while she cast another spell. He braced himself, waiting. He was almost as surprised as Mekiva when nothing happened.

Nevertheless, he couldn't wait for her to make another attempt. Evidently, the two men by the main door had decided to help search for Jaxx, they were edging closer to the bar, thrusting randomly in hopes of striking the elusive Duaar.

Jaxx crouched before the desert barbarians table, waiting for an opportunity to strike. He realized he'd need to take out the big man before he accidentally landed a lucky blow. Realizing that once he attacked, the invisibility spell would be disrupted by an attack , but figured it was worth the risk. He withdrew a throwing knife, shiny and lean as a stiletto, then cocked his arm and threw the blade. The knife struck the Orrogg low in the abdomen driving him to his knees. A second knife followed the first, hitting the brute in the chest, ending the fight.

Immediately Jaxx turned to face the two men who had joined the hunt---only to discover them kneeling side by side---the curved swords of the two unknown nomads resting against the back of their necks. The skinny man carrying the Sai was gone.

Scattered shouts and the rattle of armor drawing closer alerted everyone that the city watch was finally responding to reports of the brawl.

The nomads removed their blades, allowing the embarrassed men an opportunity to leave. Surprised, but grateful for the reprieve, they backed while still on their knees into the hallway and vanished.

"It might be a good idea for us to disappear too. It might be a bit difficult to explain the body. But where is Jaxx?" He looked around but could not see his friend, but he could hear him laughing. Shrugging, he pointed to the rear exit.

Jaxx laughed again and everyone looked to see a row if footprints appearing in the ashes as he approached. "Mekiva, I got to admit it, making me invisible was brilliant. But isn't the spell usually broken once I attack anyone? How'd you manage to keep me invisible?"

"I honestly don't know, I've never tried it before," she replied.

"So how long will I stay this way," Jaxx inquired nervously.

Both girls started giggling but neither answered as they followed Vondal through the back exit.

Nine

"Yeowwwww----Oh! Oh! Oh!" Vondal jerked his foot off the angry Draccat's tail, wincing as razor-sharp claws dug into his calf. The rampaging feline took off, flying beneath the belly of a young palfrey tied for tacking, before darting down the barn aisle. Startled, the mare reared, her right hoof striking Vondal on his forehead, the iron shoe slicing deep into the tender flesh. Blood running down his brow from the cut over his one good eye made it extremely difficult to tell which of the two horses was real--- and which was the result of double vision. His foot landed in a water bucket as he stepped back to dodge the excited mare's erratic movement. The horse, sensing an imminent victory over the man, threw her weight forward pulling Vondal further off balance. He clutched at the side of the stall, missed and fell forward, losing his hold on the reins. Seconds later he was face down in the muck and she was trotting back into her warm stall.

Mekiva covered her mouth with her kerchief to prevent the smile she was covering from being so obvious.

Jaxx wasn't quite so considerate. His loud braying laugh rang across the courtyard. Even the frosty glare he received from the portly matron who waiting for her horse couldn't dampen his pleasure.

"Do you need me to get the big bad horsy for you?" He jumped back to remain beyond the fist that Vondal swung half-heartedly at his head.

Mekiva couldn't control herself any longer. She began giggling--- then laughing, as the bloody, muck-covered man stomped back into the barn after the unwilling mare.

"Gwendolyn," she asked between bouts of laughter, "don't you think it's funny at all?" When no answer came from Gwendolyn, Mekiva realized her friend had disappeared. Where had she gone?

Gwendolyn took a moment to steady her nerves, and then ran for the shadows near the closed door. So far so good.

Inch by inch she crept closer until she was close enough to distinguish the sounds of voices, but she couldn't make out the much of the conversation. Her heart began to beat faster when she heard one name she recognized: Vondal. I need to get inside, maybe I can hear what they're talking about.

It was too dark to get a clear view of her surroundings. The only window she could see was higher than she could reach. A quick search produced nothing she could use as a ladder or anything she could stand on that was high enough to make a difference. Two futile attempts at free climbing the uneven surface of the wall left her with bloody fingers and a long scrape down one knee, but no closer to her goal.

I've got to build up my strength or get Mekiva to teach me a spider crawl spell. This isn't going to work. There's another warehouse that backs up to this one. Maybe I can find a way up there.

A rickety wooden lean-to built against its backside

looked promising. She was certain she could climb to its roof, and then by jumping, she could reach the edge of the taller building. It would be simple to drop down onto the first warehouse from above. Even better, she spotted a large barrel that held rainwater near the back corner of the wooden shed. Her feet were cold after she removed her boots, but she climbed better without them. Getting up on the water barrel was no problem. Praying that the brackets that held the iron drainpipe to the side of the building would hold, she scaled the wall, then pulled herself up over the lip of the roof.

While lying spread eagle on the rooftop to catch her breath, Gwendolyn started to have second thoughts about what she was attempting. Her parents were city-bred; they'd be aghast at the idea of their adoptive daughter scrambling about on rooftops like a squirrel. The fact that she had crawled around exploring caves with her older brothers wouldn't matter, only what the neighbors thought.

Oh well, at least I'll have an interesting story to tell everyone back at the inn. She crept across the roof then dropped down onto the warehouse below, landing with a soft thud. A ten count later things were still quiet, so she allowed herself a brief rest. Satisfied she was still unobserved, she worked her way from shadow to shadow until she was directly above the open window, the one that was not lit. Grasping the edge of the roof, she stretched downward with her foot, easily reaching the small window she'd chosen. Praying she'd not lose her balance, she slowly lowered herself down until her entire weight was resting on the window ledge, and then she squatted, sliding her hands along the sides to help her balance. Success!

She froze, holding her breath, but the room remained silent. The window was a tight fit but with a little wiggling, while going over the sill, she managed to scramble inside, dropping down to the floor without incident.

Her luck was holding, except for several cotton sacks labeled grain flour and two unlit lanterns hanging on hooks near the door, the room was empty.

Gwendolyn listened at the door for the sounds of activity. Hearing nothing, she cracked open the door and slipped out into the hall.

Lights were spaced evenly along the entire hall, enabling a clear view in both directions. She counted two closed doors between her and the narrow stairway leading down, and one at the opposite end of the hallway. Silently she made her way to the staircase, thankful for her stocking clad feet. She stopped and listened at each door, checking to see if any would open as she went past them. Both doors were securely locked and there was no sound from inside. Thank you, Tyche. Steady, you can do this.

One by one she descended the stairs, checking each one for a weakness that would creak before resting her weight on the same spot. Once she reached the final stair, she waited once more, listening. It was darker on the main floor but there was still more than enough light for her to see. This part of the warehouse was open space except for a boxed off area she thought might be an office. She could hear angry voices coming from inside that room. She used the shadows to move closer, only a few more steps and she'd be able to hear everything they said.

The sensation of cold steel against the back of her neck removed every trace of smugness. Her heart began pounding and her muscles trembled as she tried to remain still. Then two muscular hands grabbed her from behind.

Jaxx leaned casually against the pole, cleaning his nails with a small thin-bladed knife, one of four that he carried hidden within his clothing. Like a cat watching a mouse hole, he never looked directly at anything, but always kept an eye on everything going on around him.

"Please Gwendolyn, I've got to know. Tell us how you came to be trussed up, gagged and deposited on the Inn's doorstep like a holiday bird?"

Gwendolyn cut her eyes at the smirking Duaar. She thought seriously about pushing him into the nearby watering trough, then she realized the angle was wrong and he'd miss it completely. Sighing deeply, she continued her story.

"It was the delivery man from the dance hall. You were all busy with the mare when I spotted him. I know I should've let someone know, but I was afraid it might be our only opportunity to see where he was going."

"You could've been killed. You should've told us. I can't believe you'd do such a foolish thing." Mekiva wasn't willing to discuss any possible rationale her friend could have for taking that kind of chance.

"Mekiva, you're being unfair," Gwendolyn protested, her eyes misting over with tears. "There was no time, I had to make an immediate choice, and my choice was to follow him. To be honest, I've never been so scared in my life," Gwendolyn confessed, her voice trembling.

Jaxx rolled his eyes. How old was she? Drassted robe covers everything but her eyes. At times she seems like an old wise woman, other times she's as naive as a child. He'd never been that green, even fresh from the hold.

He tossed a handkerchief to the teary-eyed girl, plopped down on a bench by the barn and propped his boots up on a bale of hay. Gwendolyn wiped her eyes and gave him a brief smile of appreciation. She wondered why he didn't smile back, then stopped when she realized he couldn't see her mouth through her niqab. Feeling wicked, she stuck out her tongue.

"Could you recognize him again? It was dark after all. We'll understand if you didn't get a good look at his face." Vondal tried to act like it was unimportant, but this was the first real clue as to why someone was trying so hard to kill him. It might even lead him to identify who it was.

"Yes, of course. I don't think I'll ever forget those eyes." She answered promptly, eager to help now that everyone had stopped teasing her.

"Describe him to me. Take your time and be sure, it could be important to us all."

Gwendolyn thought for a moment and then described the man that she'd followed. He was taller than Vondal, but not as heavily built. His arms felt like iron bands when he clamped down on my arms. And he was fast. I didn't even see the knife, and then it was there. He moved like a dancer, effortlessly." She seemed to shiver and stopped talking to take a drink of water before beginning again. " My mother would describe him as handsome, but his face was too strong for my tastes. His hair is light, not grey but so pale it is almost white, and it was pulled back into a warriors topknot. But the thing that stuck out the most was his eyes, blue, but so light a blue it almost looked white. Cold....not exactly evil, more dangerous. I hope I never see him again."

"I've seen him about town." Vondal nodded to show

his approval of Gwendolyn's detailed description. "Castillo's his name. He's Samsara's second in command. Rumor says he's also an assassin. He's got one fearful reputation, mostly based on second-hand descriptions of his torture techniques since no one has lived long enough to describe them first hand. He's not the kind of man you want to make mad, even the city guard gives him room to pass."

"Gwendolyn, are you sure he's the man who brought me the letter?" Jaxx asked.

"Oh yes," she proclaimed. "He made it very clear that he didn't appreciate my following him. In fact, he implied if I ever did it again, he'd hamstring me, and then he'd leave me tied up to the pier at low tide for the crabs instead of on the Inn's front porch. I've never been so afraid in my life." She gave an involuntary little quiver and moved closer to Mekiva.

Mekiva held her friend tightly, offering her arms for comfort. "I forgive you this time." She paused then threatened sharply, "but if you ever do it again---- you'll wish he'd left you to the crabs."

Vondal vented his frustration, kicking the chair leg each time he passed it. "This drassted room is too small. I can't relax. I need to get out and walk. I think best while I'm moving."

After watching Vondal complete several passes, Jaxx decided he'd seen enough pacing for one night. "You're making me crazy, all this marching back and forth like some type of demented soldier."

He worked his body up to a sitting position upon the cramped bed, placing his legs on either side of Gwen as he did. Gwen passed him a handful of walnuts, and he began cracking them, feeding her bits of the sweet meat inside. She used her veil to catch them, before slipping them underneath each time she was successful.

"How else can you expect me to act? Someone tried to kill us…twice. Then my uncle asks me to meet with him to discuss a business matter, and it's delivered by one of the highest-ranking members of Samsara's band. It's foolish to think that the two are not related. This might be my only chance to find out if my uncle was involved with my fathers' death." Somehow, he needed to make them understand that it was important that he keep the arranged meeting, even with the possible dangers.

"And the lamb walks meekly into the Wyvern's den." Jaxx carefully cracked another nut, and then picked the meat out of the shell with his knife. He tossed the shelled meats to the girls, aiming for their mouths and laughing at their attempts to catch them each time he missed.

"I agree, he's up to something. I've never known anyone in my father's family to do anything out of the goodness of their heart. There's no one I'd rather have at my back than you. But this time I've got to go alone. My uncle said he'd send a carriage for me. He claimed it was a matter of protecting his image in the eyes of the community. So, help me get ready, okay?"

Vondal ran his fingers under the starched white collar, but the garments upright neckband still reminded him of a noose. Facing the hangman would be easier than this. But at least the condemned man gets a hearty meal for his trouble. He lounged uncomfortably against the red velvet interior of the carriage, tugged once or twice at the sleeves of his dinner jacket, and then adjusted his cravat. No matter what he tried, he was unable to remove the sensation of a rope slowly tightening about his neck. He closed his eyes and took a few deep breaths, trying to settle his overwrought nerves without success.

The Glass House was the pinnacle of elitist dining in Cabrell. Once the residence of a deposed noble family, after the war, it had been completely renovated and now provided evening meals in the style of the noble houses of Muut. With its extensive menu and a long waiting list for tables, the influential upper crust of Cabrell had rapidly ensured its niche as the city's most popular entertainment location. Originally a favorite of single gentlemen without their own dining halls, or those needing a discreet place to entertain visitors not considered important enough to welcome into their own homes, seemingly overnight it became the place where old nobility mixed readily with the social seeking nouveau riche.

Vondal had never dreamed of stepping foot inside, much less being able to afford a meal at The Glass House. He found himself looking forward to his meeting with his estranged uncle, if for no other reason than the likelihood of a first-rate meal. If he was luring him into a trap to kill him, then at least he'd die happy. Going by the line of carriages waiting to drop off passengers, the food must live up to its reputation.

The maître d' asked his name, then escorted him through a luxurious dining room draped with expensive fabric to an inconspicuous alcove furnished simply with a table and two chairs, a perfect location for anyone who cared to dine without being noticed. Lord Torrin Botherton was already seated in the private room enjoying a glass of amber-colored wine. The maître d' bowed respectfully to Lord Botherton and snapped his fingers for the wine attendant. A pleasant young man instantly appeared with a similar glass for Vondal. He stepped away, leaving the bottle on the table after pouring his drink. Minutes later, a waiter appeared with the first course, lowered the privacy curtains and left the two men to enjoy their dinner and conversation.

Vondal shifted in his chair, unsure if he should start the conversation or wait for his uncle to begin. He decided to sit quietly and enjoy his meal.

Lord Torrin concealed his contempt by taking a bite of his salad, a tantalizing mixture of shrimp and scallops glazed in some type of vinegary spiced sauce and served over a bed of mixed greens. Following his lead, Vondal took a bite. The flavor was delicious, enticing him to linger and enjoy each mouthful.

"I think you'll find the seafood goes well with the peach sherry. Many prefer a dry white wine. I enjoy being different." Lord Orrin poured more of the delectable infusion into Vondal's empty glass.

Vondal sipped at his wine again. This time he made it a point to savor it long enough to come up with some type of answer to his uncle's comment. A long silence ensued before he realized he'd thought of his answer, ---but he'd failed to utter it aloud.

"It's delicious uncle, quite unique in flavor. I find the bitternut and peach combination enticing. I'll have to save my money and bring Jaxx here to sample it in the future." His uncle cocked an eyebrow but didn't comment so Vondal continued. "Forgive me my bluntness. Why have you summoned me today? I'm certain it's not for my expertise in sparkling wine."

Lord Torrin smiled but his eyes darkened briefly. "So bold. My nephew has become a man during his travels." He laid his fork across his plate to signal to the server that he was finished with the course. "Are you in such a hurry to escape my company that you can't take the time to enjoy a good meal with your own uncle? It's not as if you've many family members left. As my brother's only surviving son you're my only living relative. Without the possibility of children of my own, I expect to name you as my heir."

Startled by his uncle's statement, Vondal missed his mouth with his fork, allowing his food to drop off unto the cloth covering the table. He immediately dropped his napkin over the scallop.

Lord Torrin smiled indulgently before continuing as though he'd announced nothing of importance. "Darien was my only blood relative. After his death, I searched for his children. I'm sure you've heard about the reward I've posted for information. It's been five years since you disappeared, longer for your brothers. I'd given up all hope of finding you. Then low and behold, you appear here in Cabrell, acting as though you never left."

Vondal coughed self-consciously. "You set men on my trail because you needed an heir? Not to have me killed?"

"Why would I have you killed, my boy? What possible motivation could I have for your death? No, I seek only to bring you back into the family. The bloodline must be preserved." He stopped talking as the next course was served, a small game bird stuffed with nuts and rice, flavored with mushrooms and wild onions in a lightly seasoned butter sauce. Vondal remained quiet until the attendant had departed before replying.

"My mother didn't feel that way. She wanted nothing to do with my father's family."

"Yes, I know. Their marriage was not a happy one. She was convinced Darien cared nothing for her. She was certain he married her in hopes of finding out the families' treasure."

"Treasure? We lived in the dock ward. The most valuable thing we owned was a copper brazier."

Lord Botherton signaled the serving girl to remove his plate and bring on the next course." Your late mother guarded a secret that has passed from parent to child for many generations, the location of a great hidden treasure. Helena died without entrusting anyone with the information. Had she lived, she would have passed the secret on to one of her children. You boys were too young, and your father turned to spirits and other vices. No one knows the location of the medallion, but I think clues to its location remain."

"It sounds like an old wife's tale, something to regale children with to put them to sleep."

"It's possible. Darien spoke of it several times as he believed it true. I think he loved her, in his own misguided way. I know he regretted her death," Lord Botherton said. His attention was briefly diverted by the arrival of the waiter, who removed the empty wine glasses, replacing them with crystal brandy snifters. His uncle waited until the waiter had withdrawn before he continued. "Your father claimed that as she expelled her final breath, she whispered three words, "in the hearth.""

"In the hearth? There is no hearth, our family home was destroyed in a fire two years ago."

"True. But I believe your mother was talking of another hearth. A location she felt you'd recognize. As her heart faded she tried to pass on the secret.

"I've no idea what she meant."

"It was to have been entrusted to the eldest. Had your brother returned, it would be him sitting in that chair. But you were always your mothers' favorite child. Given the choice, she'd have chosen you to carry on the family's honor." Once more Torrin smiled and again Vondal was reminded of a snake with his prey, his smile, held a fraction longer than was necessary, never quite reaching his eyes.

Vondal chose to sit quietly and listen as his uncle talked. Whatever this secret was, it was obviously the only thing his uncle was concerned with.

"Did your mother ever speak of a special place? Somewhere she'd feel safe leaving something of such value. Or possibly you saw her with a pendant, silver with an oval shape, hung on a chain? It's ornately engraved on one side."

"I'm sorry Uncle, but nothing comes to mind, so many of my childhood memories were of times best forgotten. If something comes to mind, I'll inform you immediately. To be completely honest, if my father found the pendant, he probably pawned it to buy Duaar Ale." Vondal tried his best to appear fascinated at the prospect of becoming his heir. "I'll do my best to live up to the honor you've bestowed on me. I had never imagined the possibility of being named your heir apparent! I'm pleased to find it wasn't you that tried to have me killed. Of course, that leaves me wondering who's behind the attempts on my life."

"I'll look into it tomorrow. Perhaps my standing in the city will prevail. Another question, I loaned you mother a book, ornate leather written in a language you would not recognize. Have you seen it?"

Vondal simply shook his head. His mother had never read anything as far as he knew. He didn't even know she could read.

Lord Botherton appeared piqued as the dessert course was placed before him. He tasted the rich confection, a delicate puff pastry filled with nuts and candied fruit, frowned once more, and then he rose from the table with a slight bow. "If you'll excuse me, I have a social affair I can't ignore, even to indulge myself at our long-awaited reunion. I'm afraid that I've delayed my attendance for as long as I dare. But stay and enjoy your dessert. My carriage will return you to your lodging. I look forward to our next meeting." He hurried away before Vondal could offer an excuse for him to linger further. Shrugging, Vondal returned once more to the delicious tartlet before him, each bite reminding him of how annoyed Jaxx would be at missing such delicious food.

Vondal flopped down and stretched, the tiny attic bed a welcome respite after the tiny bunks on board ship, despite his throbbing feet hanging over the ends of the rickety frame. Finally, comfortable, he gave a contented sigh as his tired muscled eased up enough to release the tension stored inside. His eyes narrowed as Mekiva moved gracefully around the room, doing the small things that women seemed to find necessary upon entering a room. After several minutes of aimless fussing, she finally sat down in the lone chair and turned to Vondal, a look of expectation clear upon her face

"Do you like Cabrell? Would you want to make it your home after you finish your training?"

Mekiva rolled her eyes at his obvious ploy to avert the impending conversation, then sighed and went along with it. "I lived on the farm until I was seven. Until then, I had never traveled farther from home than the county market. When my parents sent me to live in the city I was excited. I didn't think about how much I would miss them. It's was a great opportunity for me, and an honor to be chosen to attend Rosemount. But now--- I'm not as sure about my life goals as I once was."

Vondal nodded sympathetically, hoping this was the correct response to her statement. His taste in females usually ran to older, worldlier females more interested in his actions than conversation. Talking was an option that he often forswore, preferring his time be put to more practical use. But Mekiva was… different. She intrigued him. And she was smart, too smart for her own good, or his.

"You've stalled long enough. Tell me what happened during dinner."

Drasst! I knew it! Mekiva isn't going to let me off the hook that easily. "It was enlightening. No threats, merely dinner, and conversation." A great dinner.

"That's all?"

"He tried to convince me he was seeking an heir, but he was fishing for information. Nothing direct, but he spent most of the meal asking about my mother's family and some secret family treasure."

"Treasure?" She leaned forward, her eyes twinkling with sudden interest. There'd been a lot of wild rumors floating around about Vondal's family after the fire. If only a quarter of them were true, then his uncles' sudden interest made a lot more sense.

"Supposedly my mother was to pass on some great family secret, but she died before she could tell anyone."

"Then what's the problem? If you don't know, you can't tell him. Maybe if we ignore him, he'll lose interest and go away."

"It's not that simple. When my uncle was talking about Helena's hearth he'd a strange look in his eyes. I've seen that look before in my father's eyes, and it always meant trouble. Then when I mentioned the fire at my family's home, he looked guilty. I think he knows more about my fathers' death than he's admitting."

"It was strange, the house catching fire and burning so fast. But Vondal, your father wasn't the most popular man in the bottoms. It wouldn't have taken much…a word here, a few coins there…"

"I've wanted to run a knife into his gut myself a time or two. But why burn the house?

"I'm not sure but I bet it has something to do with your mother's secret. Too bad she died before she could tell anyone." Mekiva was puzzled as Vondal began to grin widely.

"I lied," he said. "My mother told me the family secret years ago. My uncle asked about a medallion. She talked about it, but she called it a pendant, not a medallion. And I think I know where it's hidden. Helena was also my grand-mothers' name. My grandfather was a blacksmith. Before he died, he used to joke about how the heat from his forge was colder than Helena's heart, heart not hearth. She made sure I knew all the family history, especially the stories about my grandparents. Sadly, I only know the general area in which they lived, I was six when they died in a fire."

"Then the story might be true? Something valuable could be hidden in your grandfather's old forge?"

"There little chance it's true…more likely a family fable, but worth checking it out. The old keep burnt long ago, and my grandparents are buried nearby. If my mother never told my father of the locket, it's possible that it's hidden near her father's forge. But it's more plausible my father found it years ago and sold it to buy whiskey."

"So there's no chance that you're really being named your uncles' prospective heir and becoming a rich noble?"

she speculated.

"Not very likely," Vondal replied grimly. "Not that it couldn't happen. I am his next of kin. But it doesn't sit right. I don't need to see a flame to feel its burn. The smart thing for me to do is to concentrate on building our shipping business. Maxx is right about that. But it might be worth taking a week off to check out the old homestead. If we find it, then we can decide if we should inform my uncle."

"Your uncle still scares me," Mekiva said. "And that man who works for Samsara, Castillo, he's even worse. He gives me chills."

"He might scare you, but he has no reason to hurt you regardless of his end game. You'll be perfectly safe after we leave town."

Vondal missed the sudden tears, but the quiver of her lips gave it away. She realized they were leaving Cabrell… and she knew he didn't intend to take her with him. He was in for a fight, a fight he'd happily avoid and couldn't win.

"Some plan you come up with; slip out at daybreak before your uncle wakes up and hope he didn't think you'd move so fast," Jaxx retorted snidely. He dipped the corner of his extra shirt into mink oil, liberally applying it to his boots to help keep the water out. Every time he went out in the snow, his feet got wet. Then he got sick. He took a quick look out the window at the snowdrifts in the courtyard, sighed and started rubbing the leather again.

Vondal gestured rudely with three fingers, and then ignored the surly Duaar as he continued going over the checklist. "We have plenty of trail food and enough water in our canteens for several days. We've already loaded our packs and the horses have new shoes. We both have bows, so we can hunt fresh meat on the trail. You carry your ax as usual. I'll take my sword."

"What if I preferred to use my sword?" Jaxx retorted.

"Well, that might be better," Vondal snapped. "You've already proven that ax gets you into more trouble, than out."

"Hilarious," Jaxx replied sarcastically. "It's not like you are a great swordsman. Sometimes things just happen. I seem to remember a time down in Zuballo that...."

Vondal ignored his jibe. "It shouldn't take us more than a week,-if the weather holds. The old homestead is a little over a day's travel east of Cabrell. That gives us five days to locate the medallion."

"Are you sure you packed enough?" Vondal could be a pain, always needing to review every detail. Besides the standard dried travel biscuits, Vondal had bought flour, sugar, salt lard, some jerky, dried fruit and kava for them both. Jaxx also carried most of the non-food items they would need: a length of spider-silk rope, a few arrowheads, extra waxed bowstrings, flint, tinder, and some lamp oil. At the last moment, Vondal added the spare candle from the small chest. It never hurt to be prepared. That, along with their clothes and bedding would have to do, the packs wouldn't hold anymore.

"We have to assume that my uncle will have people stationed nearby to watch us. Since we know this already, it won't be a problem to lose any tails. Once we evade his men, he has no way of knowing where we are going. We can leave when the Gates open at dawn, blend in with the caravan that's leaving for Alliance. We'll leave a note for Addie and Tula to apologize for taking off and explaining where we are going and why. They know we will be back, they have all our savings in their safe box.

"It's almost daylight. We need to go now." Vondal was like a hungry dog guarding a bone, he wasn't going to let up until they were leagues away from Cabrell.

Jaxx sighed, he knew what was coming.

The familiar morning sounds of Tula in the kitchen, as well as the hauntingly familiar smell of fresh bread, made Vondal feel a bit foolish about all the precautions he was taking. Reaching the courtyard outside, he stopped in his tracks, puzzled by the sight of their horses, saddled and standing docilely next to two unknown geldings.

Hearing familiar voices approaching, Jaxx suddenly decided he needed to fetch the pack mule from the barn. Mekiva and Gwendolyn came out of the kitchen loaded with fresh baked goods, confident Vondal had not thought to schedule any time for breakfast. Gwen shyly offered Jaxx a muffin which he accepted with a grateful smile. Then both sat back to watch the fireworks.

"You two are not coming with us!" Vondal shouted. "How'd you even know we were leaving?"

"It wasn't that hard to figure out. You spent most of the night staring at your packs. And you checked the shoes on both horses when you fed them. You would need cover to slip out of town without your uncle finding out. It was either leave this morning with the caravan or wait a week or two and give him time to post watchers."

"It doesn't change things. It's too dangerous a trip for young girls." Besides he's had men watching us since we arrived in town.

Jaxx snorted loudly, not even bothering to muffle the sound. Ha! Keep that attitude and Mekiva will soon show you how little you know about women… or their minds."

Mekiva ignored his rant. She placed two large sacks of food into the leather bags tied to the saddle of her waiting horse. There was also a bedroll and a waterskin showing the girls had come prepared. "You said there'd be no reason for your uncle to hurt me or Gwen. So, there's no reason not to come with you. Remember how you bragged about how you're always prepared for any eventuality that may occur? This is one of those eventualities."

Vondal tried once more. "But, ---you are girls! It's just wrong---it's unseemly! Wait! Jaxx, help me with this."

Jaxx grinned and laid back against his pack, enjoying the hole his friend was digging for himself. There's no way the girls were going to let them leave without them. Vondal was living in a fool's paradise.

"Jaxx knows when to keep his mouth shut. We're coming with you, and that's final," Mekiva stated flatly, swinging her leg across the big paints back. She shifted forward, settling her body into the worn leather saddle. Seconds later Twizzle joined her. He settled into a comfortable spot on top of her bedroll and promptly fell asleep.

"I give up, you can come with us. We don't have time to stand around and argue. The West gate is opening within the hour, and if we don't hurry, we'll get stuck behind the caravan." Some choice, he either scrapped his entire plan or got everyone moving before someone noticed their escape. Once more a tiny wisp of a girl had backed him into a corner with no way out.

Ten

"Rider coming in hot, Sergeant."

The rapid drumming of the horses' hoofs against the hard ground could be heard several moments before the heavily lathered animal appeared in the distance. The exhausted outrider was addressing the sergeant almost before the weary horse came to a full stop, his voice loud from excitement.

"The road's blocked ahead Sarge, there was a landslide. One man's injured, his horse had to be put down. He needs a healer now."

"How bad is he hurt?"

"Legs in bad shape. He'll have to be carried out. It'll take some time to clear a path wide enough for the wagons to get through."

"Drasst! We'll have to salvage what we can from the situation. Take a quarter turn break before you report back." A slight frown creased his weathered brow before Sergeant Axon addressed his adjunct. "Corporal Marcius! Ride out and get me an idea of what we are facing. The captain will want the pass cleared and he won't be in the mood to hear excuses. I'll be awaiting your report." He mounted, then addressed the corporal once again. "And send someone for the healer." Spurring his horse back toward the wagon's preparing to pull out of last night's camp he contemplated what he was going to tell his commander.

The well-trained troops hastened to obey. The weary corporal continued shouting orders as he mounted his own horse. Breakfast would have to wait.

Captain Anderson had just finished his breakfast when Sergeant Axon knocked on the frame of his tent. The ever-vigilant aide-de-camp beckoned him inside, warning him with a look that the Captain was not in the best of moods. Sergeant Axon steeled himself for the inevitable reprimand, the commander disliked having his private time interrupted.

"Excuse the interruption, sir! There's been a landslide about a half-mile into the pass. It's entirely blocked, I doubt a cart, much less a wagon, can get through. Estimates are at least two days, possibly three before we can proceed."

"That's not an option. We are on a schedule. I want the blockage removed by tomorrow morning. Put the civilians to work, they won't like it, but we can't afford the delay. I don't want excuses. Even the elderly and children can carry pails and water. Take care of it."

"Even with the civilian's help, it's not going to be easy to clear this mess."

"There are limited alternatives, we either clear the pass or return to Cabrell. Neither option will help the hungry men at the outpost waiting for supplies. We could confiscate the civilians' private stock to carry the military supplies and transfer the food to pack animals, but we'd have to abandon everything else."

"That's a decision I can't make at this time. Keep me apprised of your progress. And Sergeant, extend the guard line outwards. It would be injudicious of me to overlook the possibility of a trap."

Sergeant Axon saluted wearily. It had already been a

harrowing journey, fraught with hit and run attacks and costly weather delays. Now, only one day after leaving Cabrell this happens. He didn't look forward to delivering the captain's orders. Several of the merchants were instigators, looking for any excuse to cause trouble. This setback would only fuel the fires. At least it wouldn't be his responsibility to notify the civilians. He'd hate to be in the wagon master's boots when he delivered the unwelcome news.

The news turned the wagon masters face colder than the winter wind howling between the scattered wagons. He stood, paced around a bit and then spat on the ground near the sergeant's right foot.

The sergeant tightened his fists in disgust. "I realize this is putting you in a difficult position but that was totally uncalled for."

"Can't help the way I feel. Maybe I shouldn't have let my temper get away from me. I know you're simply doing your job. How long will it take?" The grizzled old drover squinted against the brightness of Omission's dual suns. Well, past midday. Another day lost. Not many more and we'll lose half the fresh food desperately needed at the fort. Scurvy sets in fast when all you get to eat is bread and meat.

"Captain says by tomorrow but that's not realistic. If the weather holds, a few days, maybe four," he replied. He tried to tell himself this was one of those things that happen on the road, but the entire situation didn't feel right. The circumstances were too favorable, what with the slide creating an obstruction exactly halfway between Cabrell and Fort Brockville. The captain was already entertaining thoughts of an ambush. Still, it wouldn't be the first time the unit found its self in difficult circumstances.

The cargo master muttered something that Vondal didn't catch before heading off in the direction of the main cook fires. Most of the caravan's population gathered there every morning to unwind and enjoy the meal together before a long day on the trail. The weary civilians, already exhausted from the daily rigors of the trek, looked dejected at the idea of a shortened breakfast and long day of work, followed by a second and possibly a third of the same.

Mekiva felt the same disappointment but accepted it as part of the consequence of being in a large party. When something went wrong, everyone chipped in to help. Vondal quickly explained what he'd overheard, including the sergeant's fears of a possible ambush. Even if the excavation went smoothly, accidents always happened, especially when people were already in a foul mood before beginning a task. Maybe it would be better if Gwendolyn stayed behind. "Why don't you stay here and rest, there's sure to be need of your healing skills soon.

She was tired, so she quickly agreed.

"When will we leave for the site?" Mekiva asked.

Vondal hesitated, debating whether he could convince Mekiva to rest with Gwendolyn, and then decided it wasn't worth the fight. "As soon as we can get our horses saddled."

Jaxx tied Panda, his paint mare, to a downed tree alongside several heavily lathered horses. He studied the slide for a moment and then made his way over to the soldier that seemed to be in charge. The young corporal seemed more suspicious than welcoming at the interruption.

"Heard you boys had a slight problem. What can I do to help?"

The two men stood staring eye to eye, then the harried soldiers scowl evaporated as it was replaced by a welcoming smile. He used the corner of his torn shirt and wiped the caked dirt and sweat from his face with a weary sigh. He'd been digging since the landslide was discovered.

"We've two scouts pinned down by debris. Between the loss of blood and the wintry weather, it's a race against time. The sooner we get them out the better chance they have of survival. If you could help with that, it'd be appreciated. Pick yourself a spot and dig in."

"There's a sergeant riding this way with a platoon of additional men. As I started this way the wagon master was forming the civilians into workgroups. I had my ax with me when the trooper reported to the sergeant, so I was able to ride back with him. I'll be over there if you need me," Jaxx pointed toward a tall blonde man chopping haphazardly at a jumble of trees and branches. Despite his effort, his short sword wasn't having much effect on the splintered trunks.

"Let me take a swing at that," he said. The exhausted soldier didn't argue. Jaxx raised the iron ax overhead, exhaling as he swung downwards. The heavy blade bit deeply into the green-wood, cracking the width of the bole of the broken tree. A second blow broke the trunk in half.

Acknowledging the Duaar's ax as the better tool, the tired soldier tied a rope from the trunk section to the horn on his horses' saddle and then used the animal to drag it away from the pile. Jaxx grinned at his new partner, and then, whistling a jaunty sea tune, returned to chopping.

Jaxx shifted his heavy ax to a more comfortable position across his back, tied his sword to the saddle and then trotted his mare behind the soldiers heading back to the campsite for a meal. It had been three days of backbreaking work since they'd left Cabrell, with only short breaks for food or sleep. Gazing around at the epicenter of the landslide in the early morning light, Jaxx realized what a tenuous situation the entire caravan faced. The Apex Pass was the only route that bisected the mountains, shortening travel time by several weeks over the flatter but much longer passage that followed the perimeter of the western side of the mountains. Many generations of traders had followed the well-traveled but arduous passage that descended at a relatively steep angle into a sheltered canyon. About halfway through the canyon, the road made a sharp turn to the right, following along the wall of the canyon until it reached a natural bottleneck along a dry creek bed, passing through a crevice between two enormous boulders. The road through the bottleneck had been completely blocked by a combination of dirt, large boulders, small rocks and shattered trees piled randomly within the close confines of the passage. It was a perfect site for an ambush.

Tucked up behind a large boulder atop the canyon rim, Castillo watched as the last of the laborers passed through the bottleneck. The mages plan was a simple one, wait until the members of the pack train were exhausted from their efforts at clearing the blockage of the valley, and then attack before they realized that there was no way out. After a week on the road, his men were no longer as easy to control as they had been when he'd led them onto the fresh trail. Delays only aggravated the situation. Lord Botherton's officious mage had left no room for error, making it clear to Castillo that if he failed to deliver exactly what he'd been ordered to deliver, it would be his last failure. Castillo rarely worried…that a woman was the source of his anxiety only made it worse.

The trap was triggered. He had no intention of letting their rabbit back out of the snare. His men were well hidden, they wouldn't be seen until it was too late.

Vondal couldn't shake the feeling of being watched. The canyon rim was heavily overgrown with scrub trees and briars making if difficult to spot any possible danger from below. An Orrog army could have been hiding there and no one would know it. The canyon itself was pockmarked with small caves and natural crevices, any one of which could be utilized to stage an ambush. The Sergeant had ordered his men to check out all the openings within sight, however, there had been insufficient time to check them all. One more day and the passage would be open. There had been no signs of movement except for an occasional rabbit and one nosy fox. So why was he so jumpy?

Dinner had been hot and filling, a simple stew with biscuits and warm cider. To the tired and hungry workers, it was a feast. Balancing her plate, Mekiva followed Kelvarr, a handsome young scout, over to a couple of rocks near where most everyone gathered to eat. Jaxx, Gwendolyn, and Vondal were already there waiting for her to join them.

Kelvarr ate quickly, using his biscuit to wipe the last drops of stew from his plate. Gwendolyn noticed how quickly the small amount of stew each had been allotted vanished.

"Here," she said, offering her plate to the hungry man." I'm not very hungry, and you always seem ravenous. All this digging must have increased your appetite along with your muscles."

"Are you sure?" his eyes betrayed his eagerness.

"Yes, I've already eaten more than enough."

"I guess I'm so tired I didn't realize how hungry I was," he said, taking the still steaming plate from the tiny Shi'i maiden. "I've got watch duty tonight and I'm already exhausted after digging all day."

Gwendolyn had felt a momentary pang of guilt as she noted the envious expression on several other faces as Kelvarr finished her stew. He slopped the last dregs of the stew from the plate with the last of her biscuit, and then washed it down with water.

Feeling slightly guilty about accepting Gwendolyn's food, he offered to wash the plates and return them to the cook tent.

Mekiva offered to help.

"Maybe it'd be better if you and Gwendolyn turned in early," Vondal prompted.

He pretended it didn't bother him, but Jaxx could tell…his friend was jealous. Both girls adored Kelvarr. One of these days Von would get tired of the taste of foot in mouth. Soon he hoped.

Vondal flinched as Mekiva's bright green eyes darkened to smoldering ash. He quickly collected himself before she exploded.

"Why should we be sent to bed like children," she snapped. "Gwendolyn's already healed everyone that needs healing. She saved the leg of that young guardsman who was caught in the slide, and she'll be able to help anyone who is injured. We're looking forward to a little fun."

Jaxx wisely chose to keep his mouth shut. It was going to be a long night, especially with both boys pulling night watch duty. He decided to go check on the horses. He pushed aside a length of briar and stepped across a rotten limb that had fallen across the deer path leading down to the creek. He never minded night watch. But being rushed by whoever was assigned as his partner always ruined his mood. It was easier to tack up his horse ahead of time. Then he could take a short nap before starting his shift.

Storm, his grey mare knew his routine. He'd examine her feet for stones, lightly brush her coat, and then slap her on the belly twice before cinching the belt. Once he'd made the mistake of jumping on a horse without first checking the girth of the saddle. It was months before his friends stopped calling him sidewinder. He missed Vondal's public flaying and his abrupt departure from the camp.

It was quiet down by the stream, just the thing Vondal needed to clear his head. Mekiva could fire him up in seconds and he didn't want to overreact. Like everyone, he was excited to clear the final few feet of the rubble and finish their journey. The last couple of days had taken their toll on the entire wagon train. Most everyone wanted nothing more than to eat, then collapse into their bedrolls for a few hours of sleep, before starting the next long day of digging. He relaxed a bit, enjoying the sounds of the night.

Despite being exhausted from the tedious drudgery of clearing the landslide, a few of the more talented people had formed a makeshift band, much to the enjoyment of those too stressed out to sleep. One man was playing the mandolin, its tinkling notes could be heard drifting on the night air amid the scattered voices of men and women.

A group of the younger children raced around the camp playing Wyverns and Weasels. The tenuous clack-clack -clack of their makeshift wooden swords drew the attention of the mothers in the crowd keen to send their tireless progeny to bed.

A trio of night watch guards had arranged two old wooden packing cases into a makeshift table and was enjoying a lively game of cards prior to starting their shift. Jaxx sat watching the card game, hoping for a chance to join in before the men had to leave for guard duty later that evening.

"I bid three stones and two crowns." Callus, one of the youngest guards, said as he tossed two silver pieces into the pot.

"Only a fool would bid three stones when two are showing on the table already." Pontus crowed. "I bid two blades and two crowns." He tossed in his coins and drew two cards. The burly old ranger laughed at the sullen expression that appeared on his young friend's face once he realized there was no possible way he could win the hand.

"I'll take three cards. The game ain't over 'til Tyche spins her wheel." Callus checked his new cards then tossed them all on the pile. "Guess I landed on black, time for me to get back to work anyway. Jaxx, you want my spot?"

Callus stood to leave, stretching languidly to loosen up his back as he rose. A sudden sharp pain flared in his chest, followed by a second one lower down. He grasped the arrow that jutted from his chest, trying to pull it out but unable to get a grip on the bloody shaft. Bubbles of red foam formed in his mouth as he struggled for breath, then the world went dim and he slumped forward onto the makeshift table.

"Inonu's bloody sword!" Jaxx rolled backward off the

log he'd been sitting on, using the underside of a near-by peddler's cart for protection from the hail of arrows. He crawled away from the line of fire, sheltering behind a nearby crate. Two brightly feathered arrows embedded in the wood inches away from his head marked out a pattern he'd hoped to never see again. *Orrogg raiders! And I left my ax next to my bedroll. A boot knife and no shield, against bowmen I might as well be unarmed. Some choice, death or humiliation.* He began to half crawl, half drag himself back toward his bedroll and awaiting ax. Two short runs and a belly crawl later, he claimed his favorite weapon and advanced on his first target, his eyes gleaming dangerously in the meager firelight.

In the shadow of the flickering fire, he could make out two blood-spattered young cadets. They were seriously overmatched, struggling to fend off the advances of three bigger and fresher Orrogg tribesmen. Two of the burly raiders kept their inexperienced targets attention, while the third circled warily, waiting for an opportunity to strike. He had to help…fast!

Praying no one had noticed, Jaxx worked his way from tree to tree until he was behind them. The nearest man, a heavily built Orrogg raider wielding a khopesh, had forced his opponent down onto one knee. The smaller man's time was running out. He swung the battle-ax. The heavy iron blade bit deeply into the unsuspecting raider's arm, cleaving it from his body. The unruly fighter staggered into his partner, throwing off his attack.

Tyche rolled black again, as Jaxx stepped into the path of the uncontrolled strike. The jagged flame blade bit deeply into his shoulder, causing him to lose his hold on the dagger he'd gripped in his other hand.

The Orrogg raider drove his blade into the side of the

young cadet before moving to assist his armless partner.

Jaxx didn't wait for him to close. He swung the battle-ax sideways, slicing through his leather breastplate and across his stomach. Bloody entrails followed the blades exit and the man dropped like a stone, dead before his body hit the ground.

For a moment Jaxx's vision blurred, and he had trouble staying on his feet. A lot of blood was leaking from his shoulder wound, he needed to find help before he passed out. The last time he'd seen the girls they were hiding under a wagon, he prayed they were still there. Maybe the Orroggs will run out of arrows. They can' have many left, the wagons look like porcupines. Unfortunately, Orroggs liked to reuse their arrows, believing the blood of dead enemies made them fly straighter. They would fight until death rather than leave them behind.

"Gwendolyn," he called out as he fell, hoping the girls were close enough to hear. "I could really use your Goddess right now."

"Pray Rheaaz has a soft spot for pig-headed Duaars," she said, crawling from beneath the wagon, to a sheltered spot near where he lay. She clasped his hand, kissed him lightly on his brow, and prayed. "Rheaaz, blessed mother, I beg you once again to heal this exasperating young Duaar so that he may continue to irritate us. I willingly accept your price." Almost instantly the goddess answered. A soft radiance began building around their clasped hands, spreading along Jaxx's arm, and upward toward his bleeding shoulder. Reaching the most damaged area, the glow intensified as the torn flesh melded together, the blood flow slowing, and then stopping entirely. Gwendolyn ran her fingers lightly over her new pink scar, amazed at the ability Rheaaz had granted her, worth any price she had to pay.

"I'm good for now, please get back under the wagon" Jazz struggled to pull his hand away, but Gwendolyn would not release it.

"You'll have to endure my company a little longer," she replied, leaning forward and shifting her weight to gently press him back to the ground. "Until I'm certain you're fully healed, you're not getting up off the ground. The fight will have to wait."

"Well girl, are you going to help the others, or continue to cower under this wagon?" Mekiva struggled, torn between fear, and lack of confidence. Her decision made, she belly-crawled to a nearby tree stump, and peered out at the fighting. The ambushers had the upper hand. Most of the soldiers were armed but many of the camp defenders were fighting with whatever makeshift weapon they could grab. Any help she could provide would be welcomed.

Crouched behind the meager cover, Mekiva began the first line of a spell she'd recently mastered. Three or four words later she knew she was in trouble. She couldn't concentrate. I can do this. Master Stolinn would never let me give up. Closing her eyes, she centered herself and began again, first chanting a few incoherent syllables, then throwing a handful of sand into the air. Finally, she snapped out the command word while striking her hands together and gestured toward a large group of raiders standing over the mangled bodies of two women and a child.

Instead of the glowing forcefield, she'd expected to see forming, a misty gray fog began to rise, an acrid cloud filling the air and making it impossible for the men to see more than a few inches in any direction. Mekiva looked down, realizing instead of sand, she had tossed crushed eggshell into the air. She grinned as the haze deepened, changing color and smelling like rotten eggs. The unsuspecting raiders began coughing, moaning and striking out at each other as they struggled to escape the malevolent sulfur poison. One ran directly at Mekiva!

"Mekiva, drop now!" Gwendolyn panicked and grabbed Vondal's bow' pointing it toward the raider but she couldn't get a clear shot. Stepping from behind the wagon wheel, the tiny Shi'i-Lakka girl released the taut string, firing with her eyes closed, with no thought of directing or controlling the arrows erratic flight. Her target, an extremely ugly warrior wearing the mummified head of a Foxbat as a headdress, grunted as the missile struck him in the chest. He yelped once and fell.

Amazed at her success, she sighted on a second attacker, who was standing and staring, frozen in shock by the sight of an armed Shi'i-Lakka draped in flowing desert dress. Even with the goddesses help, Gwendolyn was astonished when the arrow struck him, driving him first to his knees and then forward, to land atop the small boulder Mekiva was crouching behind.

Despite his injuries, he struggled to swing his sword at the unprotected mage, hoping to disrupt her spell. Mekiva ducked and the man's rusty blade passed over her head.

Gwendolyn acted on instinct, swinging the heavy wooden bow at the raider. She managed to use the edge of the bow to divert the blade away, but the blow numbed her wrist and left the weapon useless. She feared that even with an arrow in his chest, the Orrogg was much too strong for the two girls to defeat alone. She braced herself for the next blow, all the while calling for help that never came.

Chaos ran rampant throughout the camp. From his position near the main campfire, Vondal occasionally caught a flash of metal or heard muffled shouts and screams, as the spell blinded participants swung wildly at any viable targets in the dark. One by one the cries within the foul-smelling cloud died out. As the wind began to disperse the noxious fumes, he wondered if there was left alive. It looked like every raider had succumbed to the poisonous gas, or from the desperate thrashing cuts of a fellow raider trapped inside.

Vondal decided to search for Mekiva, eager to tell her how amazed he was by the results of her spell. He wasn't certain but he thought he'd spotted her standing near a boulder off to his right while she was casting. It was difficult to see her through the smoke from the fires and the remains of her unexpected spell, but she was still at the rock, looking disheveled… but uninjured. He turned to join her, but Jaxx, along with the redhaired Corporal and a few other men, was still embroiled in a savage melee against a handful of attackers over by the supply tent. Wiping the sweat from his face, he went to join them.

The two teens ended up fighting back to back, holding off the press of blades through pure determination. Vondal couldn't hazard a guess as to how many opponents there had been in the raiding party. No matter how many they took out, more appeared. There seemed to be no end to them. A strangled scream of pain drew their attention. Spotting an old man protecting his wife and child, Jaxx rushed to aid the suffering family. He swept his ax overhead, bringing it down across the back of one of the raiders. The excited old man quickly finished him off by driving the shattered hilt of a pitchfork into his stomach.

Vondal had his own problems, hard-pressed by a particularly ugly brute that fought two-handed. The Orrogg used one knife to strike upwards, and the second to jab at his blindside. Reflexively he threw his sword up to protect his head, leaving his abdomen to take the full brunt of the second thrust. He followed up with a third blow, jamming the blade forward into Vondal's groin. Vondal fell to the ground, paralyzed by pain. Unable to defend himself he closed his eyes and steeled himself for the death blow.

Mekiva screamed as Vondal fell, a loud and piercing wail that was cut short as a filthy hand was clamped over her mouth. A second hand wrapped her around the neck, choking off her air and pulling her backward toward the trees. She lashed out blindly, but her wild arcing swings did no damage. Panicked, she bit down on his hand in a desperate attempt for freedom. With a strangled cry he jerked his savaged hand away, scraping additional skin off. He thrust the bleeding fingers into his mouth to ease the sting, however, he didn't release his hold on the struggling girl.

Mekiva shrieked again, and kicked back with her foot, landing a blow but doing no harm. Annoyed by her continuous resistance, the irritated raider cuffed her. The halfhearted wallop knocked her off her feet. Arms windmilling, she fell backward, striking her head against the side of a tree. There was a sharp pain then everything blurred and faded away.

Eleven

"How are you feeling now?" Jaxx inquired anxiously as Vondal opened his eyes for the first time since being injured in the midnight attack.

"Like I was stabbed, tied to my horse and dragged for miles," he responded.

"Well, actually you were stabbed---three times if you count the bolt from the crossbow. But no horse was involved. It took Gwendolyn a while to stop the bleeding, but you're going to be all right now."

He pulled the blanket higher around Vondal's' chest and then held a flask for him to drink. Vondal took a few sips of the fiery brew, then lay back against his saddle, using it to prop upright . The pain was making it difficult to concentrate and he struggled to convert his thoughts into words.

"How are the girls? Is everyone all right," he asked anxiously, looking around the campsite for any sign of Mekiva.

Jaxx felt his face flush at Vondal's question. He hesitated, everyone knew Vondal was crazy about Mekiva even if he hadn't admitted it to himself. As for Gwen, she was much too young, too innocent, to deal with what she had faced.

"The girls are fine. Mekiva had a bad scare. She was pulled into the brush and expected to be killed. Instead the man snatched her necklace and ran. Gwen's been busy, imploring her Goddess to heal the other serious injuries. She says she'll be by to check on you once she has everyone stabilized, so be patient." Jaxx sighed wearily, the weight of his words making it difficult for him to speak. "But there's something else you should know. This wasn't a normal ambush. Captain Akon is convinced this wasn't a simple salvage foray. Someone took the time to plan this raid, waited until we were all exhausted from clearing the obstruction, and then attacked. The timing was too perfect, they knew we'd break through the rubble tomorrow."

Vondal closed his eyes. He knew Jaxx all too well. The straight-talking Duaar was not telling him something, something he wouldn't like to hear. "Out with it, whatever it is you are not telling me. Give it to me straight."

Jaxx averted his eyes as he answered, forcing the words through tightly clenched teeth in a futile attempt to evade a direct answer. Vondal had spent quite a bit of time playing cards with the young corporal, their friendship grew to the point of the trio discussing a reunion after their quest was complete. Maybe even an offer to join the business. Inwardly he groaned, wishing they had never left the ship. Drasst it all to the hells.

"We lost Mathias. It was fast, he didn't suffer. The girls aren't taking it well, they really liked him too. There's also a problem with the caravan continuing on to Alliance. All but two wagons were destroyed, they're burnt too badly to salvage. Most of the fort's supplies are ruined, and the three merchants refuse to continue onward. There is already some talk of returning to Cabrell immediately." He hesitated again, "It might be the best thing for us, too."

"I hate it about Mathias. He was an all right guy, even if he did pay too much attention to Mekiva. Returning to Cabrell doesn't make sense. We can continue without them. If we cut cross country, we can make up some of the lost time."

"Think we can convince the girls to return with the caravan?"

"No. But I'm going to try, Vondal replied." You're right about the attack. Why this pack-train? It's a military transport, with very little cargo. And none of that' was very valuable, mostly food supplies for the fort."

"I've been thinking the same thing. Even stranger, the raiders disappeared right after that Orrogg snatched Mekiva's necklace."

"Why? It wasn't valuable, just some cheap trinket she bought from a vendor during the festival. No, taking the necklace must have been a coincidence. Besides, there's no way anyone could know we're here---we decided to join the caravan at the last moment."

"I've no clue, but I'm positive there's more to it. Something bigger motivated the raiders, something that we've stumbled into. And my gut says it's related to what happened in Cabrell. His mind went back to the shadowy figures he'd seen through the curtains. Had someone been watching them? And why?

Vondal dropped to one knee to get a closer look at the tracks leading away from the camp. The ambusher's trail was faint, but clear enough for them to follow, even with their limited experience. "The tracks head up into the mountains. I say we take a chance and follow them as long as we can."

"That may not be for long," Jaxx replied, his eyes

drawn to the rapidly gathering storm clouds. Winter storms came in fast and hard this late in the season and even a light dusting of snow could erase any traces long before they caught up with the remaining bandits.

"I'm not much for foolish heroics," Sergeant Kelvarr said. "Even if I could spare the men--- what do you expect to do once you've located them? We were outnumbered before, a small group wouldn't stand a chance in a one-on-one fight."

"We have to try …Mathias would've tried." Von refused to accept the idea of walking away. They had a clear trail to follow.

"Mathias would've failed, too. Don't waste your time following the bandits. Those men know the mountains and neither of you are woodsmen. Give up your foolish thoughts of vengeance and return to Cabrell with us. There's nothing you can do by yourselves." Sergeant Kelvarr swung himself up into the saddle of the restless stallion, easing his injured leg into a more comfortable position slightly forward of the empty stirrup. "I hate the idea of turning back, but I won't endanger anyone else. Continuing to Alliance is not a viable option. With Tyche's blessing, I can reach Cabrell with my head intact, and save the lives of what's left of the traders. Try and understand, I'm a soldier first. It's my job to protect the caravan. Not to sound callous but continuing without adequate supplies is foolish. You young folks might be willing to risk it all to chase impossible dreams, but I'm heading back to town to sit out the winter."

He motioned for the dejected soldiers to mount up and prepare for the long trip back home to Cabrell. The entire trip had been a disaster. The only wagon remaining intact was carrying those too injured to ride or walk. Five of the male traders remained out of the fourteen that had ridden out of Cabrell, three of them in the wagon with the five injured soldiers. Three women survived out of a dozen. Even one of the children had been lost, a victim of a ricocheting arrow fired by his own uncle. All their dreams were gone, now they just hoped to reach Cabrell alive.

"I guess I can't blame you," Vondal replied despondently. "If the circumstances were different, I'd be returning to town with you. But the risk for me is greater in Cabrell. Jaxx and I will continue onward. The girls will be returning with you."

Sergeant Re shook his head sadly. "I don't understand the minds of young people. I've already discussed this with Mekiva and Gwendolyn earlier today. The girls are determined to stay with you. You'll have a fight on your hands if you try to send them back alone."

"I know it's probably a lost cause, but Mekiva trusted me to get them back in time for her next school session. I can't guarantee that any longer. This was supposed to be a simple trip, find my family's old homestead and then return to Cabrell, ten days, fifteen at the most. Half that is already gone. But Mathias's' death changed everything. I can't return until I've exhausted every lead."

Jaxx interrupted him. "You know that I'll back you no matter what, but you have to admit our chances are getting worse by the moment. The sergeant's right, there's no use following the raiders. It's been a day and night since the attack occurred. If there were tracks, the weather erased any traces. All we have is an educated guess about the general direction, and neither of us has any experience in tracking. We spent the last five years on a ship. It might be time to admit we are beaten and return to Cabrell. We can try again next spring."

"Then go back with the girls. I have to try. If not the raiders, I intend to check out the old homestead. It only half a day's ride from the other side of the cut-through."

"It may not matter what we decide," Jaxx stated. "We may not have a choice either way."

"What do you mean?"

"Take a look at this." He pointed toward several bright red strands that were caught on a broken branch. Even in the dim moonlight, the brightly colored swatch of material stood out against the ice enshrouded foliage, a flame-colored beacon that beckoned for their attention.

"Mekiva was wearing a red cape. This looks like it's the same material. And see how neatly the seams are sewn, Gwen's mother makes the cleanest stitches I've ever seen. I think the girls have been listening to our discussion. And if I know women, they've already decided what we are going to do."

Twelve

The second of Omission's twin red giants were slipping from sight as the quartet crested the ridge above the main roadway leading to Alliance. Vondal pulled his horse over to one side, scanning the area for any landmark that might seem familiar. The weather refused to cooperate with their search. The snowfall was increasing in intensity, making it difficult to see more than a few feet in any direction. He blinked his eyes to clear away a soft dusting of flakes. It was growing colder by the hour, a sure sign the storm wouldn't be breaking anytime soon.

There was a full moon rising, offering enough light to illuminate three distinct path choices, none of which he recognized. The first choice was simple, it was a well-traveled road leading directly to the main thoroughfare. The second choice, little more than a game trail, led off to the right, an improbably vague track that skirted the edge of the ridgeline before disappearing in the distance. The final choice was even grimmer, a sandy wash almost hidden in shadows, that vanished into what appeared to be an almost vertical drop less than a league away. If he made the wrong choice, everyone would suffer. He sighed and turned onto the game trail that followed the ridgeline.

True to Jaxx's prediction, the girls had refused to return to Cabrell without them. What was worse, Jaxx continued to rail about his decision to leave the tentative safety of the caravan on what he considered a fool's errand. He might be right, the odds of them tracking the ambushers were growing slimmer with each snowflake that fell. Despite his disparaging opinion, Jaxx had gathered their belongings, stripped out anything unnecessary, and followed him into the night without further comment. That was yesterday, today he'd voiced his displeasure at every opportunity.

"It looks like we'll be backtracking from here, at least as far as the last fork in the trail." Vondal stared at the waters raging below. The practical trail had led them directly to their current location, the rotted remains of an old rope bridge. The path was well worn and followed the natural curve of the terrain, someone was using it. It was the easiest way to reach the mountain cut… at least until the trail ended at the gorge. "It's been a long time since anyone used this thing for anything other than a scenic view."

"I knew it was too easy. Backtracking won't help. Did you get a good look at the other trail? That path is impossible. It looked like a mountain goat would slide, how can we expect our horses to manage it?"

"The horses can't. We'll be walking from there unless we missed something along the trail. Everyone needs to keep a watch out for game signs. If a deer can make it, maybe our horses can. Pray that we somehow missed the turn-off." He turned his horse and headed back along the trail.

"I vote we head back and try the scary route," Mekiva said." The drop off that we know about is too steep for the horses, but it seemed to be well-traveled. Maybe it leads to another way across, the path is too well maintained to go nowhere."

"Either way, it explains why the Orroggs were walking. Maybe we should skip the unknown trail and continue into Alliance. With luck, we can beat the storm and wait for the weather to break. There's got to be a better way in from that side of the mountain."

The girls debated a moment, then shrugged and followed Vondal.

Jaxx joined the others at the crest of the hill, not especially happy about Von's idea of backtracking. Logic said that the path should be overgrown with scrub since the bridge was unusable. The rocky sides of the canyon were steep, with many small crevices, none looked deep enough to hide a way out. Then he noticed the ants.

"Hey, Vondal. You notice any game sign?

"Except for a few crows, I haven't seen any sign of life since we entered the canyon." Vondal looked defeated.

"Don't say anything to the girls. Take a good look at that pile of bones…they're fresh, only a day or two old, the ants haven't finished cleaning them yet. There're more bones scattered amongst the scrubby brush nearby. This shortcut is something's home territory, something big… and it eats meat."

"Then let's get out of here before it notices were here and invites us to dinner."

The section of the trail they were following wound over a small creek and through a low area full of dense scrub. One or two heavy boulders broke up the overgrown vegetation. Here and there were signs of frequent landslides along the canyon wall. Jaxx motioned for his friend to be silent and listen.

"Something wrong?" Mekiva inquired, noticing how quiet the two men had become.

"It's probably nothing, just a funny feeling. You know

what I mean, it's like when you get icicles running along your skin. Let's just go," he said, nudging his mare into a trot.

The girls giggled, they were miles from the main road on an unknown trail that no one ever traveled. Jaxx could be so paranoid. Still giggling, the two girls turned their horses, following close behind them. A heavy silence fell over the group as everyone kept their senses on high alert, watching for any sign of danger.

"Hear that?" Vondal inquired suddenly, reining his horse to a stop. He stood up in the stirrups, scanning the area for anything out of the ordinary. Nothing…

Jaxx listened but he couldn't hear anything. In fact, it was too quiet. With the winter wind blowing it was difficult to make out anything specific. It was possible that Vondal had picked up something from a distance, audible because the wind was blowing just right, at the perfect time. The wind through the canyon shifted often, changing directions and bringing with it the strangled howls so often heard running before an impending storm.

Jaxx's eyes swept the sides of the canyon, catching a brief glimpse of grey just before the shadow slipped behind a pile of rubble. "Now I think you're making me paranoid," he snapped, keeping his eyes on the scattered rocks.

He kicked his tired mount into a shambling trot that quickly slowed to a walk and then to a stumbling halt, allowing it to drop its head to the ground in exhaustion. "Paranoid or not, we need to stop for a while and rest the animals before we lose them. They've been on the move all last night and most of the day. And I could use some rest myself, napping in the saddle isn't enough. We can't stay alert if we're too exhausted to ride."

"All right, let's take a break. I could use some rest myself. We should be all right here in the open for a short while, but we have to find shelter before nightfall."

He swung down off the weary horse, allowing it to graze freely on the sparse late autumn foliage. The ebon stud took advantage of his respite to roll vigorously on the ground, and then joined his herd mates in foraging for edible plants buried beneath the snowy blanket. The twin geldings stood quietly while the girls dismounted, more interested in rest than the minimal forage. Only the mule stayed on alert, its ears constantly moving.

The weary teens sprawled out under a stunted hickory nut tree that still held a few of its leaves. It was too wet for a fire, so the meal consisted of bread, cheese, and hard sausage, washed down by water from the nearby stream. After scraping up a small mound of newly fallen leaves that were not completely covered in snow, Jaxx stretched out on his cape, enjoying a short nap before the storm hit. Unable to sleep, Vondal was cleaning his sword, oiling the blade in preparation for any future trouble they might run into. A ragged squeal brought him to his feet, sword in hand.

Startled from his impromptu nap, Jaxx caught a glimpse of a dark form leaping from the bushes directly at Mekiva's horse. Vondal must have noticed about the same instant, his voice rising in warning as the massive beast struck the unlucky animal. Like ants, adolescent Wyverns poured out of hiding, rising from both sides of the canyon in a well-planned ambush.

Mekiva threw her hand up before her face, instinctively blocking vital areas as she fell sideways, out of the path of the panic-stricken animal's desperate charge. Bleeding freely from two deep gashes and encumbered by the weight of the massive predator, the frightened horse plunged directly into the oncoming pack. Seconds later he screamed, an almost human appeal for assistance, before silence.

Vondal somehow managed to swing aboard Tempest seconds before the animal realized the danger. Mouth-frothing and sweat-soaked, the terrified stud fought to get away from the gnashing teeth and razor claws. None of the wyverns were old enough to fly, though one or two had mastered a short gliding hop that enabled them to reach some of the higher rocks. Vondal struggled to stay in the saddle as he pushed Tempest into a ragged gallop back along the trail, directly into the largest grouping. He muttered an apology to the faithful steed before diving from its back, abandoning it to the hungry pack in hopes of buying the others time to escape. He knew he'd hear Tempests last scream of agony for the rest of his life, that's if they somehow managed to escape the trap and survive. Right now, things didn't look so good for any of them.

For the moment, the Wyverns seemed content with the fresh horse meat, but Vondal knew there were hungrier mouths waiting, and only a few freshly killed bodies. It wouldn't be long before the ravenous pack came looking for more.

Panda went down as one large grey brute tore into her rear hamstring, ripping flesh and muscle before he'd a chance to react. The terrified mare struggled valiantly to scramble back to her feet before an older cagey female tore out her throat. One of the younger males, a dark-scaled half-grown wyrmlings weighing about two hundred pounds, ignored the feeding frenzy beside the mare, thinking Jaxx an easier target. Heart pounding as adrenaline coursed through his system, Jaxx kicked out, landing a sharp blow to its ribs that gave him time to snatch his ax from his back. He swung randomly at anything that moved, landing more than one lucky hit before grabbing his bow and quiver from Panda's bloody body. Two quick slices with his boot knife and the saddlebags were free . Then he used the bow to keep the smaller wyverns away as he ran, reaching a cluster of large rocks that offered momentary cover. With his back protected from immediate attack by a large flat-faced rock, he turned to face the oncoming horde, hoping to hold them off long enough for the girls to reach safety. One or two of the adolescent wyrmlings made halfhearted attempts to get at him before the heady smell of bloody horse meat proved more temptation than a possible future meal of stringy Duaar. The ebony-scaled male gave few more halfhearted snaps before he raced to join the others beside the warm carcasses, eager for his share of the fresh meat.

Safe for the moment, Jaxx used the opportunity to check on his friends. Vondal and Mekiva were pale and shaken but neither looked hurt. They were moving in his direction, using whatever cover they could find. However, he didn't see Gwendolyn or her gelding. He called out, but she didn't answer. Jaxx knew his mind had been occupied during the main attack, but he couldn't remember hearing her, or her horse, scream. It wasn't much, but even the slim chance that she'd escaped the attack was better than the other--- more realistic prospect.

Gwendolyn had been digging in her pack for something to feed Twizzle when the Wyverns attacked. Instinct took over, and she'd somehow managed to swing astride the trembling horse in the seconds before the remainder of the hunting pack arrived. Twizzle took to the air and Brownie took off running back toward the old bridge. By twisting, he managed to evade the first wave of Wyverns by taking the bit in his teeth and running away, but he had been too tired to keep up his frantic pace for long. He slowed and stopped shortly after his followers gave up the pursuit.

Safe for the moment, Gwen stood beside the dark bay gelding, stroking his silky ears and murmuring soft words of encouragement to keep him calm and quiet. The gelding shuddered and shifted his legs restlessly, the heady scent of the freshly killed horses only intensifying the fear. The excited animal jerked his head around at the slightest noise. Gwendolyn could feel the heated moisture of his breath as he panted. She knew it was only a matter of moments before one of the hungry animals decided it'd waited long enough and made its move, and both would probably die.

When the attack came, it was from an unexpected direction. Somehow, one of the Wyverns had managed to slip around behind the boulder, scramble to the top, and then dropped down onto the back of the terrified gelding. His mate struck as the panicked animal rose to his hind legs in a futile attempt to throw the heavy Wyvern from his body. The desperate horses ragged breathing became even more labored as he strived unsuccessfully to escape the sharp teeth tearing at him from every side. Brownie was still alive, his eyes wide with terror, as they began their gruesome meal, razor-sharp teeth tearing out chunks of steaming flesh. He continued to struggle, legs churning as though he was still running, finally slowing…slowing… then stopping.

Gwendolyn turned to run, knowing it was already too

late. Her father had spoken of Dire-Wyverns, describing them as devil's spawn. They were distantly related to dragons but were intelligent and much, much larger. The reality was much worse. Even young and half-starved wyrmlings were much bigger than she'd imagined---and much faster.

She screamed as one young male drove his teeth into her calf, the flesh tearing from the weight of the young wyvern as she tumbled and rolled, a rolling, sliding kind of tumble that stopped as her body slammed into one of the large rocks scattered across the dry creek bed. She heard her left arm snap, followed by sharp pain and a rush of warm blood. One scrawny wyvern sensed her weakness and rushed in, certain of an easy kill. She kicked out at the wyrm's head, landing a solid blow that seemed to daze him, allowing her to a chance to limp away.

Searching desperately for anything she could use to defend herself, she finally spotted a jagged stone that looked small enough for her to hold, but still large enough to use as a weapon. Grateful to be right-handed, she swung, landing a clean blow to the crown of the wyverns head, splitting the skin around his eye. Blindly she continued, swinging wildly until tiny slivers of bone protruded from the injured socket. Half blinded by blood and in severe pain, the defeated hatchling snapped uncertainly once more, deciding it was better to relinquish the hunt and hope to share his sibling's kill.

Gwendolyn didn't wait for him to change his mind. With her calf injured, she couldn't run, and her left arm had long since gone numb. It was a bad break, the shattered bone protruding through the skin and she was losing a lot of blood. She needed to find a safe place to rest and pray. Jaxx had mentioned a small cave about a quarter of a mile back along the trail, marking it as a possible location to camp. If she could reach it, she was certain the others would be able to find her once they began their search. Gritting her teeth against the pain radiating down her leg as she stood, she began to move away from the feasting animals, beseeching Rheaaz to let the meat last until she reached shelter.

Gwendolyn lay slightly inside the opening to the small cave, concentrating on any movement she could still make out against the rapidly darkening landscape. Tatrias had set long ago, and while Fariki was still visible, the twin sun was only a slim red sliver of color against the starless backdrop. It would be at least an hour before Pheros rose into the southern sky, offering its dim but welcome light to the bitter darkness. Unconsciously she rubbed her left arm, an occasional twinge of pain and the new pink scar her only physical reminder of how close she had come to seeing Rheaaz face to face.

The others were alive and just as she expected, they were slowly making their way toward the cave. She was lucky to have noticed them, the wind had been blowing steadily for several hours, an eerie whistle that covered any sounds the travelers might have been making as they inched their way along the deserted streambed. Jaxx was leading, with Vondal and Mekiva following close behind. Twizzle had returned from one of his numerous forays and was now fluttering anxiously over Mekiva's head. There was no sign of the pack mule that had passed her during her flight. One of the pair was hurt, how badly she couldn't tell, but their erratic movements, coupled with the way they braced their bodies against each other, was evidence of some type of injury. The dense brush along the path obscured them from view as she was about to call out to them. Fortunately, it didn't hide the three greyish brown shadows that appeared just as they entered the remains of an old slide near the canyon wall. She whistled, and Jaxx looked up.

Mekiva slipped and fell amid the scattered rocks, scraping her shin and banging one elbow hard enough to make her cry out. Struggling once more to her feet, she guiltily signaled her need for a rest… and soon. Her breath came in ragged gasps and her calves burned from the stress of maintaining the constant pace. She was distraught over Gwendolyn's death, but she never complained, even when Vondal told her they had to keep walking.

Jaxx was unable to keep the fear he felt from showing on his face. He no longer felt individual pains, instead, it was one continuous ache that prevented him from concentrating. Breathing deeply, he slowly regained some measure of control. Every second they wasted cut into their meager lead, allowing the young wyverns another opportunity to attack. He knew they wouldn't be able to continue much longer, the terrain offered little respite from the weather, which seemed to grow worse by the moment. Unless they found a defendable shelter, and soon, the weather would provide the wyverns with a ready source of fresh frozen meat. He'd noticed at least four of the oversized reptiles pacing them as they walked along the trail, glimpsing one dark form moving along the canyon rim, then another. The rim sloped gradually downward, there had to be a way to the canyon floor somewhere nearby. He'd be willing to bet there was also another way out of the canyon from the ridgetop. Despite his warm clothing, he could still feel the chilled sweat running down his back. He remembered spotting a small cave in the ridgeline about a mile out from the shattered bridge. It was as likely a bolt hole as they were going to find, the opening high above the trail, in a spot that would be difficult for the Wyverns to reach.

Mechanically he stretched out his fingers, each muscle's response the perfect combination of strength and dexterity developed through years of evolution. Great idea hands, they leveled the playing field. He often wondered whether this was due to random chance or some divine beings' grand design. His shoulder was sore, the bleeding had stopped. At least he could still hold onto his ax. He was worried about the others.

Mekiva and Von were both in bad shape and getting worse by the minute. Both had lost a good bit of blood, Vondal could barely grip his sword and Mekiva's thigh was in tattered strips. This cave might be their only chance of survival. Then a sharp whistle broke the silence…

Jaxx's eyes were drawn to the whistle. He couldn't believe it, but it looked like Gwendolyn had survived. What he could believe was the pair of adult Wyverns he spotted flying in their direction. It would be a race.

"Go," Jaxx shouted, "I'll be right behind you. Run for the side of the canyon, there's a narrow ledge about six feet up the face that leads to that cave we talked about this morning. I don't know how she survived… but Gwendolyn's inside. She can help you up to the opening."

He knew their only chance was convincing the Wyverns they were all still moving along the dry creek bed. It would not be easy, the sky was cloudy but there was still enough light to see. The young wyverns eyesight was undeveloped, they depended on scent more than sight at this age. So he began to lay a false trail, dragging his foot and falling completely flat to add his scent to the trail. As he approached the pair feeding off Panda he gave up his feint and took off toward the cave. The temperature was dropping, and it was becoming harder to see. Once he thought he heard Mekiva cry out in pain, followed by Vondal swearing loudly. He hoped she had simply bumped a boulder in the dark as they made their way through the rubble near the canyon wall to safety.

The snow would make it harder for the reptiles to follow his trail. He was armed and lightly injured, but that hardly mattered if the entire pack attacked. The wyverns outnumbered him, were stronger and better positioned. Somewhere in the darkness was the main pack, with others were scattered along the rocky terrain. The ones on the rim didn't matter, it was the ones he couldn't see that determined his fate. Chances were he'd not live to reach the bolt hole, but at least he'd given Von and Mekiva a slight lead. Wyverns were intelligent. There was no way the two adults had missed the cave in their territory. At any moment they might decide to attack, and that was the most compelling motive to keep moving he could think of. A slight glimpse of movement in the shadows was all the warning he received.

With a snap and a flash of long white teeth, the first wyvern attacked. Jaxx somehow managed to raise his ax, the charging wyrmlings momentum driving the sharp spike that adorned the poll into its own chest. He fell against one rock, turned and stumbled over a second, falling to his knees and somehow avoiding the leap of the second predator…but not the third. The sable female was smaller and faster. She managed to drive her teeth through the tough leather gauntlet into his forearm.

Jaxx screamed. His fingers went numb and he lost his grip on the heavy ax which fell at his feet in the snow. He stayed on his feet, somehow managing to draw his long knife from his belt with his left hand before driving it upward into the females' chest and into her heart. He swayed, weak and delirious from loss of blood, struggling to keep his mind from drifting into unconsciousness as the wyrm's venom overcame his body. Then he felt something touch his shoulder.

Vondal rose up from behind a nearby boulder and forcefully drove his sword into the body of the returning grey male before it realized he was there. For now, Jaxx was still alive but dying from the wyverns venom the ravenous reptile had injected into his wound.

"Vondal…" Jaxx whispered. "I'm done for…I'm dying."

"No Jaxx, I won't let you do that. I know it hurts, but you're going to have to walk now. You can't give up. Let me help you." Vondal sheathed his sword, then, with one arm supporting his friend, the other carrying Jaxx's precious ax, the two boys stumbled through the darkness to the safety of the cave.

Thirteen

"They're still out there."

"I'd hoped they would have given up by now," Vondal replied guiltily. "I was supposed to relieve you, why'd you let me sleep?"

"To be honest, I must have passed out. I recall thinking I needed a drink of water, then I was waking up alongside the girls. I don't remember moving." Jaxx stretched, wincing at the slight ache still present in his right shoulder after he'd almost been the main course on some half-grown Wyverns dinner menu. He rubbed his neck uneasily, fingering the freshly healed ridge of skin that was all that remained of the nasty gashes. They'd all need to drop a few coins in the tithe box next time they were near Rheaaz's temple. Somehow Gwendolyn had managed to not only heal his wounds---something only a high-level cleric should have been able to do--- she'd healed him without leaving scars. In fact, one or two of the scars he'd received from an earlier injury were also missing.

His gaze ranged over the nearby landscape, spotting and mapping the position of three more of the Wyverns. Despite their position of relative safety above the restless pack, the exhausted group realized their hideaway was far from idyllic. For one thing, the Wyverns were not going away anytime soon. Dire-Wyverns were intelligent animals, and they knew their prey would either risk leaving the safety of the cave or die of thirst or starvation. Often the vindictive animals would maintain a rotating vigil, taking turns to hunt or seek water. They seemed to enjoy knowing the trapped adventurers were suffering within their chosen prison. It became a contest to see which would happen first, the Wyverns would grow bored and leave or the prey would make a rash attempt to escape the trap. These Wyverns didn't seem bored.

Earlier a few of the more aggressive males managed to leap from one of the nearby boulders to an irregular ledge below the entrance of the cave, however, after a couple of half-hearted attempts, they determined there was no way for them to maneuver on the narrow span. All the angry pack could do was pace back and forth below the opening and howl in frustration.

Ideal or not, the small cave offered a welcome respite from the inclement weather. Gwendolyn had managed to save her backpack so they weren't hungry, however, the only water they had was from the small bola Vondal carried on his belt. Even with rationing, it wouldn't last more than a day. They had flint, but nothing to burn, one blanket, and a candle.

Mekiva stroked the fuzzy draccat fondly, her nimble fingers enticing a low rumbling purr of appreciation. She'd awakened to find the adventurous Twizzle in his usual spot, curled beneath her blanket, his head nestled comfortably against her chest. He was evidently unharmed but exhausted after his late-night foray into the tiny fissure at the rear of the cavern. Despite the icy weather outside, the interior was comfortable, in fact, Mekiva was convinced that there was a warm breeze coming through Twizzle's crevice.

"Alright", Vondal grumbled after she mentioned it for the third time. "I'll check it out." He noticed the smile of approval on Mekiva's face. A hundred thoughts raced through his mind, each one centering on the young mage. Several of them would have gotten him slapped…or worse.

The crack was too narrow for any of them, however, the scratches around the opening showed something had passed through it, and recently. Since there was no sign of Twizzle, he was the likely culprit. He'd noticed Mekiva's lap was empty, the cub had vanished once again.

He tossed a pebble as far as possible into the crevice. There was no sound to show he'd hit anything. If it wasn't Twizzle, then whatever laired inside was either not at home, or too far back for the stone to disturb it.

"A least we won't freeze," he noted wryly.

Jaxx nodded. "It's clear we won't be leaving the cave any time soon, at least not the way we came in. There's a good possibility the fissure opens into another cavern. I can try to enlarge the opening. Something's got that flying mousetraps attention, let's go see what it is."

"We've got a problem, and a serious one," Vondal stated flatly as he kicked the bloody body of the young wyverns out of the cave. " It took them five tries but the parents figured out how to drop their wyrmlings onto the ledge outside. But now we've killed three of their babies. They are not only intelligent, they are also vindictive. They seem to have given up on starving us out."

"With both of us digging, we double the chances of reaching a secondary cave, possibly one with an exit we can all fit through. Then we can block the entrance behind us. Even if there's no other exit, we might get lucky and find water."

"Where's the little rat now," Jaxx asked. "One minute he's here, the next he's gone."

"He's not a rat and you shouldn't make fun of him, he's more like a cat anyway."

"Fly 'in cat, fly 'in rat, not much difference. All it does is eat and sh--."

"That's enough Jaxx!" Vondal interrupted before he managed to get both girls upset. "Leave Mekiva alone, she loves Twizzle. The Draccat may have saved us all if we can locate the way he is getting out of the cave. You know as well as I, we wouldn't have considered that tiny crack if he hadn't checked it out."

"Whatever you think is best is fine with me. It will give Gwendolyn more time to rest. I'll meditate and study a few of the defensive spells in my spellbook." Of course, they may not work. First-year students rarely get to do anything except elementary cantrips, I can make fire, levitate small objects, or make a light. Magic Missiles or Ice Storms are way over my head. Mekiva knew her meager knowledge might make the difference between life and death, so she focused her mind and concentrated until she was certain she could recall each spell if needed. The day ahead was filled with many possibilities, some of which were danger-ous and quite terrifying.

Jaxx grunted. There was no doubt in his mind that their only possibility of escape was waiting beyond the rock wall. He just wished he felt better about their chances. "You can sit here like old ladies and debate our options, … I'm going to knock down a wall." He studied the back wall, raised his ax, and swung. The blow landed solidly, break-ing a chunk of rock about the size of his fist away from the cracked face. Two more blows offered similar results. There might be a room behind the cave wall, but the rock surrounding it was solid. It wasn't going to be as easy, nevertheless, he felt an eagerness that he'd forgotten as he dug into the unyielding surface. This was what he'd been born to do! His clan was miners and metalsmiths, and he'd not realized how much he missed it until now. His ax spike wasn't the ideal tool, but he could make it work. Whistling jauntily, he swung again.

Vondal had to admit he was impressed by his friends' mining skills. Jaxx had widened the tiny crack, now there was an opening large enough for any of them to crawl through. He was impatient to see where the newly discovered passage would lead. Warm air now flowed freely through the much wider opening, and he could smell a slight but distinctive sulfur odor.

Jaxx had disappeared into the darkness of the tunnel to make a brief examination of the nearby area before the others entered. The girls had packed what little remained of their equipment and were now feeding bits of leftovers to the ever-ravenous draccat.

Von was curious about what they were whispering but knew neither would give him a straight answer if he asked.

The sound of stones falling against a hard surface followed by a second, much louder thud deep in the dark recesses of the new cavern drew his attention away from his musing. What now?

Jaxx blinked once…then blinked again. Where was he? The strident bray of Vondal's laughter was followed by the equally shrill tone of Mekiva's sharp retort. Vondal would think his fall amusing. Apparently, neither girl shared his point of view.

Totally oblivious to the bedlam he'd created the Drac-cat was perched in the middle of his chest, calmly playing a game of cat and mouse with his nose. After one particularly sharp claw swipe, Jaxx tossed the kitten toward the rear of the cave. Several sharp pains instantly reminded him of the thirty-foot drop, followed by the graceless flat back landing he'd recently experienced. He groaned.

Gwendolyn pushed a stray lock of hair from Jaxx's face, noting how pale the usually robust Duaar appeared. Vondal shouldn't laugh, Jaxx has twice the guts and three times your brains… usually. Climbing that rope without help was reckless but it could have been worse. At least he landed on the sand.

"What happened," Mekiva asked. Her eyes kept going back to the distant light streaming through the new hole in the back of the cave.

"I broke through the ceiling with no problem. I was curious to see if the area around the opening was clear, so, I stuck my head out. Then something licked my face. That's all I remember."

Gwendolyn knelt beside the injured Duaar to get a better look at his injuries. Then she sat back and sighed. "Your ankle looks worse than it is. It's just a minor sprain. Your shoulder will be okay, it's out of its socket, you must have grabbed for a hold when you slipped. It's going to hurt but we can put it back into place without magic.

"What about my back? Am I going to be paralyzed?"

"No silly, it's not broken, just bruised. It might slow you down, but it's not anything serious. I finally found something harder than your head; Duaar bones."

"Will Rheaaz heal him," Vondal asked. "I won't leave him, and our food won't last more than a few days."

"I don't know. Rheaaz may feel she's done enough, that I don't appreciate the blessings I've been given." Why hadn't she taken more time to thank Rheaaz? The goddess had already been more than generous with her blessings. What if next time I prayed for her benediction she didn't answer? Someone might die!"

"Don't think like that. You're the most faithful, the most pious person I know. Rheaaz will have to recognize that! Jaxx is depending on you." We're all depending on you!

"Von, would you please go block the entrance? It might be a while before we can move on."

Vondal nodded and walked back toward the light.

Mekiva moved out of Gwen's way, so you could get comfortable on the ground beside Jaxx.

Gwendolyn still looked hesitant, but she nodded. Taking a deep breath, she moved to a more comfortable position at Jaxx's side, settled back on her heels and laid her hands upon his damaged shoulder, imploring Rheaaz to heal his injury…. and Rheaaz answered. The warm glow of the earth goddess's grace spread rapidly down Gwendolyn's arms and into Jaxx's torn muscles, knitting the torn tissue and removing the swelling and irritation. Tears flowed down her cheeks as the pain vanished from her friends' eyes. But she knew Jaxx was still far from whole. Praying that Rheaaz would continue favoring her petition, she moved on to his foot and ankle. She allowed a slight smile as the stubborn Duaar started twisting his ankle, unconsciously verifying the healing had worked. And then she screamed.

Opening his eyes after the world around him had once more become solid, Jaxx let his vision return to normal before dragging himself into a sitting position. His back no longer hurt, and his arm felt better than it did before he injured it. In fact, his entire body felt invigorated, all feeling of fatigue had vanished. Though his recent pain was now a fading memory, the sound of Gwendolyn's scream haunted him. He'd have to find out more about Shi'i healing from Mekiva.

"You always did have a way of making an entrance," Vondal taunted him as Jaxx sipped the water Mekiva had passed him. "Why'd you leave your ax in the ceiling? Afraid you couldn't find the spot again?"

Jaxx ignored his comments as he eased his body into a more comfortable position, turning so that he could look up at the tiny opening high above. Light streamed through the small hole his ax had created in the thin layer of rock. It was an easy climb to the narrow ledge located below the new opening. A few more blows and the hole would have been large enough for them to exit the cave… hopefully without the wyverns knowledge. "I think we should get out of here before the wyverns figure out our new escape route."

Vondal frowned. "They're probably sitting outside the exit waiting. I had hoped the snow would drive them into their holes. There's no telling where the fliers are." He sighed. "Nothing has gone right on this trip. It's taken fourteen days to reach this point, on a trip that was supposed to take ten at the most. We underestimated everything, supplies, water, especially travel time. I thought we'd be back in Cabrell by now, we haven't even made it halfway to the hold."

"Poor, poor Vondal, nothing is going his way," Jaxx retorted. "Everyone realizes the trip hasn't gone according to expectations. But it's time to stop moaning about it and get back on track. We've hit a few bumps in the road, and our great adventure has turned into a series of tragedies. We survived. End of discussion."

Izabal stepped away from the window, allowing the heavy drapery to fall back into its usual position. Her expression, when she stepped forward into the dim light radiating from the fireplace was intense, so much so that it startled the unprepared man into taking two reflexive steps backward.

Castillo struggled to remain calm, to reason away the uncharacteristic apprehension he was experiencing. He was unsuccessful. The list of things he feared was very short, the sorceress Izabal topped the list. The diminutive mages' small stature was inversely proportionate to her power. Power that was now radiating base condemnation his way.

"Tell me everything, leave out no details. Make me understand----or at least give me a reasonable excuse for their escape. Not that I can imagine one." Her icy eyes were fixed on his, cold and featureless orbs that drew him deep inside without offering an opportunity to escape.

For a moment Castillo was tempted to run as he realized he had no explanation for the failed raid. He stood frozen, unable to utter even the smallest of sounds as he desperately searched for something…anything…any response that might soothe her rage. Nothing came to mind.

What could he say that would make the slightest difference? He wisely chose to remain silent, realizing after many similar experiences it was better to allow the mage to rant, and simply not comment. He chewed at the side of his mouth, biting back the bitter acid that surged upward from his rolling stomach. His ice-blue eyes turned even colder, and fear appeared for the first time on his face. He was an experienced fighter, leader of one of the largest bands of raiders in the territory. And this tiny woman scared the hells out of him. Why Samsara chose to work with her was beyond his comprehension. Everyone knew of her alignment with that upstart Lord Botherton. It would be better for all if Samsara stuck to what he knew best. He might not ever get rich from smuggling, but he didn't risk being turned into a toad for his troubles either.

There was nothing he could add to the earlier conversation that would change the situation, the damage was already done. He'd been given one simple objective, eliminate all male members of the pack train except Vondal Botherton. Despite overwhelming numbers, his men had failed. Now, the survivors of the canyon massacre were nearing Cabrell, and at least five men could identify Castillo as the leader of the raiding party. One eyewitness could be removed, five voices were impossible to contain. No, his time in Cabrell, as well as his value to Izabal…and Samsara… was rapidly diminishing. And once it was gone…he did not want to think about his chances of surviving the mages wrath.

"So, two half-grown boys and a pair of schoolgirls got away from Castillo, the famous brigand chief," Izabal scoffed, openly sarcastically. "Why did I bother giving Samsara my gold? I could have visited the docks and hired the first drunken sailors I came across. The result would have been the same."

"You didn't mention the mage girls' magic." Castillo snarled, then flinched as he realized the rashness of his action. Tired as he was, he was smart enough to realize this might not be the right moment to nitpick.

"A mage? She's little more than a child, merely a first-year student of that half-wit Stolinn at Rosemont. Inexperienced, but I'm told she does show potential," she stated flatly, a predatory curl of her lips showing her displeasure at his excuse. "The boy's a strapping fellow, but he is barely seventeen, and favors one eye. The Duaar might be trouble, but he can't have been out of his hold for more than a few years himself. And the other girl is a seamstress, not even a novate Shi'i-Lakka, who tagged along for a lark. If I'd not witnessed your attack, I'd think you made up the entire story." Her fingers trembling against the stem of her crystal wine glass was the only sign of how angry she was.

Castillo's temper made him careless. Usually cowed and deferential in the presence of the imperious sorceress, he realized he'd little to lose by meekly accepting her chastisement, deciding instead to argue back, fully expecting it to be his last defensive diatribe.

"You dare blame me? The information you provided was incorrect. There were three times as many soldiers guarding the supplies than you stated, as well as several families with their own mercenary guards. We arranged the ambush exactly as you planned, started the landslide and attacked during the chaos. Your plan failed… and my men died."

The diminutive woman was silent for a moment, and then her laugh rang out, bringing with it a familiar tinge of bitter disdain.

Castillo flushed, his aggressive nature vying with his

instinct to stay alive at any cost. Instinct won, he gritted his teeth and held his tongue as the enraged sorceress swept across the room coming to a halt directly before him. "I'll drink their torment like I drink this wine," she said. She downed the remaining burgundy, the ruby liquid staining her lips the rich color of blood. "This fiasco ends now, she declared, this is what you shall do…"

Castillo listened in silence, nodding occasionally as she talked. After she finished, for a long moment he stood there, eyes closed.

At last, he whispered, "It shall be done."

Fourteen

The climb up the rope had proved to be trickier than Gwendolyn expected, and she was trembling by the time she reached the ledge below the opening. Muttering a silent plea that she'd be able to hold on, she swung out and up, somehow managing to grasp the edge of the overhand with three fingers. Her arm throbbing, she gritted her teeth against the pain and then slowly, one foot at a time, she pulled herself up through the new hole. Then she collapsed on the canyon rim, out of breath and shaky, until her breathing returned to normal.

"We need to keep moving," Mekiva said after Gwendolyn caught her breath. "Jaxx thinks we've deceived the wyverns for now. But they're smart, and we know they scout along this rim. It's dark now but the suns will be up soon. We will stand out against the snow. They won't stay fooled for long." She grinned at Vondal as his head popped through the narrow opening. He made it all look so easy. Of course, he was too pigheaded to admit anything as simple as climbing a rope could ever be challenging. They'd already decided to follow the path back toward the old bridge. It was clear the wyverns had developed a system of herding potential targets entering the blind canyon. They would have posted scouts near the entrance. Heading away from it would offer the best possibility of remaining undetected for the longest time. A silence settled over the group as they walked along the rim of the canyon, each alone with their own thoughts. Everyone knew it'd only be a matter of time before the wyverns discovered they were no longer trapped inside the cave. Once the pack realized where they were, it would turn into a race, a race they had little chance of winning.

The early winter wind had favored them, blowing from the west to the east, it had prevented their scent from being carried to the pack. Unfortunately, it wouldn't matter for long. Directly east of them, the pale light of Omission's second sun was rapidly rising. Once they lost the darkness it would be harder to move without being seen. Dire Wyverns were not strictly nocturnal, they hunted whenever the pack was hungry. The horses were long since devoured by the ravenous pack elders and there was little chance the younger members of the pack had managed to find sufficient game for all within the last few hours. Scouts would be out, it would be wishful thinking to expect their escape to go unnoticed. The path paralleled the ravine, gradually descending toward the bottom of the ridge, the game trail meeting the old road in an area thick with scrub-brush that they had overlooked earlier.

Less than twenty feet later they came across the remains of the pack mule. Both men wasted little time, immediately scavenging for anything salvageable from the scattered remains. They were able to put together a small bundle of food, a cooking pot, two empty canteens, and two ripped but still usable bedrolls. Then Jaxx moved the carcass and pulled out a blood-covered lantern and two flasks of oil. Gwen had spotted a quiver of arrows , still partially full that had fallen a short distance back along the trail. She debated looking further but decided it wasn't worth the risk.

Vondal tensed and perused the area. He'd noticed Jaxx

turn once or twice for a quick scan of the rim of the canyon behind them. Jaxx had heard something. He listened, and he could hear it too, the faint sound of nails against the stone, carried to them by the natural acoustics of the canyon.

"Which way are they moving?" he whispered.

"The wrong way. And they're coming faster than we can run," Jaxx replied.

Vondal swallowed, took a second to settle his overwrought nerves, and then made his decision to tell the girls the truth.

"The wyverns have found our trail. It'll only be a matter of minutes before they find us. We need to keep moving, ---and fast.

"But that's a dead-end," Mekiva replied. "Shouldn't we look for another place to hide?"

"No time", Vondal responded, he tightened his belt and drew his sword. "If they surround us before we get to cover, we don't stand a chance, run!" They'd been lucky to escape the hungry pack once, they couldn't count on their luck holding again. With the rope bridge out, they had one option. And the girls weren't going to like it.

Jaxx had been carrying Gwendolyn's pack and his own. Now he began throwing anything non-essential to the side. He tossed a length of rope to Vondal who tied one end around his waist, the other end to the pack, leaving about twenty feet of rope between them. He noticed Jaxx had done the same thing with the other packs.

Mekiva looked at the dark water at the bottom of the ravine below them. "Are we going to let them think we jumped into the river to get away?"

"Something like that," Vondal answered. Sometimes Mekiva asked too many questions.

"What do you mean?" she questioned. There were no obvious places to hide and the wyverns were getting closer. The old bridge didn't look like it would support the weight of one, much less all four of them. And there were at least twenty feet missing from the center. Did Vondal think they could get across? Is that why he tied the rope to the pack? She turned to look at him and froze as his hand clamped down on her arms. Von was edging closer to the rim.

"We're going to jump into the river to get away," he replied.

"You are crazy! It too far, we won't survive the fall. Forget it! We need to hide!"

"It's the river or the wyverns. Unless we go now it won't matter, we'll all be dinner. Now hold my hand…. Jaxx, Gwendolyn's with you. When I count three, we jump."

"No Vondal, wait… Gwendolyn …"

"One ----."

"Wait. You must listen to me. Gwen…"

"Two---."

"But Vondal, It's important!"

"Jaxx will take care of Gwendolyn. Just trust me."

"Jaxx wait! She can't sw---."

Vondal stepped forward, pulling the reluctant girl with him. He could hear Gwendolyn's scream echoing Mekiva's as Jaxx mimicked his movements, dragging the protesting Shi'i maiden with him.

"…aiiiee!!!!" Gwendolyn screamed as she fell toward the river below. She managed to gulp in a large mouthful of air before striking the frigid surface, barely remembering to hold it in as she slid beneath the icy water into the murky darkness. It seemed like forever before her feet struck the bottom of the river. She thought she could make out Jaxx in the dim light that filtered down from above, close enough to reach out and squeeze his hand. Bracing her feet against the bottom of the river, she pushed upwards, kicking her feet frantically as she struggled to reach the surface. As her head broke through the icy sludge, she inhaled great gulps of air before the weight of her water-soaked robes dragged her beneath the turbulent froth once again. The choppy river tossed her like a bit of driftwood, flipping her body through the water as she flailed helplessly against the current. She was thrown against a large rock, the sharp pain forcing an involuntary cry that released the last of her air in a stream of tiny bubbles. Panic edged into her thoughts as her straining chest screamed out for air. All she could think of was how long it had been since her last breath. She closed her eyes, praying that the goddess would grant her a calm acceptance of her circumstances. The cold water sapped her strength, numbing her body and making her impending death much less uncomfortable then she'd expected. She vaguely remembered spotting something shiny flashing by, then pain exploded in her head and everything went dark.

Jaxx surfaced and looked around, but there was no sign of the diminutive Shi'i girl. Mekiva and Vondal were already on the rocky shoreline. Vondal was encouraging her to stay out of the frigid water, but she was arguing, a look of devastation showing on her face.

Gwendolyn had screamed something about not being able to swim. I thought she was joking. The waters like ice!

It's my fault. Where is she? There! That shadow might be her. Before he thought about it, he was swimming toward the shattered tree half-submerged in the frigid water. Just as he thought, Gwen's robes had caught on a limb, keeping her from reaching the shore. That same limb had probably saved her life, as it also kept her from being pulled under the water, but she had been in the cold too long. He needed to get her to shore now.

"Sorry Gwen. You can yell at me later. It's the only thing I can do." He pulled his boot knife and began slicing away the waterlogged robes. Even though it only took a minute, the icy water made it feel much longer. Finally, he was able to pull her loose and begin the swim toward shore.

Mekiva watched, her heart pounding as Jaxx struggled to free the semi-conscious girl despite the surging water. Her eyes flooded with tears as she watched Jaxx dive again and again beneath the foaming water in a futile attempt to free her from whatever was pulling her down. Once, she thought she caught a glint of steel in his hand, and then he was gone, beneath the surface once again. Vondal pulled her close and held her but instead of making her feel better, it only made things worse. His eyes were soft and full of compassion, but she didn't want to be held. She wanted Gwendolyn.

"Let me go," she gasped. She threw her weight against his arms, breaking free and running toward the rushing water. And that was when she saw Jaxx rising out of the water, carrying a limp girl dressed in a torn white shift in his arms. He somehow managed to carry her the last few feet before collapsing beside her on the rocky shore.

Jaxx and Mekiva held Gwen to share body heat as Vondal bustled around the new campsite using scrub and driftwood to build a fire. Everyone was cold and wet; unless they were able to warm up soon, it wouldn't matter that they had escaped the wyverns. It was too cold to out in the weather and Gwen was in no condition to walk. In no time Von had a lively fire going but everything they had managed to save was still wet. He carried the shivering girl closer to the fire, and the three huddled together, enjoying the limited warmth of shared heat. It was going to take a bigger fire to warm them, and Jaxx had already collected most of the loose wood nearby.

Mekiva pointed to a decaying stump half-buried in the sand near the water. "Can you drag that over to the fire?"

Von looked at Jaxx and raised one eyebrow.

Jaxx shrugged and moved to examine the stump. It was long dead but still connected to the taproot. His ax had survived the water, tied to the pack, so that wasn't a problem. "I'm reasonably certain the two of us can drag the stump to the fire, but it might be hours before the petrified wood catches fire and burns."

"Don't worry about that, just get the wood. I'll make sure it burns."

Jaxx nodded and the began moving the sand away from the stump. Cutting the taproot was easy. Two blows and the stump was free. It was easier to roll the stump instead of carrying it, but they were able to retrieve the wood in a very short time.

Mekiva motioned for them to move back.

Jaxx was skeptical, but he helped Von move all their supplies and Gwen away from the fire.

Mekiva nodded when they were far enough away. Then she closed her eyes, concentrating on the words of the fire spell she had memorized earlier. The existing cam fire made it easier. She snapped out the last word of the spell and gestured. A blast of heat warmed the air around them as the small flame grew to a roaring bonfire. The old stump was engulfed.

Jaxx grinned and moved Gwen near the heat. The warmth from the fire had already dried the front of his clothing. The back was damp but a hundred times better than before Mekiva cast the spell. He dug an oiled slicker out of his pack, passing it to Mekiva. She helped Gwen into the thick canvas cape, knowing that the soft-spoken girl would be hesitant to mention how uncomfortable she was wearing only the thin cotton shift. There was a spare change of clothing in Gwen's pack, so she dug it out and spread it near the fire to dry.

Vondal stretched the two remaining bedrolls over a stunted tree in hopes they would dry faster as Jaxx did the same with all the additional spare clothing. Most had been lost during the wyvern attack.

In a very short time, all four were warm and thinking about what their next steps should be. Mekiva was stirring something up in their only pot; giggling and dodging Gwen as the young Shi'i snuck a taste, adding her own bits and pieces to the mixture, before tasting it again. Whatever it was that the girls were cooking up, it would be a welcome treat after the trail mix and cold jerky of the last few meals.

With the advent of winter, the days had grown shorter and it wasn't long before the shadows deepened into the rich darkness of night. Mekiva sat watching as the light from second of Omissions' twin suns gradually diminished, fading bit by bit before finally vanishing over the northern ridge.

Vondal had dropped the last load of firewood next to the fire pit. Jaxx had somehow retained his dice during the escape, and he challenged Von to a round of Flokker, the latest craze in dice games making the rounds of their favorite taverns. Even though he wasn't familiar with the rules of the game, Von enjoyed shooting dice and figured he'd be able to follow the process enough to learn the basics after a short time. His concentration was broken by Mekiva's announcement that dinner was ready. He had sneaked a peek at the girls' special concoction and grinned. The fish stew looked delicious. The outside layer of flour had been damp but useable, so Gwen had made journey bread with it, wrapping the remainder in a section of the dress Mekiva had been wearing. The dress had been torn by the wyverns claws, so Jaxx had cut it off into a tunic, and she was now wearing it over trousers from Jaxx's pack.

The fresh bread was worth fighting for; and considering the way everyone was drooling, he might just have to. Before long everyone settled around the fire with a hot drink and a small bowl of Mekiva's stew.

Jaxx groaned, rubbing his overstuffed stomach contentedly. There was nothing like a hot meal, followed by a long nap. Mekiva offered to take first watch, accompanied by the ever-playful draccat she set out to walk the perimeter of their camp. Twizzle, besides being excellent company, made an outstanding night scout since he preferred to sleep during the day. Also, he loved hunting once the forest grew dark.

Jaxx had been puzzled at the young girls offer but didn't make an issue of it. Mekiva was just entering adolescence and like most teenagers, she seemed to never need rest. Gwen had made an early night of it, heading for her bedroll as soon as the evening cleanup was complete. Nodding as she left, Jaxx threw a couple of more pieces of wood into the pit, hoping that the meager blaze would be warm enough to enable them all to get some sleep. Even cuddled close together to share body warmth it was going to be a long cold night

Fifteen

The way-station was empty and from the look of the blacked stones, the building hadn't been used in ages, possibly since before the waterway dried up. It was disappointing, after walking along the waterway for hours everyone had hoped for a chance to bathe and clean their clothes. It had been a long day. With the way-station closed, they were now faced with another choice; to continue to follow the old creek bed or turn off onto the overgrown path that horses had at one time used to draw the ferry along the water.

Vondal insisted his mother had emphasized following the creek, so they continued onward. The dried wash continued for over a league through a rugged ravine that looked as if a giant's ax had cut into the steep, brush entangled hillside leaving an uneven gouge. At one time the creek had been a tributary of the Parma River, flowing out of a lake in the valley below the keep, now a quick search upstream had revealed an impassable cul-de-sac.

"At least it's not another canyon," Mekiva stated wryly as she scanned the sky for wyverns.

"Ha. Funny. Give me a minute to think. I wish I'd paid more attention to her stories," Vondal said as the others sat despondently staring at the back wall of the ravine. There wasn't much to see, the dried creek ended in a sand-covered basin at the base of a jagged stone outcropping.

The face of several rocks was scored by small abrasions, indications of the waters erosions over the centuries. "I remember something my mother told. Wait here, I want to try something."

Vondal walked directly up the path to the back of the ravine, paused for a moment to look at the rocks, looked back at the others, waved and then disappeared from the view of his friends.

"What the…, Jaxx said, a confused look on his face. "That sly devil," he added as Twizzle flew after Vondal, only to vanish from sight as well.

Seconds later Vondal reappeared and called for the others to come ahead. It was a great illusion, the path turned sharply into a shadowed cleft in the rocks, veering off at an angle. It was impossible to see the entrance unless you were standing directly in front of it. Nature had provided its own deterrent from unwanted visitors.

"Go ahead and follow him. I want to see if I can remove our tracks back to the turnoff. I doubt anyone is following but it can't hurt to be careful." Jaxx walked back along the trail as the two girls followed Vondal.

The passage through the cleft opened into a breathtaking valley of trees, streams and thick grass nestled beneath a light dusting of snow. Jagged amethyst peaks tipped with white-crowned the valley, while a tranquil lake of cerulean blue sparkled in the distance. The remains of a once well-traveled lane meandered westward through the verdant meadow, continuing for almost a mile to the base of a mountain, before winding its way upward to their destination, the remains of a once-proud keep.

"So that's where we are going?" Mekiva inquired. She leaned back in her saddle, following his gaze. Despite the distance, she could make out the hazy outline of an enormous stone building, perched high above the valley. She was assailed by emotions; especially the exciting news that they had finally located the homestead…anxiety over what they would find once they arrived. Somewhere up ahead lay the burned-out keep where Vondal had been born.

Over the last few days, Vondal had told them the entire story. His grandfather Olen was the keeps farrier. Helena, his grandmother, worked for the laird as a housekeeper. She was one of two women responsible for the upkeep of the interior of the holding.

Vondal had been born while his father was serving his time in the district prison. After being turned away from her job when his father was arrested, his pregnant mother had returned home, seeking help from her parents. The wizened old sorcerer Ammaonth had been enchanted by her beauty, welcoming her into his home and doting on her young son.

"It was the best time of my life," Vondal had said, "I can't remember ever being happier. Then my father returned, and everything changed."

Mekiva smiled. She hoped he wouldn't be disappointed. Reality rarely lived up to our memories. Some said Ammaonth was powerful but sadistic, a conjurer ruled by self-indulgent desires. Others claimed him a broken-hearted romantic who'd secluded himself away from civilization after a necromantic spell failed to revive his wife lost in childbirth. No one remained that knew the truth.

I'm certain of one truth. I was sick of setting in a classroom listening to old biddy's drone on and on about dead people and archaic spells. I wasted an entire year and still only have a basic understanding of magic, and absolutely no control. Her instructors refused to discuss why her spells kept going so terribly wrong, implying she would gain control with experience. Well… I bet this trip is one experience they never expected.

Glimpses of the scarred and desolate battlements of the abandoned keep could be seen in the distance, standing in defiance of the extreme conditions. A narrow, overgrown trail of scrub bushes and stunted grass led upwards, winding through the wind-worn rocks, like broken teeth in a two-copper hag's mouth. Vondal was surprised that any of the old buildings still stood, given the force of the wind that never ceased its relentless howling. Night was rapidly approaching, and the distant keep was slowly fading from view. Jaxx suggested they make camp for the night, but he assured them that they'd easily reach the keep by midmorning. He'd been pleasantly surprised to find even an overgrown path to follow. Most seasoned travelers avoided the Alaoreauna Mountains as their dark and foreboding crags were the home of the Feyriian witches.

Gwendolyn shuddered as Jaxx talked about them. It was hard for her to believe the dainty creatures dancing among the flowers in her favorite painting were based on the vile, sadistic creatures Jaxx described. She found herself peering into the shadows as they walked, watching carefully for any movement.

"I agree," Vondal said. "I could use the rest. Let's set up here for the night, get good night's sleep and then start the climb in the morning."

Jaxx nodded. "I'll search for wood to build a fire if one of you will cook. I really could use a hot meal."

"I'll join you," Gwendolyn offered. "I'm not in the mood for cooking. Mekiva can handle it."

"I think I can manage. First, something hot to drink," Mekiva declared. "I think we still have some kava. We'll have to drink it plain, the sugar melted in the water, but it's better than nothing in this weather."

Gwendolyn shuddered and her smile faded. She could handle the cold and the wetness. She could even handle the aching muscles from walking all day. But kava without sugar was wrong!

Vondal studied Jaxx as the usually dour Duaar, and the tiny Shi'i girl walked away to gather wood. They were best friends, as close as brothers, but no matter the circumstances they never pried. If Jaxx wanted him to know something, he'd tell him. He'd been acting oddly for the last two days. Now he was whistling. During their last dice game, his attention hadn't been focused on his throws. He didn't want to consider the possibility that they were growing apart. It had to be something else. He sighed. Whatever it was, it would work itself out.

Vondal delighted in the clear blue skies that deepened all too soon into the rich darkness of a moonless night. He sat watching as the last bloom of light from the second of Omissions' twin suns gradually diminished, fading bit by bit before finally vanishing over the northern ridge of the distant purple mountain. The sight of his friends as they bustled around the new campsite, smiling, even whistling as they worked to make the clearing a bit more comfortable was a welcome change. Mekiva was stirring something she had cooking in their only pot, giggling and dodging Gwendolyn as the young girl snuck a taste, adding her own bits and pieces to the mixture, before tasting it again.

Jaxx dropped the last load of firewood next to the fire pit before challenging Vondal to a round of Fokker, the latest craze in dice games making the rounds of their favorite taverns. Gwendolyn drifted in their direction, eager to join in if the opportunity presented. She wasn't familiar with the rules of the game, but she enjoyed games and figured she'd be able to follow the process enough to learn the basics after two or three rounds. Her concentration was broken by Mekiva announcing that dinner was ready.

Vondal snuck a peek at the girls' special dessert. While searching for firewood, Jaxx had spotted a hava tree still heavy with the late fall fruit. Despite the lack of sugar, the fruit and nut cobbler looked delicious. He was tempted to forgo the main course and dive straight into dessert but only tempted. Hot venison stewed with root vegetables and wild onions and Mekiva's fresh bread was worth fighting for. Considering the way Jaxx was drooling, he just might have to take him out.

Gwendolyn offered to take the first watch. Just after sundown was her favorite time of the day. She enjoyed the faint whispers of nocturnal activity; the solemn hoot of an owl seeking prey or the soft rustling as squirrels and chipmunks foraged in the underbrush. Jaxx had enticed Vondal into a game of dice earlier. She wasn't sure what the two had wagered, but from the self-satisfied grin on Jaxx's face, something would be lighter tomorrow, either Jaxx's load or Vondal's pockets. One way or another, the trek up to the keep would be entertaining.

Vondal was puzzled at Gwen's offer but didn't make an issue of it. Nearly drowning was traumatic. He was surprised she slept at all, but Gwen showed no sign of distress after her recent ordeal. He could imagine Mekiva's reaction, she'd have tried to turn them both into toads…

or something worse. The thought made him smile. Mekiva had slipped off to sleep earlier, curling up in their only blanket as soon as the evening meal was complete, leaving him to do the cleanup. He called out to Gwen before she stepped away from the light, "I think I'm going to lie down myself. Don't forget to wake me for my turn at watch."

"Sleep well. Jaxx, you should join them." Gwendolyn grinned. "I'm too hyped up to sleep anyway. The Wyverns are miles away and I doubt the young ones can swim. Jumping into the river may have been the smartest thing we've done since beginning this mad adventure." Accompanied by the ever-playful draccat, she set out to walk the perimeter of their camp. Twizzle was excellent company; he listened without comment and never repeated anything he heard. Plus, he made an outstanding night scout. Besides staying up all night and sleeping during the day, he preferred hunting once the forest grew shadowy… though it was better not to wonder what mystery meat he was enjoying. The first watch gave her a chance to think and she had a lot on her mind.

Jaxx had a lot on his mind, too. He tossed a few more chunks of wood into the pit, hoping to build the skimpy blaze into a fire warm enough for them to get some sleep. Without tents or blankets, it was going to be another long cold night. Mekiva usually claimed the lone blanket, and Gwendolyn had her heavy robes. But even when everyone huddled together to share body heat, the ones on the outside were never warm. They had begun to build two fires to sleep between, and it helped until the fire burnt down. Not that he expected to get much rest. Every time he closed his eyes a vision of dark curly hair and doe brown eyes wouldn't stay out of his mind. The fact that those heavy black draperies she called clothes covered such a perfect little body kept distracting him from whatever he was doing all evening. Despite everything, I don't regret coming at all. This treasure hunt hasn't been the golden opportunity I expected, but overall, it's been fun. Chances are, all we'll get out of this adventure are a few scars and a lot of memories. Tomorrow, if we're lucky, we'll find out if it was all a waste of time.

Sixteen

Dawn brought with it a dense fog that made it difficult to see much beyond arms reach. An ominous iron-gray haze blanketed the mountain, offering occasional hints of sunlight but never enough to brighten the dreary day. The moisture-laden air felt heavy and chill, bringing goosebumps to any exposed skin. Rime coated trees emphasized the eerie feeling, the icy wind twisting their stunted limbs into a fog-shrouded dance. Everywhere the land appeared faded, as though the very life itself was being stripped or sucked from it by the onslaught of winter. Overnight the welcoming vale had developed a malevolent atmosphere, initiating a heated argument over whether they should delay the climb until the imminent storm had passed.

"The climb is difficult in good weather," Vondal said. "I'm certain there are icy patches remaining from the last squall. You know what winter is like in the mountains, it could be weeks before the sun warms enough to melt them all. We can't afford to wait."

"I hate to admit it, but Von is right," Jaxx replied. "We stand a better chance if we leave now. There's no shelter here and we are running out of fuel. Despite the fire, there must be one or two usable rooms in the keep. The smart thing is to go there."

"But the fog is so thick, don't you worry about falling?" Mekiva asked.

"I worry more about freezing," Jaxx stated. "We have nothing to protect us from the snow. And it will be much worse if it's an ice storm."

Realizing Jaxx was right, they resigned themselves to a difficult climb in inclement weather. Everyone gathered what remained of their supplies and readied themselves to begin the descent.

Vondal fidgeted impatiently, eager to get started. If he could find the pendant and return it to his uncle, he could finally put his ghosts to rest, along with the dubious honor of being named Lord Botherton's heir.

Equally anxious but for entirely different reasons, Gwendolyn and Mekiva waited nearby for Jaxx to lead off. Even encumbered with the additional weight he was stronger and easily the best woodsmen of the group. The trail would not be easy going, but knowing he was the leader would somehow make it seem that way.

Jaxx was doubtful, finding it hard to believe that that the decrepit manor on the ridge crest was hiding a secret worth killing for. He was certain they were doomed to disappointment, but he decided to keep his own council and wait and see what might develop.

Gwendolyn sniffed a bit, then sneezed. She was fighting a cold, and the idea of getting caught halfway up when the snow, or worse, ice storm began, scared the hells out of her. Still, once Jaxx started climbing, she fell in behind the others, hoping to reach the sheltered plateau that the old keep had been built upon before the storm broke.

"Are you scared," she whispered to Mekiva.

Mekiva shook her head. "I passed scared a long time ago."

Resigned to her fate, Gwendolyn gave Mekiva a brief

smile. Logic told her that neither boy would allow her to come to harm. But she couldn't shake the feeling of impending doom.

"I can see why you loved this place." All her anxieties of the past few days now seemed foolish. Recklessly, Mekiva perched at the edge of the cliff, the wind blowing her hair around her face, her fingers stretched overhead as she exulted in the cool afternoon breeze. She motioned for Vondal to join her, indicating the view with a wave of her hand.

Vondal peered over the edge, and then pulled her back a step, making a conditioned effort to respect the safe boundaries Jaxx had designated on the crumbling cliff edge. Noticing his step back from the corner of his eye, Jaxx nodded his approval, pleased that Vondal was finally starting to acknowledge his far greater experience when it came to stone or rocks.

They stood close together, taking in the view of the twin suns on the distant horizon, enjoying the slight warmth as the twin suns dried out the clouds that had beleaguered them for days. The storm had followed the valley, leaving only a light dusting of snow on the high plateau that was rapidly melting in the late afternoon suns light.

The view from the top of the cliff was magnificent, stretching all the way across the forest and out to the open sea many day's travels in the distance. She could see the snow-covered remains of cultivated fields in the valley below, the unkempt rows spiraling outward from the natural boundaries of the mountain and lake. From above it was easy to make out sections of overgrown stone walls and long-neglected roads. One road led off to the east, possibly leading to Alliance as Vondal had surmised. The gusting wind was blowing from that direction, the steady breeze carrying the pungent smells of salt and fish.

Vondal sighed. He loved the free and easy way that Jaxx and Gwendolyn worked together and hoped to someday realize that same degree of companionship with Mekiva. He'd never hid his attraction to the young mage, but he wasn't sure about taking the next step. For now, he pulled her close against him, enjoying the feel of her warm body against his. Tipping her head up, he melted into her eyes, sinking into their jade green depths. When he finally spoke, his voice was low and even, tightly controlled, as if he feared to speak.

"Looks like it's almost over now," he whispered. "Soon enough it will all be back to normal, Gwendolyn back home with her parents and you back at school." He wondered if she was feeling the same way. So much had changed in the past weeks. He felt years older.

Mekiva's eyes darkened.

Von could tell she was thinking, but she didn't seem happy with her thoughts. She was smiling, a warm kind of tender smile, but as he watched a single tear slid down he face. When she finally answered, her words were filled with passion and a real sense of despair.

"Life goes on, but at least we are still moving forward. We've made very little progress, but at least it shows we've made an effort. I'm happy that we've had this time together, but I've resigned myself to ---", she paused, "let's agree that all good things come to an end."

Startled by her statement Vondal stepped away, uncertain what he should say next. He struggled to find the words, but he couldn't think of anything that would loosen the tightness he was feeling as he looked into her teary eyes. His usual response was not to answer at all. Somehow, he knew that wouldn't work with Mekiva. When he spoke, his words were extremely gentle, if he hadn't been standing so close she might not have even heard them.

"Don't cry, it makes your eyes go all puffy, and I don't have a silk handkerchief handy."

Mekiva sniffed noisily, trying not to laugh as she pictured Vondal with a silk handkerchief, dabbing ineffectively at the tears flowing down her face. Failing this she covered her face with her hand and then replied between giggles, "I'm not crying, that would be weak, and I so despise weakness." Her voice was harsh, but as she looked up he could see that her eyes were soft and moist, sparking from the laughter she unsuccessfully tried to hide. Red-faced, Vondal laughed too and then turned her around to enable her to look directly into his face.

"Of all the girls I've ever known, you're the last that need ever worry about being weak. I've been breaking my back to impress you. Instead, I've barely managed to keep up with you. I think we're both trying too hard. It'll work out, I know it will." But the fear was never far away.

Jaxx was ready to get moving. If Vondal was right—and so far, Jaxx had seen little to prove he wasn't, then the 'family treasure' was hidden somewhere nearby. Scorched timbers and heat shattered rocks strewn amongst the burnt-out remains of the decrepit keep offered few hints to a possible hiding place. One decrepit tower still stood, but it looked like a strong wind could change that at any time.

Oh well, it is called a treasure 'hunt'. He shrugged, then turned to Mekiva, "I don't suppose you know a spell that will help us locate this thing? If we need to search through this wreckage, it could take weeks to find it."

"Magic doesn't work that way. It will be years before I'm good enough to cast that type of spell without a scroll or at least a written version to study first." She shifted uncomfortably. I should have researched search spells before we left Cabrell. I packed everything I thought I might need for the trip but never thought about the actual search. Gwendolyn and I never talked about anything except how much fun we would have. So far, we haven't had much fun.

"At least we won't be out in the cold. Vondal said his mother mentioned a caretaker's cottage." He looked toward what remained of the fire-damaged keep. "It must be beyond the tower. It's the only thing large enough to hide it."

"If we're in the right place, and if Von got the story right, and if it's still standing, you're probably right."

"That's a lot of ifs," Jaxx replied. "Let's just go and see. We can worry about the rest later." They made their way around the tower, then stood absorbing their surroundings. There was a cottage. The quaint bungalow was made of stacked stone, probably scavenged from the scattered remains of the old keep, with a thick thatched roof and a small wooden door in front. There were two small windows on either side, edged by stout wooden shutters to keep out the weather. The building appeared to be relatively new, the roof thatching was free of mildew and the chinking around the stones had not cracked, neither had seen more than one or two of Omission's unpredictable winters. Someone had started building a fence, but something must have interrupted the work before it was complete, the carpenter's tools were still lying nearby as if he'd return at any moment to finish the job.

"Careful," Vondal cautioned the two girls; who were now eagerly walking in the direction of the tidy building. "We don't know who's living there. They may not want to be disturbed."

"Nonsense, anyone this house proud can't be a bad person. Let's knock and introduce ourselves. Come on Gwendolyn," Mekiva said. Gwendolyn wove past Vondal and Jaxx with a nonchalant wave. They walked directly to the door of the tiny cottage and knocked loudly, waited, but there was no response from inside. Gwendolyn tried shouting, and then knocked again with no better results. Frustrated, she gave the men a glare of pure exasperation as her efforts continued to get no response.

"Jaxx, you're tall enough, look inside and tell me if anyone is in there." Mekiva pointed to a window a bit higher than her head.

Unless he did as she requested Mekiva would make his life miserable. He pressed his nose to the small shuttered window, the building was silent, there was no fire burning in the hearth, nor any sign that one had been there for some time.

"Look's empty to me. I don't think anyone lives here anymore," Jaxx said. "Maybe the cottage belonged to a Caldarean family and they moved to a safer area when the war started." Sounds good to me.

"It's possible, but the cottage was built out of stone from the old keep. Whoever lived here had to be familiar with the secret entrance to the valley…or it's someone who lived here before the fire. Perhaps they intend to return in the spring."

Jaxx, as ever the impatient one, went to the door and

jiggled the handle. It swung open easily, allowing the young Duaar to enter. Just as Vondal said, the building appeared to have been vacant for months, if not years, as dust covered most of the surfaces and the ashes in the hearth were old. But it was a great base of operations to work from as they began the hunt for the medallion.

Gwendolyn ran her finger over the well-crafted wood furniture. It wasn't ornate, but someone had lovingly sanded and polished each piece until all the rough edges were gone, then carved delicate flowers and other ornamentation to highlight the smooth surfaces. An enormous straw-filled bed sat in one corner of the room. "It shouldn't take long to get this place into usable shape," she announced. "It will be nice to cook on a real hearth again."

"Speaking of cooking, I'm afraid that this poor thing is all I'm able to provide for our evening meal." He tossed a scrawny brown rabbit to Gwendolyn. "Do you think you might be able to come up with something out of this?"

"Don't be daft," she chided. "With a few of the dried vegetables in my pack, we will soon have a fine meal. I think I might even have some salt left, and maybe some other spices." He doesn't need to know Twizzle had already produced two rabbits and most of the meat was salvageable. "Maybe you can convince Vondal to spare the time to look around for some wild onions. There might even be tubers and carrots if he can remember where the keeps garden was. One more thing," Gwendolyn pleaded. "We need firewood. I don't trust the weather, we may have to stay inside a day or two if it starts snowing again." Her smile brightened. "It will be nice to be warm and dry for a change."

"I really wanted to get started looking for the key before dark," Jaxx mumbled, he was already moving toward the door before he realized he'd unconsciously begun following the order as soon as Gwendolyn had given it. "The chain of command around here could use a little bit of work." He colored self-consciously as Gwendolyn's expression made it clear that his comment had not been received kindly. Perhaps it might be better if he gave Vondal his orders, then gathered the wood, and hope she'd forget his snide remark by the time he got back to the cottage. From the frown on Gwendolyn's face, he'd better hurry.

"Over here! I think I found it." Vondal scraped away the burnt wood and ash left behind by the fire, looking for signs of the old keep's foundation. Underneath it was the clear outline of a blacksmiths hearth, the partially melted anvil sticking out of the rubble.

"It looks like a ring of stones to me. You're sure this is it?" Jaxx used his ax to move aside another burnt and partially melted scrap of metal, all that remained of an ornate enameled urn. "A forge fire shouldn't have caused all this damage."

"I'm kinda blurry about the details. I was young, around three I guess. All I really remember is my mother waking me in the middle of the night, wrapping me in my blanket and running out into the darkness. There was fire everywhere. Everyone was searching for someone, running around in the dark randomly screaming out names of missing relatives. My grandparents never made it out. Neither did the old mage Ammaonth. Not that anyone missed him. Over the years I've heard many stories about that night. One favorite talks of how Ammaonth summoned a demon... one too strong for him to control. It broke his binding and destroyed the keep, taking the sorcerer back to the nine hells when he departed. Another tells of a vengeful dragon, taking back the gold that had been stolen from his hoard. I think my mother's version is closer to the truth. She believed it was more likely a bitter husband or father, firing the castle after gutting the lecherous old goat in his sleep. Old Ammaonth often took his "noble" rights, regardless of whether the girls were willing or not."

"What are we looking for?" Jaxx asked, turning over another piece of blistered wood and finding nothing of value beneath. "It's all ashes and melted metal. If there was anything of value left after the fire, it was scavenged long ago--- or destroyed by the weather.

He studied the one tower that partially remained. About thirty feet of the tower still stood, a silent reminder of how grand the old keep was at one time. "It would be easier if I was certain which tower of the four that is. I know that the forge was near the north tower by the stables, which would make it the south tower. We played along the battlements above the stables. There have to be stones or metal from the stables remaining to mark the north tower's location."

Jaxx brushed off the remains of a little girl's doll, scorched almost beyond recognition. It was still grasped in the charred bones of a small child's hand. A single tear slipped from the stoic Duaars' eye before he dropped the remains back to the ground, the hand shattering into individual bones as it hit the hard soil.

"Let's find the medallion and get out of here as soon as we can."

Gwendolyn scowled as the tiny fire struggled to stay

alight. The cottage had been left in a clean and orderly condition, except for the old ashes left inside the hearth. Jaxx had been in too much of a hurry to remove them before lighting the tinder. On top of that, birds had recently nested inside the flue, the remains of their old nest were mixed in with the wastes the birds had deposited, keeping the chimney from drawing correctly. She'd have to start over and make sure it was done properly.

Mekiva let the ragged scrap of fabric drop back across the window. "They look so serious. I hate to interrupt their hunt."

"Nonsense, they're like children, they'll keep looking until it's too dark to see, or until their stomachs remind them to stop."

"We could always charm them, we might actually get something done. But then we'd be stuck with them underfoot until the spell wore off."

Gwendolyn was certain she could see the twinkle in Mekiva's eyes as she talked. "It'll be easier to do it ourselves. Help me to build up the fire and we can get started cooking a hot meal. We'll use whatever's left in the wood box. Jaxx will just have to bring in more. She swept the ashes into a pile with an old broom that had been left behind, then used the broom handle to knock what was left of the nest from the flue. Twigs and feathers rained down, along with a cloth-covered bundle that clanged as it struck the hearth floor.

"What the…?" Lying nestled in the faded material was a flat, tarnished, oval-shaped, chunk of metal hanging from a chain. "Want to bet this is the medallion?" she said merrily, "It was hidden in a hearth. Just not the hearth Von was thinking about. Guess who won't be doing the dishes tonight? It'll be dark soon, let's go and rub it in. I'm sure it's going to change their plans for tomorrow." Whistling merrily, the medallion swinging from her fist, she headed out the door.

Jaxx threw down his ax in exasperation. "I can't believe we spent the entire day digging through the rubble and the medallion was hidden inside the cottage the entire time."

Gwendolyn was enjoying this. "If you'd taken the time to clean the chimney before you built the fire, you'd have found it. That's what happens when you rush through a job."

Vondal laughed. Tyche had a wicked sense of humor, they'd spent most of the day looking for a pendant that had literally fallen into the girls' hands.

"I've been trying to remove some of the corrosion," Mekiva said interrupting her friends' banter. "It's not very fancy, there's hardly any ornamentation. The front shows a castle with four towers. The back's engraved with a lot of flowers and swirls. I can't understand why Lord Botherton wants it. There are no inlaid jewels. It's not made of gold or platinum, I think its silver. Could it have been planted to throw off the hunt?" She held it up for the others to look at it, now that it was clean.

"Someone went to a lot of trouble to hide it if it's a fake," Jaxx remarked. He tried to bend, then bit took the pendant. "It's not silver either. Too hard…maybe mithral?" He held the softly burnished medallion closer to the lamp. "Take a look at this. I think these are words engraved in the swirls. Maybe that's why your uncle is determined to get his hands on it"

"Looks like gibberish to me. You girls want to look at

it?" He held the pendant out to Mekiva, who looked but then shook her head.

"I'm no help," she replied, "I think its words, but it's not like any language I've ever seen."

"Let me try," Gwendolyn asked, taking the small pendant back from Vondal. "It looks familiar but… like Lakkadoa, but older I think, than my mother's tongue. "Wutheh Ghaatiil Olin – Iilor Tel Sharr Morv Levarithin Thraen- Ikwe telwyverna," she muttered.

"What?"

"Oh…sorry, I forgot you didn't understand… it's not exact, but it reads: 'To find your heart's desire, the hidden path lies beyond the Wyverns claw.'"

"That does not make any sense at all," Mekiva pondered wryly.

"Regardless, that's what it says. It's not worth arguing about it." She started to return the pendant, then paused, "If no one cares, I'd like to keep it and study it a bit more."

"Fine with me," Vondal said. "Is dinner about ready? It smells great."

Jaxx helped her clip the pendant around her neck and then she slipped it under her tunic. At first, she was strangely disturbed by the touch of the cold metal against her skin, but gradually that feeling was replaced by a warm comfortable sense of belonging.

"Almost," she said with a smile, "although Mekiva and I had to hunt for the onions and root vegetables ourselves.

Both men had the decency to blush.

Vondal sighed. Dinner had been great, a baked rabbit pie with a mixture of tubers and wild onions, courtesy of Twizzle, plus warm bread fresh from the oven. It was followed by a sweet pie made from dried apples and the sugar Mekiva had discovered, forgotten in the back of a cupboard. In fact, there was quite a bit of staples remaining in the cabinets, leading him to wonder what had happened to the caretaker.

Equally content, Jaxx yawned and stretched. "How about another cup of Kafka? The sugar you found really tops it off. And maybe a bit more of… his train of thought unraveled as something bumped lightly against the door. His hand went to the pommel of his knife as he settled into a defensive position and then he hesitated, realizing it might be the owner of the cottage.

Kettle in hand, Gwendolyn turned away from the firepit as Jaxx's voice trailed away. The door to the cottage opened, and a large man stepped boldly inside. He paused to stomp his feet on the jam to remove the light dusting of frost that had developed after the sun went down

"Castillo," she whispered recognizing him instantly. Her hands began to shake, and a cold chill passed over her … like someone was pouring ice-cold water down her spine.

Vondal rose, his hands coiled tightly around his knife and his mug, ready to use either as a weapon if necessary. Jaxx, ashamed that he'd been too intent on the excellent food to hear him coming, pulled his ax closer but remained seated as he studied their unexpected visitor. Gwen seemed to recognize him, but her expression did nothing to ease the overwhelming sense of danger he felt.

Unperturbed by his indifferent welcome, Castillo crossed over to stand by the fire, leaning close to warm his hands. "Thank the gods you're safe. I've been following you since the remnants of the caravan returned to Cabrell with news of the attack. Lord Botherton was distraught when he realized you were not with them. It wasn't as easy to follow your trail. I lost it by the river…lost one of my horses too." Castillo's voice was clear, almost musical. The contrast between it and his outward appearance was startling. "This valley is quite beautiful, and so well hidden. No wonder no one was able to locate it."

Jaxx grunted, but Vondal chose to ignore Castillo's comment. He turned and muttered something to the Duaar, who frowned, but kept his tongue in check.

Castillo soon realized no one else intended to speak, so, he asked another question. "Lord Botherton said you are treasure hunting. Have you had any success in your search?"

"We located the remains of the old smithy and started tearing it apart today. But we didn't find anything of note in the rubble."

Jaxx was unsurprised that Vondal failed to mention that they'd found the medallion in the cottage. Outwardly calm, the Duaar scout was coiled tight as a spring, ready to react at the slightest provocation. He kept his eyes on Castillo's hands, watching for the slightest movement.

"Then I may be of assistance. Samsara uncovered some additional information after your abrupt departure. The city is on high alert, suspecting the group that attacked the caravan to be Caldarean mercenaries looking to recoup their losses after the war. I personally think them wrong. Many of the local thugs have gone missing. I know of one or two that worked the seaward that no one has seen for weeks." His smile was friendly as he sat down in the chair that Mekiva had vacated, motioning for Gwendolyn to fill a cup for him also. Leaning forward he addressed Vondal directly, his eyes growing dark, his expression stern. "Lord Torrin wants that medallion. He's spending a lot of gold to ensure he gets it. He's counting on you. I'm here to expedite that delivery."

Jaxx listened carefully. Vondal wasn't lying, he was answering Castillo's questions truthfully but leaving out anything of importance. It was good to know that Vondal didn't trust Castillo or his uncle. He shifted his weight in the chair, balancing lightly on his heels in case he needed to move fast.

"We appreciate my uncle's offer of help, however, we're doing all right on our own. Please give him my regards when you get back to Cabrell." Von dismissed him as unnecessary.

Jaxx couldn't stand it any longer. Vondal wasn't going to ask, so he would. "It would help if we knew more about this medallion we're looking for. What does it look like? I mean, are we supposed to search blindly for anything that could be it or just take a wild guess?"

Castillo smirked. "I see Vondal has told you something of his quest. Good, that will make it easier for us to talk. I've never seen the thing myself, it was lost a long time ago. The medallion is silvery in color, with some type of glyphs or writing on it."

Mekiva's eyes widened at his description, but Gwendolyn's elbow kept her from blurting out anything about their find.

Vondal stood, stretching with a yawn. "It was probably melted down and sold for ale before I was born. It's late," he said sleepily, "and we've had a long day. You're welcome to bed down in here with us, you've got a long ride ahead of you tomorrow. Maybe the new day will bring us all a change in fortune."

Castillo walked over and pulled out a chair. " Sounds good to me. Is there any of that pie left?"

Castillo slipped silently around the room, careful not to make any loud noises that might awaken the youths sleeping nearby. He'd become quite deft at reading faces over the years, they were hiding something from him. The slumber moss he'd tossed onto the fire would keep them asleep until morning. He expected the draccat was hiding nearby, the malicious creature had laid open his calf when he'd slipped outside to give the moss an opportunity to work. It disappeared into the shadows before he had a chance to pull his knife. Should have kicked it instead.

Carefully he searched the small cottage looking for any likely hiding spots. There was a hidden cache behind the third stone down of the hearth, however, it contained little of value. Just a small stack of coins and an ivory-handled knife that had seen better days. He pocketed the coins and tossed the knife onto the table.

Searching the packs would be harder. One pack was entangled in Vondal's arms, the other one the Duaar was using as a pillow. Kneeling beside Jaxx, he gently pulled the battered bag aside then rummaged through the contents. No luck, the sack contained only the usual items carried by travelers. He ran his hands over the sleeping Duaar, noting a neck blade and second knife in a sheath near his left ankle. For a second his hand lingered on the hilt of his belt knife, a simple twist and just like that, one factor eliminated from the equation. No, that would encourage Lord Botherton, and he really enjoyed tormenting the pompous fool. Instead, he moved on to Vondal, repeating the process with similar results.

He resigned himself to the distasteful act of searching the sleeping girls. Which one first? The Shi'i-Lakka had been nervous at dinner. What was she hiding?

Hands gently tracing the outline of the Shi'i girl's body, he searched for a hiding place. It was surprisingly easy to locate. The girl wore it on a chain around her neck, hidden by her hair and the high neckline of her robe. He dropped the medallion into a muslin pouch, and then placed it carefully into an inner pocket. Quietly gathering his own possessions, he slipped away into the night.

Seventeen

"Slumber moss! And we invited him to sleep by the fire. I feel like such a fool." Vondal was devastated. Castillo had played his ego like bard played the lute, using his own arrogance against him. Now he had the medallion and was probably halfway back to Cabrell.

"You need to stop blaming yourself," Jaxx stated, shaking his friend by the shoulders to emphasize his point. "It's not like we could have prevented it, there's no remedy for slumber moss. At least we only slept like the dead, it would have taken him seconds to cut our throats." Guilt overcame his insolent attitude. It had been his responsibility to stay awake and keep an eye on Castillo. Instead, she'd slept so soundly, he hadn't noticed when the pack was pulled from beneath his head.

"I agree with Jaxx, it's no one fault," Mekiva added. She poured herself another cup of the strong beverage Gwendolyn had brewed that morning. "Castillo brought the slumber moss with him. Let's stop wasting time and get on with the search."

"He didn't fool me, I've felt his knife on my throat," Gwen added. "I didn't think about slumber moss, it only grows in the Delamarra bogs."

"We worked so hard to find the medallion, and it was

all for nothing." Von snapped as Mekiva fought back tears.

"Big deal… we lost the medallion. You're starting that whining thing again. I'd hoped you left it behind on the Sirens Breath. We've still got our stake. We can head for Alliance, buy a team and wagon, and join up with a pack train bound for Cabrell at first thaw."

"Castillo won't take it straight to my uncle, he'll take it to Samsara first. Samsara will either keep it and cheat Lord Botherton or stall him until he figures out why the medallion so important.

"Vondal, your uncle was never honest with you anyway. I think he sent you on this quest expecting you to fail. That was his first mistake." Gwen grinned and removed a scrap of rolled-up parchment from her pocket. Inscribed in minute detail was an ash rubbing of the medallion, showing both front and back. Next to each rubbing, she'd made notes, little observations and reminders to help them along the way.

"He didn't count on you being so methodical," Vondal replied. "No one else would have thought to make drawings of the medallion."

"That was his first mistake. Leaving us when Castillo is involved, there is no such thing as being too careful. I can still feel him drawing his dagger along my neck. He knew it too." Gwen shuddered and Jaxx squeezed her hand.

"Do you think the picture on the medallion is of the old keep that burned down," Mekiva asked.

"Yes. Once there were four towers. Take a closer look at the rubbing, the north tower had a flag on it."

"A flag, what's that got to do with it?" Jaxx inquired.

"Maybe nothing, …maybe a lot. I was always certain Ammaonth's coat of arms was a dragon and sword entwined. What if I was wrong? Think about it, a small boy might see a flag with a picture of a wyvern, and believe it a dragon?"

"It's possible…yes," Mekiva answered. "They do look similar. Do you think the medallion is only a clue, pointing the way to something much more valuable? That means there might be more to the story than your uncle told you."

"Let's find out. It's already too late for me to start the winter session. So why not do some exploring?" Mekiva smiled as everyone nodded. She could care less about a treasure, it gave her an excuse to spend more time with Von. She pulled out her spell book and began studying. It was always better to be prepared…

There was one obvious place to begin their search. The roof of the remaining tower had caved in and the walls had several big cracks, but the stone steps were clean and free of ash and other debris from the fire. Jaxx noticed that the mortar around several of the stones at the base of the tower was lighter in color, proof that someone had tried to repair the damage. They had also repaired the entrance, a new iron-banded door was in place, complete with an intricate-looking lock.

"I can chop my way thru, "Jaxx offered.

"Give Gwendolyn a chance first, Mekiva says she's really good with locks. After what happened last night, I like the idea of a locked door at our backs."

The boys stepped back, allowing the tiny Shi'i-Lakka girl access to the door. She knelt, studying the cast-iron lock carefully prior to her attempt at picking it. Then she unrolled a small leather pouch, removing several tiny strips of metal.

"Do you think you can open it?" inquired Vondal as

Gwen twisted a thin metal strip within the keyhole.

The soft click, accompanied by a barely audible sigh of self-congratulation, signified how quickly she'd been able to remove that minor obstruction to their entrance. The room inside had been used for storage, possibly by the missing caretaker. There were several bags and a stack of boxes. The two women began an immediate search, looking for anything usable. Unfortunately, other than a small bag of ground cornmeal, there was nothing they could easily carry with them. Jaxx removed an oil lantern hanging on a peg by the door. He checked, finding it full of oil. A good find, especially since they had lost theirs during the wyvern attack.

"Stairs seems strong enough. Watch out for traps," Jaxx called over his shoulder, signaling for the girls to space themselves behind him. "Step where you know I've already stepped. Sometimes these old stairways are rigged to drop out from under anyone stepping in the wrong spot. "

"Thanks," Mekiva muttered sarcastically, "another thing to worry about." Despite their skepticism, both girls attempted to mirror his steps as they made their way up the winding staircase.

Vondal, following just behind them, thought it more likely the stairs would fall because of Jaxx' weight, than that of the slender girls. He noticed that many of the pavers were discolored and cracked from the intense heat of the fire. Several of the stones were brittle as if extensively or repeatedly burned and many pieces were fractured in place, held together by a combination of mortar and ash.

"This fire wasn't an accident, someone coated the steps with oil or resin to make it burn hotter and spread. You can see the bristle pattern of the brush they used to apply it. An accidental blaze would have died out without fuel once it had consumed all the burnable material. This one literally climbed up the stone stairway to reach the floors above. Maybe my mother's theory was correct, it does look like someone wanted Ammaonth dead."

The first two floors had suffered the most damage, the flames had consumed everything burnable, leaving ashes and melted lumps of metal behind. The third floor was different. The oak framework bore occasional scorch marks, but no hint of catalyst marked the stones. One room showed signs of recent use, the floors were swept clean and several woven tapestry rugs hung on the walls for additional warmth against the wind that blew a chill throughout the old tower. An ornate bed with eiderdown mattress, ink-stained desk, a couple of cushiony chairs and a fire brazier for warmth made the room feel homey. Remnants of old meals could be seen, as well as ashes and partially burned wood from two or three different fires. It was evident that someone had used this room often, and from the lack of dust, not too long ago.

"It's waiting just like the cottage," Mekiva said. "It's like they went to buy supplies and never returned."

"People disappear every day, think of all the bones in the Wyvern canyon. We can't assume they're not coming back. We can start our search here. This room is as good a place as any.

"It's not very large, so it should not take us too long to search," Gwendolyn pointed out as she started pulling out drawers in the old desk. "I don't see anything that even resembles a dragon or a wyvern."

Mekiva smiled fondly at Vondal who was methodically searching behind one of the large tapestries featuring two dragons flying above a castle. "If this is the right tower," she said. "And if you translated it correctly. We also have to face the possibility that the treasure was lost in the fire."

"That's a solidly made desk Gwendolyn…look for a hidden catch in the carving," Jaxx interrupted. "Rich people are fascinated with secret compartments." He ran his hand across the molding around the door. "And check out the parquet on the floor, maybe one of them is loose."

The girls looked at each other and smiled, then everyone began to search for anything that seemed remotely out of the ordinary. Vondal gave up on the tapestries and decided to concentrate on the floor, dragging his dagger along the cracks, hoping to trip a hidden catch.

"Tyche's blessings," he called, "I think I may have found something." There was a brief bang, and a small puff of dust rose up from between the floor tiles.

Startled, Mekiva fell back against the wall, her hand clutching the edge of an elaborately carved stone mantle as she struggled to keep her balance. As she fell, the weight of her body shifted the small dove carved into the side to one side. There was a faint clunk, and then a grinding noise, then the wall beside the mantle swung open on concealed hinges, revealing a staircase leading down into the darkness. Carved into the lintel above the door was a tiny wyvern!

"Our first treasure!" Vondal declared, proudly showing off the small bag of coins he'd found in the hidden compartment beneath the floor tile, then his mouth fell open as he realized what Mekiva had accidentally discovered.

"Well, do we go in, or not?" Vondal asked as he joined the others gathered around the dark opening. He peered down the stairs into the unending gloom. "It's too dark to see where it leads. We'll need lights, several of them if we're going to explore."

"We have the oil in the lantern," Jaxx surmised, "and I think I can rig up a torch from the tapestries and a leg off that small table in the room next door. We have our packs with us, and everyone is carrying water. Besides, Twizzle just disappeared into the passage. We have to find him."

Mekiva decided to stay out of the boy's way, instead looking thru the small cache of coins that Vondal had found. She knew a simple cantrip to call up light, but maybe it would be better to not mention it. Jaxx might think she was demeaning his offer. Men were touchy about such things.

It didn't Jaxx long to fabricate two torches after they decided to save the lantern in case it was needed in an emergency. Vondal took one and passed the second to Mekiva before he entered the dimly lit passage. He took two steps, brushing a cobweb away from his face. The light from the glowing torch lit up the narrow corridor, causing thousands of spider webs to dance in the shadows from the breeze blowing through the open door. Other than the pawprints in the dust left by the exploring draccat, no one had passed that way in years. "I'll go first, followed by Mekiva, and Gwen. Jaxx, grab Twizzle and keep him with you. That way we can make sure he won't set off any traps." And be sure that the steps don't collapse until after the girls have passed.

"Missed him!" Jaxx snorted and reached for the elusive draccat that immediately flew down the open passage. "Hold your hand against the right wall and let your fingers brush against it. That way if we come across any side passages you won't miss them in the dark. I'll keep a watch on the left side. I can see reasonably well in the dark, but to be certain I'll drag my fingers the same way. It can't hurt to be extra careful seeing how overconfidence got us into so much trouble back in Zander."

"Yeah," Vondal conceded, "but that involved a mother and a daughter, one very angry banker, and the city watch. I don't see how you can compare the situations."

"It's the first thing that popped into my head. It was a major mess, and we were overconfident going into it."

"Well, just don't mention it to the girls. I don't think that it will seem quite so funny to them."

"Don't mention what?" Mekiva asked. She wedged one end of a small bench she and Gwendolyn had found against the far wall, keeping the sliding mechanism from closing. "This should keep the door open behind us, we might have to come back this way in a hurry."

"Don't mention how dirty it is in here, or Gwendolyn will have us cleaning it before you come in," Vondal interjected before Jaxx had time to make some type of smart remark and get them both into trouble.

"We're not that bad, are we?" she inquired.

Vondal and Jaxx decided it might be better if they just kept quiet.

"I wonder what kind of spider spun these webs," Vondal said, sheepishly brushing strands away with his torch. Unlike many people living in the downs, his mother had been a stickler for cleanliness. They might have gone to bed hungry, but they were always freshly bathed. He'd bravely confronted a pack of starving Wyverns… but the idea of a tiny arachnid brought chills to his spine.

The group had been descending steadily since entering the ancient stairway, deeper and deeper into the depths below the burnt-out building. Tensions were high as each passing moment led them further from the safety of the familiar lands above. By the time they reached the last step and stopped to rest in the small antechamber at the foot of the stairs everyone's nerves were frazzled. The stone-walled room was circular and manmade, not natural, with one doorway opening into a narrow hallway that led off in two directions.

"My aches have aches of their own," Vondal sighed as he dropped his pack against the nearest wall and slid down beside it.

Mekiva was grateful. "So nice of you to consider a poor girl's fragility. Gwendolyn and I lost feeling in our legs about a thousand steps ago." She yawned and stretched. "I need to rest… and something to eat, lots of both." Twizzle hovered just overhead, alert and attentive to the mention of the possibility of food, any thought of exploring immediately forgotten.

"We've been lucky so far. I spent most of the climb debating our chances of surviving the long drop to the bottom of those old staircases had one collapsed while we were on it."

"Well, I'm not climbing back up until we are certain there is nothing hidden. Let's hurry and find it. For all we know Castillo is still slinking along behind us, just waiting for us to find the treasure like we found the medallion."

"You think?" Jaxx snapped. "So, which do we go now, O wise one? I've been looking but so far I haven't seen anything that even hints at a drassted wyvern." The usually confident Duaar appeared anxious as he slowly rotated the handle of his ax in his hand.

Vondal sighed. "I don't have a clue. We don't know where Castillo is. We all assumed he returned to Samsara or my uncle, whichever one is pulling his strings right now. But we could be wrong. It's frustrating, we've come too far to turn around now."

Neither choice looked promising. The left passage showed signs of structure deterioration, including several rather large sections of the ceiling that had collapsed sometime in the past. They decided to check out the right passage since there was no obvious damage. Not that they could see very far in either direction. The stone of the hallway was cut from some type of obscure semi-porous rock that absorbed almost all the light from their makeshift torches. The narrow passageway continued onward for some time, appearing to get darker as they went along. Soon the light from the torches grew so dim they left most of the floor unseen, both before and behind them.

Gwendolyn didn't like the uneasy feeling the dark hallway gave her. No one had walked this hall in ages. Dust covered the floor and she could feel the remains of broken spider webs across her face as she walked along behind the others. There were lamp brackets set into the wall at intervals, but no lamps were to be found. Someone had removed them, along with anything else of value when the keep was abandoned. No one was prepared when the passageway ended suddenly in an ancient brick wall, an apparent but quite unexpected dead end.

"Well expert, Vondal mocked, what do we do now? I seem to remember you telling us all, 'I'll lead, Duaarien delvers never get lost."

"Who's lost?" Jaxx retorted. "I know exactly where we are. Why the tunnel ends this way is another matter. It doesn't make sense."

"Something made them block it up." Vondal looked around as if he expected that thing to appear at any moment.

"Let's go back," Mekiva coaxed, hoping to forestall further discussion. The boys could spend hours puzzling over the reason for a dead end. "Maybe we missed something. Perhaps there was a secret door or passage along the way."

"She's right." Vondal turned and started back up the corridor without waiting for the others to follow him.

Jaxx ignored him. "Vondal is being a jerk. Building this passage would cost a fortune. Why stop in the middle of nowhere? There's got to be something we're missing." He began examining the bricked up passage.

"I've no ideas," Mekiva offered. "It's possible they were still building when the fire started, and just quit."

"Not a chance, Jaxx stated. This stonework was put in intentionally. There would have been no reason to do it after the fire. Vondal's mother would not have known about it."

"It looks like the stonework in Cabrell, down in Old Towne," Gwendolyn added. They tried to match it to the main tunnel, but the color is slightly different.

Jaxx continued to study the end of the corridor. There was something about it...something that didn't fit, ...just a feeling he had. Oh, well. Vondal wasn't waiting. He had to hurry, if he left Von alone for long he was sure to blunder into something that would get them all hurt. Shrugging in resignation, he turned away, then stopped. The shadow! It was moving.

Jaxx allowed a grin to show for just a second, then his usual stone-like expression returned. He stepped away from the door and took a good look at it from a distance. Kneeling on the floor he drew his fingers lightly along the center of the tunnel. While at first glance all the stone blockwork seemed the same, by running his hand along the floor he could tell there was a faint indentation in the stone of the floor leading up to it, as though many feet had traveled up and down the tunnel over a long period of time.

"Step back away from the wall," he ordered smugly. Then he swung the back of his heavy ax head at the wall. The mortar in old stonework crumpled and the feeling of moving and increased. An additional few well-chosen blows opening a gap big enough for them to climb through. The corridor continued behind the broken wall into the darkness.

"I knocked! Nobody's home, he quipped snidely, think we ought to wait?"

Neither girl thought to dignify Jaxx's comment with a reply.

"Mekiva, would you fetch Vondal back? He can't have gotten far working his way back up the tunnel. Gwendolyn, you stay here and let me check it first. Once I'm sure it's safe, I'll call out for you to come ahead."

Mekiva agreed, knowing Jaxx could hardly contain his own curiosity. Luckily Vondal heard the stones falling, and was returning on his own, Twizzle flying above his head.

Jaxx enjoyed his best friends' chagrined expression for a moment, then stuck his head through the opening. Spotting nothing dangerous, he squeezed through the hole, followed closely by Twizzle and the much taller Vondal. There were the sounds of things being shifted around, and a yelp from Vondal as he struck his knee against something in the dark, and then Vondal stuck his head back out the hole to let Mekiva and Gwendolyn know everything was safe inside.

"The torches aren't helping much," he said. "It's so dark I can't make out anything but shapes. Even Jaxx is having a little trouble."

"In that case, I may be able to help," Mekiva answered, rummaging through her pack of spell components, she removed a silver coin and started rubbing it back and forth between her palms, muttering some strange sounding words as she did. "It won't last long, maybe two candle-marks at the most, but it will be much brighter than the torch if this works." The small coin began to glow dimly, then gradually increased in intensity until the area around the crumpled wall was lit as brightly as a summer day.

Ignoring the astonished look on Vondal's face, she passed the brightly glowing Ryl to Jaxx, who in turn passed the smoking torch back to her. Everyone held their breath as Jaxx held it up inside, lighting up the chamber beyond and allowing them all to get a good look around. Beyond the wall, about twenty feet further down the hall was a heavy door, barred by a thick metal beam.

"Think that's the exit?"

"There's only one way to find out," Von said. "Help me with this bar."

Eighteen

It wasn't an exit.

Once a workroom or study of some sort, the room was littered with a lifetime's collection of paraphernalia and assorted trophies from someone's life. The remains of a once opulent teak bedstead filled the center of the room. A traditional ceramic brazier and an oversize desk took up most of the right side of the room. Atop a stack of books sitting on the desk was a lamp which had seen better days, the glass chimney was cracked, and the linen shade was in tatters. Jaxx lit to see if it was worth taking along. It smoked for a moment then glowed with a steady warm light.

Whoever had used the room had appreciated books. Of different colors and sizes, they were stacked haphazardly on every available surface of the workroom. Besides the desk, the walls held an assortment of shelves overflowing with even more of the heavy, leather-bound tomes as well as a large collection of vellum scrolls.

Mekiva moved around the room, her excitement growing, as she thumbed through one or two that caught her attention, many of them were works of magic! If the grimoire lying open on the desk was similar in age to the others, the tomes were ancient, most dated hundreds of years before she was born. She stroked the worn leather cover of the old book. Most of the red had faded from the binding but it was apparent someone had put a lot of effort into crafting the ancient grimoire. Master Stolinn was going to be so excited when she showed him what she had discovered! The other two were interesting, but this one she somehow knew, was special. She immediately placed the three book in her backpack, removing the bag of cornmeal so she could have room. When Jaxx wasn't looking, she slipped the heavy meal sack into his backpack.

Her curiosity aroused, Gwendolyn eagerly joined in the search, looking for anything relating to medicine or healing that might be available among the stacks.

The men had no interest in the books. Enraptured by one intensely fascinating find after another, they were moving about the crowded room examining random items that caught their attention.

Vondal was drawn toward the far wall. The entire back wall was cluttered with examples of every type of weapon he has ever seen and quite a few he hadn't. Someone had spent a lot of time putting this collection together, the selection ranging from fanciful daggers with ornately decorated pommels, to heavy swords for stabbing or slashing and thin, easily bendable epees designed for fencing. Larger weapons, such as halberds and spears were mounted on clever displays along another wall. He found himself admiring one gold embossed spear topped by a razor-sharp metal tip, but his attention quickly turned to a display of swords mounted just beyond.

He couldn't take his eyes off one, a hand and a half sword with a curling dragon pommel. He swung it a few times, appreciating the balance and weight of the beautifully crafted weapon. The sword was exceptionally well balanced and weighed almost nothing in his hand. He ran his finger down each side of the blade, admiring the keen edge and even temper. The weapon was an exquisite example of what a sword could be if crafted with skill and finesse. Forged from Zarrni steel, it had been folded and refolded until the slender double-edged blade reached the maximum degree of hardness possible. Yet it was perfectly straight and honed razor sharp. The sword's grip was simple, a slender braided chain of tiny mithral links wrapped around and around from end to end. It was designed for fighting, with a slender curve of metal to protect the wielder's hand, and a slight tracery of runes decorating the blade. Vondal was smitten, he' never imagined owning anything of this quality. Even Jaxx, who preferred an ax, was envious of his best friends find.

"If no one else claims this, I'd like to keep it for my own use."

Jaxx jibed, "Maybe a good sword will help you hit your target." He dodged backward a few steps, managing to stay just out of his friends reach as Von swung the flat of his new sword his way. Then he moved off to explore more of the assorted stacks and piles scattered around the large room.

"If you claim that, then I claim these," he declared, holding up a matched set of throwing knives that he found wrapped in a moldy piece of cloth. He brushed the dust off, then held one up to the light, enjoying the way two tiny rubies sparkled as the lantern's beam brushed against them. The rubies seemed alive in the flickering light. That's weird, he mused quietly to himself. He decided to move closer to the lantern but instead of being easier to see, the jewels seemed to be getting darker. His interest kindled, he changed directions, moving back toward the area Vondal was searching, the glow intensifying with each step until it was almost unbearable.

Twizzle was bored. The half-grown kitten had been sitting quietly on the desk corner, aggravated and pouting after missing the excitement of the wall coming down. He was hungry and no one had mentioned food. Instead they were playing with toys. There... a faint noise. Was it a mouse? His ears perked forward listening for any further sounds. A few seconds later he flew off into the dark.

Vondal's search had produced little of value besides the weapons along the walls. All he hadn't checked was a pile of trash in the corner, dry and crumbling from the passage of time.

He idly stirred the pile with his foot. Startled, he jumped and almost fell on his knees as a human skull rolled out of the pile directly into his foot.

"I think I may have found what's left of our host," he called out to the others. "Hey, are you even listening ...to ...me?" The hairs on his arm and head were on end. Step by step he edged backward until the rear of his boot bumped into an overflowing crate of books sitting in the middle of the small room.

The sound of the books...and Vondal crashing to the floor finally caught Jaxx's attention and he let a thin smile break the determined expression he displayed while searching. Vondal looked sick, almost ghostly pale. He kept a watchful eye on him as he regained his feet. .

Vondal kept his eyes on the corner, motioning for Jaxx to join him as he backed slowly away. Every nerve in his body was alert and screaming. He couldn't shake the sudden feeling of imminent danger. He was viably shaking.

"You okay," Jaxx asked, taking a firm hold on his ax with his other hand.

"Much better than my new friend here," Vondal responded, motioning to the moldy pile of bones that were now emanating a soft green glow. Jaxx blanched. He immediately joined Von as he continued to back slowly away from the corner. They had almost reached the area where the girls were searching when Gwendolyn noticed the strange way in which they were behaving.

"Jaxx, is everything all right? You look like you just saw a ghost or something."

"Well, you got the 'or something part' right anyway. It's a Gorrdul." The light from the glowing gems in his new knife's hilt illuminated the dim outline of a man now sitting with his back against the wall, formed from the scattered bones of the skeleton. Remnants of his clothing still clearly visible, though in shreds from the time that had gone by since he passed away. Slowly the figure began to take shape, gradually becoming more and more solid with each passing moment. The eyes glowed red in the darkness, a strange radiance that increased in illumination as time passed.

"What's a Gorrdul?" Gwendolyn asked. She moved closer to Jaxx and looked in the direction he was pointing. At first, she could not make out anything in the dim light, then the newly animated figure rose to its feet and began shuffling in the direction of the two young men.

Jaxx brandished his ax in the direction of the rapidly solidifying lich, hoping to provide his friends an opportunity to get away through the opening in the bricks.

"That's a Gorrdul. A walking bag o' bones! Call it a

lich if you want to. Hells girl, you can call it anything you want. But unless one of you can turn it, you girls need to run…now! Start edging your way toward the hole while I distract it." He swung his ax at the emaciated arm extended his way. "It seems to like me."

Mekiva couldn't take her eyes off the brightly glowing eye sockets, a malevolent radiance burning within that awoke shivers within her. She froze as it moved nearer and nearer to Von.

Vondal swung his blade at the Gorrdul's outstretched arm, removing a few fingers but not stopping its advance. The reanimated skeleton moved erratically, the bones brittle with age and loose in the sockets. His jaw bone was moving, a dry inarticulate murmur that was too faint for words to be discerned. Gradually his hands began to glow an unusual shade of green, and strange mists began to form around the bones.

"Move! Drasst it Mekiva, run!" *Ligazra drag me to the nine hells! Mekiva's going to make me pay for that. Any other time I'd be flattered she'd obeyed without an argument. Now I'd just like to stay alive.* He shoved Mekiva out of the way of the strange green mist that was slowly drifting closer. Once she was safely out of harm's way, he directed his attention back to the eerie apparition shambling slowly in his direction. Moving warily, while keeping his body facing toward the strange skeletal creature, he waved his new sword before him to ward off the ungainly monster. As he swung, streaming bands of white light followed the path of the blade. Startled by the impromptu light show, he missed the lich completely, the strength of his overextended blow throwing him into a spin. He gathered himself and tried again, noticing that whenever the sword came within a few feet of the lich, it began to glow with a warm white light that flared brightly each time it struck the lich. It would flinch, as if in pain, but the light wasn't enough to turn it away.

Mekiva had no idea how to help. Necromancy and spells against the risen dead were not covered until her senior year studies. Her one defensive weapon was a barrage of light missiles. She muttered a quick spell, but the missiles passed harmlessly through the bones of the skeleton without doing damage.

Jaxx attempted to remove the skeleton's legs. His ax struck the bones but somehow the sharp blade did little damage. The Gorrdul continued its walk across the room, directly toward the area of the room in which the girls were hiding.

Gwendolyn had petitioned for a spell to turn evil without results. Ligazra and Yaaga ruled the nine hells, neither felt any obligation to help one of their sisters' neophytes. Rheaaz had been more than generous about healing their injuries, best not to push her luck. Then she remembered something she had heard from an old mercenary riding with the caravan. That's it! Maybe I can help after all. She quickly rattled off a short prayer and then tapped Jaxx lightly on his back. As soon as she touched the Duaar, a warm glow spread over his body and he seemed to stand a little straighter and his grip on the heavy ax became even more solid.

"Thanks. I don't know what you did but I feel great. Like I just had a week to sleep, eat and relax." Reinvigorated, he moved forcefully toward the undead creature and swung his ax, the blade biting deep, causing a sizable chunk of the rib case to separate from its torso.

The lich didn't seem to notice the damage. It continued to walk forward until it stood next to the old desk and then it extended its bony arms outward, the green mist growing thicker, spreading out and flowing up along the wall behind it. As the mist struck the wall, portions of the surface began to glow green. Three times more it waved its bony arm, duplicating the gesture's pattern each time. With each pass, the glow deepened. Then, as if satisfying a compulsion, the Gorrdul knelt and bowed its head before crumbling back into individual bones and dust.

Strange glowing glyphs remained as the mist dissipated, a clear, though pale, greenish-white against the dark granite of the walls, scribed in a language that was unfamiliar to anyone in the small group. The closer Vondal came to the runes, the brighter the silvery-white glow of his sword grew. He moved a few of the scattered bones apart, then declared the danger over.

"Can any of you read this?" Jaxx asked, puzzled by the Gorrdul's' unusual behavior.

"Read it? I'm more concerned with why the Gorrdul acted that way," Von replied. He kept one eye on the remains while he studied the runes. "I think I recognize the one that means open. It's a very common glyph. I don't know any of the others."

"It looks like gibberish to me," Gwendolyn apologized. Some type of archaic Shi'i runes perhaps? The symbols are similar, but not quite the same as I was taught. "It does remind me of archaic Shi'i-Lakka hieroglyphics, but there are some differences. But why would there be Shi'i writing on a wall so far away from an enclave?"

"Maybe we all see different things," Jaxx added. "I was thinking they were similar to an old form of the Duaarien language, but that's not right either. For all we know, it could be Tabruk or Zarrni, both races are nomadic and it's possible they had a similar written language in the past."

Mekiva agreed. She felt like she should recognize one or two of them at least. Rune lore wasn't her favorite class. She probably should have paid more attention to Mistress Aberdeen but her droning voice usually sent her to sleep, and then to the headmasters' office. Why would the lich want us to see the hidden runes? What did they mean? Was this related to the medallion and the map, or just another strange find? Then the most important question of all came into her mind and she spoke the words loudly for all to hear. "How long would they continue to glow?"

"Probably not long enough," Gwendolyn responded softly as she continued to stare at the light, "I'll copy them now before they fade away. It may prove worth our time to try to figure out the meaning if we can. She walked over to the desk in search of something to write upon. "We can work on deciphering the meaning as we travel. It will give us something to do on the road back to Cabrell." There were a few old leather scrolls in a crumbling wood box. The writing was faded but the skin was still remarkably supple. She hastily mixed burnt wood charcoal and lamp oil to create a type of ink, then turned one of the old scrolls over and traced the runes upon its bare backside. Amazingly the combination of oil and light brought the discolored words on the front to the surface, the faded letters now readily seen by anyone with the skill to read what was written. There were quite a few words still too faded from the passing of time, but the gist was easy to deduce from the context inscribed on the tattered parchment.

She passed it to Mekiva to read. The writing told of the original owner of the keep, an elderly mage who had refused to divulge the location of a valuable artifact. In retaliation, he'd been sealed inside the room to die. He'd used the last of his waning strength to scratch out his story in his own blood on the now faded scroll. Then, on his death-bed, he'd cast one final spell, thus, enabling his essence to survive as a lich, albeit a weak one, until the right person… a person of honor, came along to avenge his death.

"The poor old geezer, I doubt that his death was a quick or easy one," Jaxx mused aloud. "Can you imagine? Walled up in here… slowly starving or dying of thirst… unable to escape? I'd be willing to bet they smashed his fingers to prevent him from casting any spells. It explains why they fell out so easily."

Mekiva was quick to offer her opinion too. "Take a look at his skull, his jaw was damaged, maybe broken. That would make it almost impossible to correctly pronounce the words to any complex spell, like pass-wall or teleport. I barely manage the correct pronunciation of the first level incantations without an injury."

"It had to be a nightmare. With damaged hands, he'd be unable to hold a knife, much less use it to scratch the mortar from the bricks. No sound except his own voice. It would have driven him crazy long before his food ran out or he died from dehydration." Gwendolyn shivered, "it would explain the piles of books around the room, too. He probably broke apart sections of the bookcase, and then used the wood for heat. I don't see any coal."

"Perhaps that is what drove him to become a lich, a slow buildup of hatred for the ones that enclosed him in the room and left him to die."

"It's something we'll never know for sure. The Gorrdul didn't speak to us. Not that we gave it much of a chance," Vondal added.

They all looked at each other, overwhelmed by emotions that left them at a loss for words.

"Oh great," Jaxx moaned. He pushed at the dusty

bones with a chunk of the wood from the shattered bookcase. "Now you're going to start feeling sorry for the creature. It tried to kill us, remember?"

"I don't think he was trying to hurt us at all, Vondal said. We were between him and the desk area. The girls happened to be standing in his path. If he was being compelled, nothing else mattered."

No one answered. The guilty silence remained until Mekiva worked up her nerve, then skirted carefully around the now inanimate pile of bones lying before the old desk, eager to get back to sorting through the mage's spell books. Earlier she'd discovered one of the old scrolls held an assortment of spells, inscribed by the mage to enable him to carry extra protection when needed. She hoped that others would be of similar value.

One scroll spell, in particular, had caught her eye. She'd never attempted it before, but it was within the range of her powers. She decided it was worth at least a try. After finding a comfortable position on the floor, she focused her mind, staring at the runes inscribed on the scroll. The words seemed to dance before her eyes, shrinking and growing in size, as she struggled to commit them to memory. Whoever crafted this spell intended it to be used by someone advanced in their studies. A shadow fell across the page, startling her into looking away from the scroll and into the face of the man standing over her.

"What's so interesting?" Vondal asked, moving to sit down beside her on the ground.

"This spell I'm trying to memorize. If I can commit it to memory, I should be able to cast it here inside this room. It will allow me to detect magic on material objects. I feel like I'm almost there, but it still evades me."

"Perhaps you just need a break? Gwendolyn used the

lamp to make tea and we have some roast quail left from breakfast. After you rest you can try again."

Vondal's concern left Mekiva uneasy. Fresh off a ship, like most sailors, his language was often colorful and his manner brusque. This uncharacteristic behavior was a complete surprise. It also confused her. Could the sword be controlling him? It was obviously magic. Maybe she should ask Gwendolyn. Or Jaxx? They'd know what to do. The expression on Jaxx's face was troubling. He looked apprehensive, as surprised as Mekiva by the tenderness in Vondal's voice.

Jaxx noticed Mekiva's interest and quickly looked away, his face almost as red as her hair. His body shook with unreleased laughter. Yes, Vondal had changed in some manner. When Mekiva looked him in the eyes he looked back, a tender smile on his face. His friend was in love again. Drasst! They didn't have time to deal with that now.

"I think," Mekiva declared, "that I'm ready to cast the spell, or at least I think I'm ready." She grinned optimistically at Vondal, who helped her up from the ground, then motioned for the others to back away from her as the young mage cleared her mind and mentally prepared for the attempt.

Mekiva stood quietly in the center of the room and took a couple of deep breaths. The others quickly moved back against the wall near the glowing runes. Mekiva concentrated on casting. After making a few gestures with her hands, she began chanting the complex-sounding words aloud, careful to pronounce each one exactly as it had been written. At first, there was no reaction, but then all at once, everything changed.

The sword Vondal held came alive. First silver, then purple, then green colors flashed, the brilliant array shifting as they raced from hilt to tip and back again. Vondal had felt there was more to the sword than just steel after the way the lich had reacted to it, but now it was obvious to anyone watching that the sword held magic--- strong magic!

Less obvious were the various glows that radiated from several objects scattered around the room.

"Quick! We need to find them before the spell wears off." Besides the two scrolls Mekiva had already put aside to take with her, another scroll was found buried among the books stacked nearby. One of the drawers of the desk was also glowing lightly, but when Gwendolyn opened it there was nothing inside. Her backpack was glowing, but she had expected that.

"Let me look," Jaxx suggested. "There's got to be a hidden compartment." Visions of treasure flashed through his mind as he moved his nimble fingers along both sides of the wooden drawer, feeling for any slight irregularity. A quick twist, followed by a click, opened the false bottom of the drawer. Inside it lay two small objects, both giving off a slight glow in the dim light.

"Well, what was in the drawer?" Gwendolyn demand-ed, eager to get a better look at the items Jaxx held in the palm of his hand. The glow proved the items magical, what wasn't clear was what kind of magic.

Jaxx held his hand palm up so everyone could easily view the two small items that had been hidden in the secret drawer. The first one was a ring, silver in color and very simple in design. It wasn't ornate at all, solid except for a string of stars and eyes etched to circle around the middle of the band. The second item was much harder to figure out. It was a simple stone, a cat's eye opal, shaped to set in a circle of gold. There was no obvious way to attach it to apparel, no pin or clasp to string it on a chain.

Gwen took the small cat's eye from Jaxx's hand, turning it over so that she could see it a little more closely. On the back was a small piece of metal, as though something had broken off the back. The edge of the metal was slightly brighter in color than the surrounding metal, suggesting that the item had been broken after years of wear. "I think that this was a broach, with the pin broken off. See, look here," she said, pointing out the scarred metal on the broaches back. "It's really quite pretty, maybe I can have it repaired once we return to town? That's if no one else wants to claim it? And Mekiva can have the ring."

Jaxx grinned rakishly and raised his right eyebrow, leering in a suggestive way as he leaned closer to the two girls. "I'm sure we can come to some type of arrangement in trade for the jewelry," he proposed drolly, then ducked to avoid the book Vondal tossed in his direction.

"If you're quite finished," Gwendolyn retorted, "now might be a good time to eat, then start back. I don't know about you but I'm dreading the climb back up to the top."

"But we haven't worked out the details. I'm thinking the pin must be worth a backrub or two at least."

"Stop clowning around Jaxx," Mekiva snapped. "We've wasted enough time. Unless we hurry, winter break will be over. I'd hate to miss the start of the spring session, they may not let me back in school if I'm late again."

"Speaking of eating…has anyone seen Twizzle?"

The draccat had vanished.

Nineteen

"Botherton wasted all that gold for this?" Samsara asked. He continued to study the metallic necklace that Castillo dropped into his open palm. Such a simple token… to generate such lust amongst the rich and powerful. *The young ones, I can understand their interest, so eager to make their fortune. Izabal was another thing entirely. That slitch does nothing unless it benefits her in some way. So what was it she wanted? A book? It's an attractive piece of jewelry, but certainly not worth the gold that miser Botherton had spent. And why are they so adamant about the other boy's immediate removal? I agree the Duaar shouldn't be taken lightly. He might be young, but he's crafty, and he wears the clan mark of Raskurr Stoneshield. It would not be wise for us to underestimate his ability… or his bond with Botherton's nephew.* A subtle glint lit his eyes. *Izabal is troubled by him, which makes him a potential asset.*

"I'll leave it up to you to decide our next steps," Castillo replied. "The youngsters were surprised to see me at the cabin, as we expected. They had no defenses prepared." He paused, "I understand why I must continue our little charade with Lord Botherton, however, Izabal has no idea I'm associated with you. She wants the location of that spell book, and nothing else matters to her. It must contain powerful spells. Spells she will pay a fortune to get her hands on. May I make a suggestion? Lord Botherton has never seen the medallion. Perhaps a copy with a modification, close but with a few minor changes?"

"Hmmm… yes, if only to jamb another thorn in Izabal's side. Contact Loric and have him return immediately. He's the best for this kind of project. You make the arrangements. The mithral will be no problem, we have sufficient in the vault."

"I've already ordered Loric's return. Once he's completed the duplicate, I'll deliver the fake medallion to Lord Botherton. For the moment I think we should leave the boy alive. The young Duaar pup thinks I'm hiding something but he's unsure what it is I'm hiding. He's convinced I'm working for Vondal's uncle and has no idea you are involved. I admit the Shi'i girl's presence was a surprise. She's the same one I caught in the warehouse last week."

"That's unexpected. I need to think about how it changes the game. For now, I agree we should change our own plans and keep the medallion. We'll give them the copy as you suggested. Even if its discovered to be a fake, Lord Botherton cannot prove it wasn't substituted for the original long ago. We're risking everything if anyone discovers the substitution but for now, I'm enjoying the game."

"And then I should resume my search?"

"Yes. If there's something of great value to be found, I want you to be the one to find it."

Chapter 20

The faint clink of metal against stone was all the warning Jaxx received, they were no longer alone in the tunnels. He hesitated, unsure if it was Twizzle returning from another of his rambling jaunts or even more likely, his futile attempt to catch something to eat. The adolescent draccat tended to vanish without warning and return the same way, often with no explanation for his absences except an occasional bloodstain around his mouth. Usually, he'd answer Mekiva's call, but sometimes, especially if he was feeling petulant, he'd ignore her requests until he'd decided she'd waited for him long enough.

Of course, it was better to be safe than sorry. He held one hand up to Vondal while placing a finger over his mouth in a silent warning of imminent danger. Vondal stopped walking immediately and signaled for girls to remain still and quiet. Gwendolyn quickly closed the light shield on the lantern, shrouding the hallway in darkness.

Satisfied that the others would remain still and silent, Maxx crept cautiously toward the entrance to the stair landing, pausing to listen just before the arched doorway. He could clearly make out distant voices as well as the heavy footfalls of several bodies fumbling along in the dark. Despite his limited vision, he could make out movement on the steps far above. Whoever it was, they were stealthily making their way down the winding staircase. Unless their small group moved quickly, they would be trapped between the stairs and the passage to the hidden room. Their only escape was the unexplored partially collapsed hallway.

"We have a problem," Maxx whispered to Alex as he rejoined the group. "There are at least eight people approaching. It's too dark for me to see if it's Castillo, but we need to assume its trouble. There's no way we can get past them on the stairs. With the exit blocked we either stand and fight or take a chance that the damaged side of the tunnel leads to another exit. We don't know anything about it, it may be just like this side, continuing for a while then ending at a wall. Or even worse, we discover that it's completely blocked by fallen stone. Not that we have a lot of options. There're too many of them for us to fight."

"I vote we try the other tunnel," Vondal said. "Don't worry about Twizzle, he's sure to be hiding nearby, hoping to snatch a snack when they're not looking. He will be right behind us once he realizes there's no food to be pilfered. With Tyche's blessing, we can slip past the doorway in the dark and be well down the other tunnel before they reach the landing."

"Let Jaxx go first, Mekiva argued. He can see the best in the dark." She took Jaxx's left hand, carrying her pack in the other. Gwen placed her right hand on Mekiva's shoulder, then stepped in behind so it would be easier on her. Von tried to convince Jaxx to let him lead, then gave up and moved into position behind Gwen.

Jaxx shouldered his pack, then he moved slowly down the tunnel to just before the arch of the open doorway. There he stopped. Signaling for the others to remain quiet, he lay on his stomach and inched forward until he could check the downward progress of the party on the stairs. They were still at least ten or twelve landings above the bottom. The absolute darkness of the corridor made it impossible for the group to be seen from so high up. He signaled for them to go ahead and followed.

Silently they wove their way around the rubble blocking the opposite passage, trusting Vondal to find the safest path in the darkness. Entire sections of the tunnel had fallen, scattered stones blocked portions of the passage leaving only small areas to squeeze through. Once they had to move a large stone before they could proceed.

Then Jaxx took the lead. Somehow he managed to spot potentially dangerous segments before the girls had to cross them.

Vondal stayed in the rear, keeping a watch over his shoulder as they fled, looking for any sign that the brigands were following. As he walked he silently mumbled a prayer to whatever god might be listening, asking that the men would follow the easier path to the chamber at the end of the passage, thereby wasting much needed time. They might get greedy once they discover the hidden chamber, and waste time clearing it out. So far Tyche had been with them, but the twin moons mistress had always been a fickle lady, that advantage could change at any time.

Gwendolyn didn't want to complain about walking, but her legs had gone numb long ago. Mekiva appeared to be just as tired.

Jaxx decided they needed to rest. The area was reasonably stable, and they could stretch out.

Mekiva made her way over to an open spot and slid her back down the wall until she was sitting on the ground. Once Jaxx was sure she was settled, he went back to help Gwen. As she slipped to the ground her legs started to tremble. She couldn't remember ever feeling so weak.

Jaxx knew it was too dangerous to stop for long. "We need to keep moving, it won't take them long to explore the other end and realize they have us trapped. I'll light the lantern, but we need to keep it partially closed. And don't talk unless you've to, voices carry a long way down here."

"Do you think that this tunnel is a dead end too?" Nikiva whispered. "I'd hate to think we made a big mistake by running instead of fighting."

"There's an opening somewhere ahead, Maxx reassured her. I've felt a steady, cool breeze on my face for a while now. If the air can get in, we can get out, even if we have to dig a tunnel to do it. Someone built this tunnel for a reason, just keep your fingers crossed it's a back exit."

Jaxx didn't want to scare them but he wasn't certain it was a way out. The passage had a gradual downward slope, the other didn't, that might not be a good sign. Of course, right now it's the only option they had.

"Well, the odds of finding a way out are much better than the odds of staying alive if whoever's trailing us wants us dead," Vondal said. "By now they've realized we slipped past them. They'll be coming fast, they can't be far behind us. Our only chance is to beat them to the end of this tunnel."

"I'm starting to worry about Twizzle. He's usually back by now," Mekiva said.

Vondal wasn't worried. The draccat was small but quick, no one would catch him if he didn't want to be caught.

"Pack up anything that even resembles a book. I want it delivered to the warehouse immediately. Then clear out anything that might be of value." The Tabruk mercenaries did not comment as they immediately began packing up everything in the hidden room.

Callisto turned to the druid shaman standing by the door. " Is there anything you can do to slow them down. There is no way we can know how much of a head start they have."

The old shaman shook his head. "My magic works with nature. There is nothing here for me to use as a focus. The wood of the desk is no longer in its natural form."

Calisto thought for a moment then searched through his pockets. " Will this work?" he said, holding out his hand palm up.

Potuk smiled. " That will work splendidly." He spoke a few words and blew his breath upon Calisto's hand.Immediately a thin green mist began to rise. Potuk blew his breath toward the tunnel and the mist slowly drifted in the direction the four adventurers had traveled.

"How long?"

"We should give it a candle mark to reach them."

Callisto gestured to the remaining men. "We leave in one candlemark."

"I think we can risk a short break. Try and get some sleep and I will keep watch." Jaxx knew if he didn't let the girls rest they would not be able to continue much longer. No one argued. They had been walking for hours and had already put in a long day before the unexpected visitors had changed their plans to return to the cottage. He waited until they began to slip to the ground, and then he walked a few minutes back along the tunnel until he reached one of the clearings. It was a good spot, right after a heavy rockfall and provided plenty of cover as well as a clear field of vision. It was too dark to see anything through the rubble, but he hoped he might catch a glimpse of a light in the distance or hear someone talking as they approached the blockage. It had taken them the best part of a candle mark to wiggle their way through the twists and turns. He figured that would give him time to wake his friends and escape before the pursuit managed to work past it.

Gwendolyn stretched out using her pack as a pillow and immediately fell asleep. Mekiva lay down beside her but despite being exhausted, sleep would not come. She wanted to remain cheerful but the stress of the last few days was catching up to her. As the tears welling in her eyes began to slide down her cheeks, she curled up into a ball and pretended everything was going to be okay. Twizzle landed beside her and immediately began licking the salt from her face. As though sensing her mood, the tiny fur-faced dragonet curled around her neck, softly mewing in hopes of cheering her up.

Vondal allowed himself a brief smile, every time he watched Mekiva's miniature sidekick it reminded him more and more of the kitten he had raised by hand. Necessity had forced him to leave her on board the Sea Wyvern, as it could little afford the loss of its ships-cat. Good mousers were more valuable then deck hands any day.

Most of the time the miniature draccat spent her time weaving in and out among the rocks looking for lizards to eat. Occasionally she would break away from her dance; suddenly darting out from behind a pile of tumbled stones in a playful attempt to startle whichever victim she had de-cided needed chastisement--- or a good laugh. Witnessing the draccat make such a valiant attempt to rouse Mekiva from her depression only make his resolve stronger. But until they were all safe and they were once again on the road, he could not truly relax.

He yawned and stretched. It had been a long day. He

must be sleepier than he thought. He decided to close his eyes for a moment and rest.

The eerie green cloud of chilly mist sent fingers of cold along his nervous system, slowly zapping any strength from his already overwrought muscles. Jaxx concentrated on the distant torch, but the flickering flames did little to ease his affliction. His focus wavered, at first he could think clearly, but gradually it became more and more difficult to maintain even the smallest amount of attention. He struggled to stay awake but failed, his eyelids growing heavier and heavier. Resolutely, he jerked himself alert. Whatever was causing this strange lethargy, he could beat it. Valuable seconds passed as he struggled for a solution. Then, almost without conscious thought, he drew his dagger and jabbed himself in the thigh. Sharp pain lanced through his body; then abruptly, it was as if the murky cloudiness dissipated and his mind was once more his own. Unfortunately, he wasn't sure how long that was going to be true.

He needed to alert the others. He grabbed his ax and went running back toward the sleepers. Every step grew slower until he was barely walking by the time he reached the others. Stealing himself for the pain, he jabbed his leg once more with his knife. As before, the pain snapped him out of his fugue state.

"Wake up! Everyone needs to wake up now. We need to get moving they are almost to the blockage."

"Huh ..what wrong?" Vondal yawned and turned over to go back to sleep. Jaxx kicked him and he sat up. "Drasst it Jaxx, that hurt. What are you thinking?"

"Somethings wrong. I almost fell asleep standing up. There's something in the air . We need to move now." He reached down and shook Gwen awake. She looked up at him and went back to sleep.

"We will either have to hurt them or carry them. You need to carry Mekiva's pack. I'll get Gwen's. We need to hurry."

"So what should I do?"

Jaxx gritted his teeth and muttered an apology to Rheaaz for what he was about to do to her novitiate. Then he slapped Gwen across the face.

" Wha..?" she sputtered as she woke up. Her eyes grew dark as she contemplated what he had just done.

"No time to explain. Just start running as quickly as you can. I will be right behind you. Von has already started that way. He's carrying Mekiva."

"Why didn't you carry me?"

:Because I'm going to try and slow them down." His eyes were on a key support beam. If he could weaken in enough, he could bring down another section of the tunnel.

"Jaxx! That's dangerous. It might come down on your head."

"Not if I do it right. Just go. Tell Von to keep moving. If you stop you might all fall asleep again." He watched her until he was sure she was out of danger then he began chipping away at the support keystone. It was going to be close. He could see the lights of their lanterns in the distance. They were still working their way through the rubble, but it was only a matter of minutes before they were past the blockage. Once they were free it would not be long before they caught up.

He hadn't been entirely honest with Gwen. Normally he would not consider blocking the path behind them. But there was good airflow coming from the direction they had been traveling signifying the possibility of a larger chamber nearby. And an even better possibility of a way out. The tunnel they were following sloped slightly but was easy to walk until I made the turn; then it narrowed quickly to a crevice that appeared barely passable. That's where he intended to drop the keystone.

Removing a keystone in an existing tunnel is difficult, doing it in a tunnel that had already been damaged and already unstable could be suicidal. Every rock you remove from the pile bringing with it loose dirt and small particles of rock. At any time the ceiling could collapse again. Also, the passage behind you could become clogged with debris from the digging efforts, often making the exit equally as dangerous as the extraction had been. He should be taking his time and doing it right but that was a slow and tedious process. Instead, he intended to force the keystone from its position to collapse the section behind him.

His hands shook and he stopped working to calm his nerves. At least one of the followers had made it through the blockage. By now they would be moving toward his position, moving carefully in the dark so he would not hear their approach. It would not be long now. He could feel the change in the vibration of the rock. One or two blows and the keystone would fall out. The only question was would he have time to escape the collapsing tunnel before it fell.

He hit the keystone twice and watched as it shifted position. It was going to collapse at any time. He began backing up the tunnel, keeping his eyes on the tunnel behind him. He could hear men talking and it wasn't anyone he recognized. In fact, he couldn't understand a word they were saying but they were getting closer. A small shiver ran down his spine and he started edging slowly backward.

The rumbling grew louder, and a small amount of dirt

trickled down from the ceiling overhead. The last thing he saw as he backed slowly into the darkness, was a profane look of shock on the unknown man's face, then with a loud roar, the entire ceiling of the tunnel collapsed.

What was taking Jaxx so long? He should have rejoined them by now. She turned to Vondal,

"Do you think we should go back and check on him?"

"Give him a few more minutes. If he has not caught up by then, we will go back." Von didn't mention the possibility that Jaxx had not escaped the cave in. They were at least a quarter league past the narrows, and they had felt the force of the fall. If Jaxx had been caught in the collapse, he may not be coming. He was reasonably confident that if the wily Duaar had survived, he would dig his way free and rejoin them within a candle mark. Then he could help them figure out what to do next.

He joined the girls, watching the dark tunnel for any sound or movement. Just as he expected , it was only a few minutes before he caught the first glimpse of movement. Von drew his sword and prepared to defend the girls of it turned out to be one of the pursuit.

The shadowy figure inched closer, moving slowly. As it limped into the light of the glow stones, they could see that it was Jaxx. And he was hurt.

Von ran forward and helped him hobble to the clearing.

"How bad is it?" He asked.

"Rock came down on my knee. Its banged up but I can still walk so I don't think its broken. We need to keep moving, that collapse might slow them down, but it won't stop them for long. Of I sit down it might stiffen up and that could be a problem.

"Well, we have a bigger problem. The tunnel ends in about fifty feet."

"Ends? What do you mean?"

"Its blocked up like the other end." He helped Jaxx hobble along the last of the tunnel. The girls followed, carrying the packs.

"Well, at least it's not a dead-end," Jaxx acknowledged as he examined the blocked off wall.. "I can feel the air moving through the cracks. I don't suppose you know any spells that would transport us all out of here?" After miles of walking through the narrow passage, they were once more facing a roadblock.

Everyone looked at Nikiva hopefully, however, the young mage shook her head.

"No luck here either," Gwen added. "Teleportation's a major spell and only high-level clerics attempt it. I've no idea why I can do healing spells, there's no way I'd try to teleport."

"At least we have good, solid rock under our feet and the ceiling appears to be in great shape. Whatever caused the structural damage back in the tunnel didn't affect this area. I can tell by the way the stones are set in the mortar that experienced masons built the wall, but it was a long time ago. See how light the mortar is, and how the dust has gathered in the cracks and on the face of the stones? No one has touched it for a very long time, years longer than the wall that was closing off the hidden room… maybe hundreds of years longer."

Von was already shaking his head. "It's so old I feel guilty about what I'm about to ask you to do, but unless we want to face off against whoever is tracking us, we'd better get to work knocking it down." He used his sword pommel to start chipping away at the ancient mortar. Just as Jaxx had suggested, it was old and dry, breaking apart with little effort. With Jaxx beside him working on the opposite side of the hole, the men soon cleared an opening large enough for everyone to squeeze through. He kneeled, preparing to make the crawl when a blur of fur slipped by, slapping him in the face with his tail as he passed.

" Drasst it Twizzle. Move out of my way."

Mekiva grinned, happy that the elusive draccat was with them once more. She hurried to follow Vondal through the hole. Gwen handed Mekiva the lantern and crawled through, then Jaxx followed.

The light from the bulls-eye lantern enabled everyone to see. They were in a small cave. Through the opening they could see stars twinkling in the clear night sky. Below them he could see a well-traveled roadway, worn down by the passage of many feet. There was a hand hewn stairway cut into the face of the mountain, a narrow but easily traveled path to the bottom.

Jaxx grinned. They had made a big circle and were now back on the same road that they had left a week earlier. They could be back in Cabrell in a week!

Mekiva was experiencing an entirely different emotion, ---despair. The men following them would not be delayed for long. The very idea of another staircase was more than she could handle. She slowly slid down until she lay prostrate at the feet of her worried friends.

"Drasst," Vondal cursed under his breath, berating himself for overlooking the young woman's condition, concern showing on his face. She was too stubborn to admit how tired she was. He dropped to his knees beside her, raised her head to his chest listening for her breath, then relaxed noticeably as she moaned a soft sigh and snuggled deeper into his arms. Mekiva's breathing was shallow but steady. There was already a warm color returning to her cheeks. Lazily she opened her eyes and smiled up at Vondal, a look so innocent and pure that he felt immoral holding her.

"Don't hover over her like that," Gwendolyn snapped crossly, give her some room to breathe."

"What happened?" Mekiva asked drowsily, burrowing deeper into Vondal's arms.

"You fainted." He maneuvered her body into a sitting position without releasing her, fearing loss of even that small concession. Gwen shot him an exasperated look and then smiled after she realized Mekiva was holding him just as tightly.

Until now, Jaxx had not truly realized how scared the two young girls were. Other than the Wyverns, they'd calmly faced any of the myriad obstacles that they'd encountered along the way. It appeared the girls were better at hiding their true feelings than he'd realized. Both were exhausted, somehow, he needed to find a way for them to get some rest soon. But in the meanwhile, …he picked up the small bags Mekiva and Rhianwen had been carrying and added them to his already heavy pack. "We'd better keep moving," he said. If they catch us on the staircase, we'll be slaughtered. There're dozens of positions for archers to fire down at us, and numerous sections where there's no cover at all. Once we reach the bottom, the way is open and easily passable. We'll start making good time after we get off the stairs."

"I wish Twizzle would show back up," Nikiva said. "I've been trying to reach him. All I get is a general feeling of safety and curiosity. I know he's all right but that's about it."

"We are out in open now, there's nothing to prevent him from tracking us. He's probably stalking something edible. Hopefully enough for all of us to have dinner."

"Dinner sounds wonderful." She glanced at the opening. "Give me a minute, I might be able to slow them down some more." She spoke a few words in a strange language and pointed at the stone. Colorful lights began to gather and spread until they covered the entire stone wall. " If they have a mage with them he can probably dispel the barrier, but it will stop them until the mage catches up.

Descending the stairs proved to be much faster than anyone expected, the stonemasons had crafted the steps to a universal height and smoothness that allowed them to practically run down them. The rapid pace allowed Mekiva to stretch her long legs, almost crying after the slow, bent back crawl that she'd endured most of the morning. You could almost feel the relief after the small party reached the bottom without hearing the first signs of pursuit.

Now, by the lantern's light, they could see the ancient road, stretching off in two directions… one way went to alliance, the other back to Cabrell.

Jaxx looked at Von and Mekiva. "Choose, left, or right?"

"I always preferred to go left," Nikiva said with a quirky grin.

"Why is that," Von asked. "Most of the times I choose to go right. And that's the road to Alliance."

"That's the reason. Given a choice, most everyone will choose right. I'm hoping the men following us will too."

"Left it is. We head toward home. Should we leave a trail for Twizzle?" Gwen asked.

"No, Twizzle's fine. By the strength of his 'I'm ok', I expect we'll see his furry face very soon. He'll be able to track us without any problems."

"Unfortunately, if they have dogs or anything else with a good nose, the others will too," Jaxx added.

"Then let's get as much distance between us and them as possible. That fort is not getting any closer."

He was whistling as they began walking.

A native if Atlanta, Georgia, Victoria Sanford had a long career in Information Technology as a Systems Engineer.

Prior to relocating to the North Georgia Mountains, she authored many Technical guides for the Federal Government as well as the public-school system.

Since retiring from the Centers for Disease Control she has split her life between working with teenagers in her area to better ensure their chances of reaching their own personal goals in life and her own love of writing.

She shares her life with her husband Tim, her spoilt white four-legged best friend Tweet, and her husband's Lil' Princess, a 250-pound miniature pig that did not get the message.

V C SANFORD